Peril in Paris

Peril in Paris

RHYS BOWEN

BERKLEY PRIME CRIME
New York

BERKLEY PRIME CRIME
Published by Berkley
An imprint of Penguin Random House LLC
penguinrandomhouse.com

Copyright © 2022 by Janet Quin-Harkin
Penguin Random House supports copyright. Copyright fuels creativity, encourages
diverse voices, promotes free speech, and creates a vibrant culture. Thank you for buying
an authorized edition of this book and for complying with copyright laws by not
reproducing, scanning, or distributing any part of it in any form without permission.
You are supporting writers and allowing Penguin Random House to continue to
publish books for every reader.

BERKLEY and the BERKLEY & B colophon are registered trademarks and
BERKLEY PRIME CRIME is a trademark of Penguin Random House LLC.

The Edgar® name is a registered service mark of the Mystery Writers of America, Inc.

Library of Congress Cataloging-in-Publication Data

Names: Bowen, Rhys, author.
Title: Peril in Paris / Rhys Bowen.
Description: New York: Berkley Prime Crime, [2022] |
Series: Royal spyness mysteries; 16
Identifiers: LCCN 2022029120 (print) | LCCN 2022029121 (ebook) |
ISBN 9780593437858 (hardcover) | ISBN 9780593437865 (ebook)
Subjects: LCGFT: Detective and mystery fiction. | Novels.
Classification: LCC PR6052.O848 P47 2022 (print) |
LCC PR6052.O848 (ebook) | DDC 823/.914—dc23/eng/20220623
LC record available at https://lccn.loc.gov/2022029120
LC ebook record available at https://lccn.loc.gov/2022029121

Printed in the United States of America
1st Printing

This book is dedicated to the best next-door neighbor in history, Kim Press. Not only does she bake wonderful bread and scones and bring me honey from her bees, but she loves my books!

Peril in Paris

Peril in Paris

Chapter 1

WEDNESDAY, MARCH 25, 1936
EYNSLEIGH, SUSSEX.

Spring has finally arrived in our neck of the woods. Primroses are
dotting the hedgerows. Birds are singing like mad in the trees,
which are sprouting new green leaves. After a long wet winter it
feels like coming out of a cocoon.

"It's spring at last!" I exclaimed to nobody in particular as I pulled
back the heavy curtains and looked out of my bedroom window
across the grounds and saw the sun sparkling on morning dew, a
group of rabbits in the meadow and in the distance a lone deer.
Through the open window (windows are always open in bedrooms—
it's a rule of the upper classes, however freezing it is outside) a deafening birdsong came to me, the sweet notes of the blackbird and
thrush competing with the harsh calls of the rooks. I felt a great
surge of hope and anticipation. New life was bursting all around us

and I could look forward to my own new life sometime in July. Yes, it was true—Darcy and I were expecting a baby!

The last few months had been rather bleak. The year started with the king's death and the whole country in mourning. It was hard to believe that my cousin David was now King-Emperor Edward VIII. He was really the most unlikely king (unsuitable king, his mother would say) but the public seemed to have embraced him. He did, after all, have an abundance of charm. It's just that he didn't much like the thought of hard work or duty. He had been inclined to go off and enjoy himself on a yacht or at a country house rather than stick to the task at hand. I wondered if becoming king would sober him and make him realize the enormity of the job.

And then there was the problem of Mrs. Simpson. Strangely enough the average person in England knew nothing of her—since the British press had a gentlemen's agreement not to mention her. I was now convinced that David wanted to marry her. He was besotted with her. But I didn't see how this could possibly be allowed to happen, since the king is the head of the Church of England and the church forbids divorce. Mrs. Simpson would be a twice-divorced woman, when the second divorce had gone through. He could keep her on as his mistress, of course, quietly in the background. That had been quite accepted for kings of England. His grandfather, King Edward VII, had kept an abundance of mistresses. But if you know Mrs. Simpson, you would know that she isn't the type of person who will agree to stay quiet and out of sight. She adores the limelight, and I think she has set her heart on marrying David. And from what I could gather, she had actually set her heart on becoming queen. Oh dear. I was afraid it would turn into an awful mess before long. Poor Queen Mary must be so upset, I thought. And then a second, more terrifying thought crossed my mind—golly, I hope she doesn't send for me to cheer her up!

I had been lying low since our Christmas at Sandringham when I saw rather too much of the royal family and their troubles. No travels, no entertaining and certainly no visits to my royal cousins. My excuse was that there is a little O'Mara on the way. Actually my pregnancy had been rather ghastly until now. For the last few months I had been horribly sick. They call it morning sickness but it struck me equally at any time of the day. One mouthful of the wrong type of food and it was a quick rush to the nearest loo! So for a while I hadn't wanted to eat anything except cream crackers and clear soup. My housekeeper, Mrs. Holbrook, had tried to pamper me, serving me tempting little morsels. But then you realize that my cook is none other than my former maid Queenie. Yes, that maid. The walking disaster area. Actually as a cook she's not at all bad, but her repertoire is limited to the sort of foods she has grown up with. Meat suet pudding, boiled cabbage and spotted dick do not go down well when one is horribly nauseated.

Darcy had been quite concerned about me, treating me as if I were made of the finest porcelain and suggesting we hire a nurse to look after me. I pointed out that women all over the world have babies all the time and work in the fields until they are ready to give birth, but I thought it was sweet that he was so concerned. To tell you the truth, I was a little concerned myself, worried that all this nausea and vomiting might have a bad effect on the baby. But a couple of weeks ago I awoke one morning suddenly feeling better. I didn't have to sprint to the nearest loo. And it had stopped raining. I could take the puppies for walks in the fresh air. Suddenly I realized I felt positively blooming and healthy. Rather larger around the middle as well!

Now I felt ready to get up and out to do things again—only there was nothing to do. The house ran like clockwork (apart from the odd disaster coming from Queenie in the kitchen). Darcy had become horribly busy with his own activities, popping off now and then on assignments he couldn't tell me about. And at dinner last night my grandfather announced that he thought he should be going home for a while. He had been staying on at Eynsleigh since Christmas to keep me company and I had cherished his comforting presence around the house. So it came as a shock when he told me he thought it was about time he went home.

"But, Granddad, I wanted this to be your home now," I said. "I don't like the thought of you living alone and having to shop and cook for yourself. And I like having you here with me."

"I know, ducks," he said, reaching across to pat my hand. "And don't think I'm being ungrateful or nothing. I do like it here, but it don't seem quite right, being waited on hand and foot and not being useful. I wasn't born to do nothing like your aristocrat friends. I need to keep busy."

"But what if we could find you something to do here?" I suggested.

"Like what? Manage the croquet games?" He shook his head.

"Maybe get some chickens and put you in charge of them?"

He chuckled then. "What would I know about chickens? I've lived all my life in the Smoke, love. Them chickens would probably peck me to death. Besides, I don't like the thought of my little house in Essex being unoccupied for too long and I miss chatting with my old neighbors."

I did understand. He felt out of place. He hated being waited on. Of course living in a big house in the country was quite foreign to him. He'd grown up in a humble London two-up two-down terraced house and been a policeman on a beat until he retired. (In case you are confused by this revelation, perhaps I should explain that while my father was the grandson of Queen Victoria and the Duke of Glen Garry and Rannoch, my mother had been a famous actress from humble beginnings she chose to forget.)

I was upset to see him go, but I couldn't beg him to stay just because I wanted company. I knew I'd be lonely without him. The truth was I didn't have any real friends nearby. I had met most of the neighbors by now, been to tea and dinner at their houses, gone to watch the local hunt, though not to ride in it as we had no horses, and anyway I was pregnant. They were nice enough people but I hadn't really connected to any of them yet. They led intensely social lives, always doing things together, mainly outdoorsy, hearty sorts of things like pheasant shoots, hunts or organizing pony club and Boy Scout meetings—things I could not really take part in at the moment. My dearest friends were far away. Princess Zamanska, our dear Zou Zou, was never in one place for more than two seconds. She was even threatening to fly to Australia in her little two-seater plane and thus set a record.

Belinda, my best friend from my school days, had grown tired of being rich and idle (having inherited property from her grandmother) and had returned to Paris to continue studying haute couture with none other than Chanel. I received the occasional letter from her, describing life in Paris, to which she seemed to have adapted rather well. Lots of parties and nightclubs that all seemed so far removed from my own lifestyle that it was like reading a fantasy novel. Don't misunderstand me. I didn't envy her, exactly. I was extremely content with my new life as wife and future mother in the British countryside. But I just wished . . . I'm not sure exactly what I wished. For something exciting to happen, I suppose. Although in the past few years too many exciting things had happened to me, not all of them pleasant.

So everybody was busy except me. My one task was to try and tame the two very exuberant puppies we had received as Christmas presents. One was a black Lab and one yellow, a boy and girl, both equally sweet and horribly naughty. We had found it a challenge to

come up with proper names for them. We had tried several dignified names: Castor and Pollux, Arthur and Guinevere, but they
simply didn't look or behave like dignified beings. Darcy had first
suggested we call them Victoria and Albert.

"You can't call our dogs after my great-grandparents!" I said.

"Well then, how about Gin and Tonic?"

"Be serious." I slapped his hand playfully.

He laughed. "I know. Bubble and Squeak."

"Darcy, I am not standing on the village green yelling, 'Squeak,
Squeak!'"

"Well, you come up with names, then," he said, pretending to
be offended.

"I hope we don't have this much trouble naming our child," I
said to Darcy.

"No problem. I've already picked out the name," he replied.

"You have?"

"Yes. Marmaduke Archibald," he said. "Old family name. We'll
call him Marm for short, like the queen."

"Darcy, you can't . . ." I began. Then I saw his face and hit him
as I burst out laughing.

"You're not allowed to tease me. I'm in a delicate condition."

He wrapped his arms around me. "It was good to see you smile
again. You've been looking really down recently."

"I've hated not feeling well," I said.

"But that's all behind you now. And you'll forget how bad
you felt."

"I do hope so," I said. I looked at the puppies who were stretched
out in front of the fire, having just been taken on a long walk.

"We should call them something Christmassy," I said. "After
all, they were our Christmas presents to each other."

"Mary and Joseph?"

He was teasing again. I gave him a stern look. "Nick, after St. Nicholas? But what about the girl?" I looked at the adorable little black male puppy, who was lolling in most undignified fashion. He was a real clown. Naughty but so adorable that one forgave him.

"I know," I said. "How about Holly and Jolly?"

"If you like those, then it's fine with me," Darcy said.

"You don't like the names?"

"I was thinking more of Irish royalty. Queen Mab. Brian Boru. Or Scottish royalty after your side of the family. Robert Bruce?"

"I don't want a dog called Brian," I said. "Or Bruce for that matter. I don't want to stand on the village green shouting, 'Bruce, where are you? Come here instantly.'"

He grinned. "I'm just teasing again. Holly and Jolly suits them just fine. And while we're at it we'll call our child Golly, since it's your favorite word."

"It's not!" I said hotly. "Is it?"

He nodded. "You do say it quite a lot."

"Oh dear. I was trying to train myself to stop saying it. But it just slips out in moments of stress."

Darcy slipped his arms around me. "Don't change. I like the way you are." And he kissed me on the nose.

Since then, most of the time the dogs were referred to as the VNPs (as in very naughty puppies). We let them have the run of the place to start with until the servants tired of mopping up puddles on the floor and we tired of rescuing any object within reach, from socks to shoes to sandwiches, from their naughty mouths. Mercifully they loved going on long walks, chasing rabbits, rolling in messes and generally having such a great time that they were exhausted for a while afterward.

I worked at obedience training. It was hard work. They were not stupid—they learned to come and sit and stay, wagging their

tails and looking adorable, until they wanted to do something
naughty and then no amount of calling would make them obey.
We had finally had to relegate them to the servant's area downstairs
when we were not actively supervising, where the floors were stone
and they could go outside easily. They thought this was a splendid
idea as they were around food and there was always the chance that
a morsel would fall from the table. They were now four months old
and I was hoping they might show a bit more sense soon. Golly, I
hoped a baby would be easier to rear. At least it wouldn't be able to
run around so easily with my shoe in its mouth!

Apart from the puppies I tried to do what expectant mothers
are supposed to: make a layette for the baby. Let me state that my
sewing and knitting skills are minimal at best. I failed sewing at
school. We had to make a white blouse and mine ended up an interesting shade of gray with one sleeve sewn in the wrong way. I
tried crocheting a baby blanket, only I forgot to add a stitch at
the beginning of each row and so it got more and more narrow
until I realized I was creating a triangle. Luckily I knew that the
poor child would not have to rely solely on my skills. Zou Zou
would be bound to arrive with enough clothes to dress triplets,
and my mother would probably also come up trumps in her new
role as grandmother (although I wondered how she would recon-
cile admitting to grandmotherhood when she still claimed to be
thirty-five).

THE MONDAY POST brought another letter from Belinda. Darcy
and I were at the breakfast table together—a rare occurrence for the
past few months. He was busy spreading Cooper's Oxford marmalade onto toast. I was eating a kipper when Phipps, our footman/
chauffeur, brought in the morning letters on a silver salver.

"Your ladyship, letter for you from abroad," he said, handing it to me.

"Oh, it's from Belinda," I said, looking up with a pleased smile. Darcy took his own letters, opening one and thus giving me leave to read mine at the table.

Darling Georgie,

How are you feeling now? Better, I hope. That morning sickness sounds ghastly. It brought back horrid memories, but then mine was never that bad. One does soon get over it, so I hope you are past the bad part by now.

Life in Paris gets more hectic by the minute. We are now in full production for the spring fashion shows which happen in a couple of weeks. I am supposed to be an assistant designer to Madame Chanel but now it's all hands on deck and I find myself sewing, ironing, modeling clothes with everyone else. It's a truly beautiful collection (fall, naturally). Chanel's designs are stunning—her lines so simple and elegant. And you'll never guess what? She is allowing one of my designs in the collection. An evening ensemble—a backless affair with silk trousers in black and white. I am so flattered and can hardly believe my luck.

I wish you could come over and see it modeled on the runway. I miss you, darling. I know loads of people here but I don't have any real chums like you—real friends I can laugh with and share secrets with. And you know every bloody secret from my life, don't you?

You'd love my apartment not too far from the Seine in Saint-Germain. I can actually see the river through a gap in the buildings, also the Eiffel Tower if I lean out of the bathroom window. It's a lovely space with a little wrought iron balcony. All would be perfect if it were not for the old dragon who is the concierge on the ground floor. You'd think it was her building, not that she was the caretaker of it. She leaps out of her little cubby when anyone comes in, examines what they have bought, who is coming in with them, and has a horrid cat that also leaps out and bites ankles. She is always sweeping the courtyard. You hear her all day—swish, swish, swish, swish. It's a wonder there is any gravel left. I bet she flies around on that broomstick when we are not watching.

Anyway, the other residents are more pleasant, especially the chap on the top floor. He has the garret under the eaves—rather romantic, really, as he is a writer. An American called Harry Barnstable. Rather attractive in a sort of scholarly, shabby, worried way. And terribly intellectual. I've met some of his writer and painter pals and frankly I can't understand half their conversations. But he has been jolly helpful in setting up my place and making it comfortable. He knows all about flea markets (darling, they are not as bad as they sound and one can get amazing bargains in furniture and paintings there—such fun). So my flat is now très civilized and I have a great big feather bed—big enough for more than one, should the occasion arise.

Harry and I haven't got that far yet, but one never knows. I'm not sure that I actually fancy him. A little old for me and a little too shabby. Oh, but there is also a frightfully elegant nobleman called Louis-Philippe de Montaigre who seems to have taken an interest in me. Frenchmen are fascinating, aren't they? I'm not sure I'm attracted to Louis-Philippe but it's awfully nice to be courted in an old-fashioned way. He sends flowers on a daily basis, and chocolates, and champagne. Do you see me as a French countess? One never knows . . ."

"Good news from Belinda?" Darcy asked. "I can see you smiling."

I put down the letter. "You know Belinda—there always has to be at least one man in the picture. In this case there are two: a struggling American writer in the garret and a French aristocrat who sends her champagne and chocolates."

Darcy laughed and shook his head. "She certainly likes to live dangerously. I wish she'd stop all this and settle down. I thought she had finally met her match with Jago in Cornwall."

"I did too," I agreed. "They seemed perfect for each other. I hope Jago has not backed off because she's upper-class and he's the son of a fisherman. I don't think it mattered to her."

"Men are sensitive about these things," Darcy said, taking a thoughtful bite of his marmalade toast. "They want to be the provider, you know. I have to confess that it's been hard for me to accept we are living in a house provided to you by your godfather and not a house I have bought for my new bride."

"Don't be silly," I said. "I know we are both equally penniless and if Sir Hubert hadn't come up trumps we'd have been living in a horrid little London flat."

Darcy frowned. "But I don't want to be penniless. I want my family to be able to live in style."

"But we are living in style," I reminded him.

"Not thanks to me." He sighed. "I have to admit it's time to buckle down and get a proper job, Georgiana."

The fact that he used my whole name made me look up. I reached across and covered his hand with my own. "But, my darling, you love what you do. I'm not sure exactly what it is, but I know you love the challenge, the danger and the adventure. You'd be utterly miserable in a desk job. Our sort are not brought up to that kind of life."

His eyes met mine. "Georgie, most people don't have the luxury of leading the kind of life they'd choose. They go to work every day in a bank or a shop or an office because they have a family that depends on them. Why should I be any different? I want to support my family. What happens when our children are ready for boarding school? Who will pay the fees? And if we have girls and the time comes for their debut? It costs a lot to be presented at court, doesn't it?"

"That really is looking ahead," I said. "Think positively. Maybe we'll have six sons and you won't have to present any of them."

Darcy grinned then. "Make it seven and they can play in their own seven—a side rugby team."

"Hold on a minute," I said. "I feel terrific at this moment but if we'd had this conversation a month ago I'd have sworn one child was quite enough, thank you."

Darcy now squeezed my hand. "You've had a rough time," he said. "I'd like to make it up to you." He paused, as if considering. "I was wondering, would you like a trip to Paris?"

I stared at him. I suspect my jaw was open. "Paris?" I stammered out the word. "You're inviting me to go to Paris?"

He nodded, grinning at my shocked expression. "Well? Would you?" Darcy asked me again. "Do you feel up to the journey, do you think? It might be your last chance to travel for a while."

"Do I feel up to it?" I asked, a big smile spreading across my face. "Darcy, it's not a caravan to outer Mongolia. It's a ship across the Channel and then a train. Hardly taxing. And it's Paris! Of course I'd love to go, except . . ." I broke off, as our conversation of a few minutes ago came back to me. "How can we afford it?"

"Ah." I saw that wary look come into his eyes. "We don't have to afford it. You see, I have to go to Paris on a spot of business and I thought my wife might like to come with me. . . ."

"Your spots of business normally involve danger," I said. "Remember our honeymoon in Kenya? I wondered how you could afford that and it turned out that you were being sent there to uncover a Nazi agitator."

"In this case," Darcy said, slowly, "I thought we'd travel together but then you could stay with Belinda, while I got on with my . . . business. Belinda has invited you to stay, hasn't she?"

"Several times," I said. "And it would be fun to stay with her. And to see the spring fashion shows and meet her intellectual pals."

"There you are, then." Darcy looked relieved, I thought. "I think this will all work out splendidly."

I wondered at the time what he meant.

Chapter 2

MONDAY, MARCH 30
EYNSLEIGH.

I can't believe I'm going to Paris. Paris in the spring. It's like a dream come true.

This would not be my first trip to Paris. I had passed through it several times on my way to and from my finishing school in Switzerland, but it had always been a tantalizing glimpse from a taxicab window between the Gare du Nord and the Gare de Lyon. I had always just arrived on the night train and wasn't feeling too perky in the first place, but I had gazed out of that cab window with longing as I saw elegant people sitting at sidewalk cafés and strolling in parks. Those women all seemed so worldly and self-assured in the nonchalant way they draped a scarf over their shoulder or held a slim dark cigarette between their fingers. As we passed narrow side streets I had looked up to see the improbable gleaming white of Sacré-Coeur church high on Montmartre, and then, as we came toward the Gare de Lyon, there was the River Seine across a broad plaza. I longed to leap out of the taxi, shouting, "Forget about school. Now I want to live a little."

Of course, being a good, well-behaved child (until I met Belinda), I duly boarded my train to Switzerland and off I went. And now, finally, I was about to live my dream. I wrote to Belinda telling her I had the chance to travel with Darcy and could I come to stay for a few days and received an instant reply:

Darling, so excited to see you! Stay for as long as you like. Only I might not be as attentive as I should be as it's going to be the week of the revelation of the fall collection and I'll be working like a dog. I might even drag you in to help (not to model, in your current condition, but to help with chatting to the right people and that sort of thing). But we'll have our evenings if you're not off with Darcy being madly social. Harry knows such interesting people. Artists and writers—all very intellectual and intense.

So let me know when to expect you and I'll get in supplies. I have to confess that, having no maid, I tend to eat at the nearest café a lot. The food is so scrumptious in Paris, one can't go wrong. But I'll try to think what pregnant women enjoy. If you come at the weekend you can count on my being home.

It's going to be such fun! Just like old times.

With bunches of love,
Your friend,
Belinda.

I telephoned Zou Zou, wanting to tell her about it, but her maid informed me she had gone off in her little plane again and who knew where she was. I always experienced an absurd sense of disappointment when she wasn't there. I needed reassurance about what to take to Paris, what people were wearing. Not that I could compete with my humble wardrobe of well-worn clothes. Actually both Zou Zou and my mother had provided me with some fashionable outfits, but alas my middle was now too large for them. I was at that awkward stage of not being large enough to look pregnant but instead as if I had devoured too many second helpings of treacle pudding at my last meal.

So clothing was definitely going to be a problem. I'd be with Belinda and even, God forbid, Coco Chanel herself, so I couldn't look like a dumpy frumpy woman from the country. I examined my wardrobe with dismay. The long cashmere cardigan that had been a pass-on from my mother would hide my bulging front, and I could still wear my tartan skirt if I used a large safety pin at the waist. But for evenings? My lovely, fashionable dark blue culottes with the low back would not go around me. Neither would my evening gowns. Doomed, I thought—then I decided it was unlikely I'd be invited out in the evenings. And if we did go out, it sounded as if Belinda's friends were a bohemian bunch, the sort that wore patched jackets and berets, not dinner suits. So maybe I'd fit in beautifully.

One good thing was that I wouldn't have to take a maid with me. I seemed to remember that Belinda had mentioned she had no servants. Maybe a woman to clean but certainly not to live in. I'd just have to take clothing I could do up and undo by myself. My current lady's maid, called Maisie, was a sweet little local girl, ever willing to please, meticulous in the way she handled my clothing, but she had a sick mother nearby and simply refused to leave her. My alternative was Queenie. Enough said. I would not be taking a maid.

I told Maisie which items I'd be taking with me. They looked pathetically inadequate when laid out on my bed. There was not a plain black dress among them, nor any trailing silk scarves or well-cut suits. Not that a well-cut suit would button up at the moment, but I had to admit that what I was taking would be fine for a country house weekend, tramping through the heather with the dogs, but for Paris? Maybe Belinda would take pity on me and run me up a stunning outfit or two. One can always hope.

Maisie was in the middle of packing when I heard a noise that sounded rather like a herd of elephants stampeding in my direction. While I was still wondering what this could be, since we possessed no large animals, Queenie burst into my room, her face red from running, her cook's apron half undone.

"What on earth's the matter, Queenie?" I asked.

"What's this, then?" she demanded. "I just heard you're going off to Paris, missus." (She had never learned to call me "my lady" as is normal in my status and had always referred to me as "miss." Now at least she acknowledged I was married and called me "missus." I suppose that was all one could hope for.)

"That's right. Mr. O'Mara and I are going to Paris for a while. So you will be able to take a break from all the cooking—maybe use the time to work on your skills? Learn to cook new things?" I gave her a bright smile but she was still glowering.

"When ladies go to Paris, they take their maid with them, right? But you didn't even ask me. You're not taking her, are you?" She indicated Maisie, who was looking terrified. "She don't know nothing about abroad. She ain't never been farther than Brighton. And I've been with you to all them continental places, ain't I? The French Riviera and that castle in whatever it was called. . . ." She was still fuming. "She'll only panic, won't she? When foreign blokes grab the luggage and run off with it she'll go to pieces and want to go home."

"Queenie," I interrupted this rant. "Maisie is not going with me. I'm not taking a maid, as it happens, as I'll be staying in Miss Belinda's flat where there is no room for servants. But if I were taking a maid, and Maisie was willing, I would naturally take her. She is now my lady's maid and you are my cook."

Queenie's face now had a sullen expression on it. "I know I'm your cook," she said, "but I was your lady's maid first, wasn't I? I was the one who helped you out when you was in danger."

"That's very true. You have been very brave and I appreciate it. But you are of value here as the cook. The house could not run without you."

I saw the expression soften. "Yeah," she said, nodding. "That's right. I'm needed here, ain't I? They'd all starve without me." She smoothed down her apron. "Right, then. Well, that's settled. But you don't need my help getting your clothes ready? Or packing them?"

"Thank you, Queenie. We can manage," I said hastily. I remembered too many times when I had arrived with one shoe missing or my best dress wrapped around my riding boots. "Now why don't you prepare a lovely lunch for us?"

"Bob's yer uncle, missus," she said, and off she went.

I let out a sigh of relief. Running a household was still a challenge for me. I knew I should have rebuked her, told her she was out of line and as mistress I would select whomever I chose to accompany me. Furthermore, if she barged into my room ever again she would be dismissed on the spot. That is what a real lady of the manor would do. But I still wanted to keep the peace and make everyone happy.

"Oh, my lady, I'm so sorry about that," Maisie muttered as soon as Queenie had gone. "She's terribly jealous that I'm now your maid. I think it's because she's stuck down in the kitchen and doesn't see you very much." She gave me a worried look. "I do a good job, don't I? I take care of your clothes and everything."

I smiled. "You do a splendid job, Maisie," I said. "I couldn't be happier." I was about to add how relieved I was that I had a maid that didn't iron my velvet the wrong way, burn a hole in my evening gown, lose one of my shoes on my wedding day. A constant stream of disasters, in fact. But I didn't want the other staff to have ammunition against Queenie. However challenging she was, I was strangely fond of her. Instead I said, "But when your mother fully recovers I will expect you to travel with me."

"Like to abroad, you mean? Other countries? Foreign parts?"

"Well, yes. If the need should arise for me to travel in the future."

"Oh no, my lady. I don't think I could handle seeing foreign parts. They speak funny over there, don't they? And Queenie said they pinch your bottom."

I tried not to laugh. "Well, I don't think the occasion will arise for a while, Maisie, since I'm going to be stuck at home with a new baby soon."

Her face lit up. "I'm so happy for you, my lady. I'm dying to help with the little baby. It will be wonderful."

I nodded agreement. "Yes, it will be wonderful."

"When will you be hiring a nanny?" she asked. "Will it be someone local?"

Oh golly. That was going to be my next servant challenge. I hadn't even managed to hire a proper chef or cook yet—again not wanting to hurt Queenie's feelings. But the thought of hiring a nanny—an efficient, starched nanny who would bring up the young master to be a future leader of the empire. That was utterly terrifying. In truth I wanted to raise my own child, but I had to accept that my class of person always had a nanny. My own nanny had been the exception to the rule—sweet, loving, warm. A local Scotswoman who sat me on her lap and sang to me when I was little. I will try to find someone just like her!

Chapter 3

I can't believe we are actually on our way. Unfortunately we haven't chosen the best day for it!

It was not an auspicious start. There are supposed to be April showers, I know, but we set off in a full-blown April storm. I awoke to the rain peppering my window and the wind moaning through the chimneys.

"The weather doesn't look too great," Darcy said with his normal understatement as he pulled back the curtains.

"Too great?" I said as there was the rattling crash of a slate tile being blown from the roof. "It's a howling gale out there. Do you think the ships will be allowed to cross the Channel?"

"The weather may have improved by midday," he said. "And I think they sail in all weathers. At least it doesn't take long."

I didn't find this too comforting.

"We could always put it off and go another day," I suggested.

Darcy shook his head. "Oh, no, I don't think we should do that."

"You have a meeting you have to attend?" I asked.

"Something of the sort." He went off to the bathroom without another word.

A tiny knot of anxiety formed in my stomach. Darcy had never actually told me what he did for a living, but I knew it was some kind of undercover work, usually for the British government. In other words, I suspected my husband was a spy. And it occurred to me that this assignment might be dangerous for him. That desk job that he had threatened did suddenly seem awfully appealing.

Our chauffeur, Phipps, drove us to the station. We had originally thought that Phipps would drive us to nearby Newhaven, where we could take the ferry to Dieppe, but it was a longer crossing and not one we fancied in weather like this. So we opted to travel up to London and then take the *Golden Arrow* in the direct route to Dover, Calais and then Paris. The first part of the journey was comfortable as the rainy Kent countryside flashed past. But the weather hadn't improved by the time we reached the port at Dover and had to leave the train, find a porter and then make our way onto the SS *Canterbury*. We arrived on board drenched, wind-blown and out of breath.

"In my experience there is only one thing to do when facing a crossing like this," Darcy said.

"Find somewhere to hold on tight or lie down?" I asked.

"No, go straight to the bar and have a large brandy with ginger ale," he said. "Works like a charm."

He led me to the warmth of the bar, which was surprisingly empty, then settled us at a table in the corner with our brandies. I took a dubious first sip and had to admit that he was right. The drink warmed the stomach wonderfully. I'm not used to drinking much before lunch, on an empty stomach, so I was feeling quite floaty and content as we left the harbor.

"See, it's not too bad." I had hardly uttered the words when the ship gave a dramatic lurch. After that we plunged, bucked and rolled all the way to Calais. Glasses fell off tables. Chairs skidded across floors. Over the creaking of the ship came the regular sounds of crashes and thumps—and distant moans and groans. I imagined our suitcases being tossed around or drenched up on deck. Other occupants of the bar turned green and left until we were almost the only ones still sitting there. Even Darcy had gone remarkably quiet. Strangely enough, having been horribly sick for three months I now felt perfectly fine.

"Is there anything to eat?" I asked.

Darcy looked at me as if I'd gone mad. "You feel like food?"

"As a matter of fact, I do. It's been ages since breakfast."

"Some crisps?" he suggested.

"A bacon sandwich, maybe? A meat pie?"

Darcy shook his head in disbelief but staggered to the bar, grasping at pillars as he went, and came back with a sausage roll. "It was all they had in the circumstances," he said. "The cook isn't feeling up to cooking."

I tucked into it, relishing every mouthful, and had only just finished when the violent rolling stopped.

"It feels as if we are coming into port," Darcy said.

We went up to the embarkation deck, passing prostrate bodies, lying in deck chairs and on benches, all looking as if they were at death's door. Some groaned as we passed them. There was vomit on the floor and a horrid smell that made me reach for my handkerchief and keep it pressed to my nose as we went out into the fresh air on deck. It was still raining. A stiff wind was still blowing, but it was no longer a gale. In fact it felt fresh and bracing, reminding me of my childhood in Scotland.

What's more, we were passing a row of pastel-colored houses on a seafront, and the Calais docks were ahead of us. We joined the stream making our way down the gangplank. Our luggage was located and transported to the waiting train and we walked down the corridor to find our seats. As we reached our compartment door Darcy slid it open for me. Before I could enter, a man came toward us, wearing a trilby hat, the collar of his raincoat turned up.

"Excuse me," he said, edging himself past Darcy. "Rotten day for a crossing, what?"

"Not the best," Darcy replied, "but we made it, didn't we?"

And he stood aside to let me enter the compartment first. Having done a small amount of sleuthing in my time I had sensed something: a vibration between that man and Darcy. For all their polite remoteness I could have sworn that they knew each other. Had that man been one of the only other occupants of the bar? There had been a lone man behind a newspaper in a far corner. And then I tried to picture something else. Had his hand brushed Darcy's and had he passed something across to him?

I gave my husband a questioning look, but he only responded with an encouraging smile.

"I can't believe how well you survived that crossing," he said. "I have to confess I felt a tad green myself and I'm usually a wonderful sailor. And that ship looked like one of Dante's seven levels of hell, didn't it?"

"It was pretty awful, wasn't it?" I agreed. "In fact I—" I broke off with surprise, my hand going to my stomach.

"What is it?" Darcy was instantly alert. "Is something wrong?"

I smiled, shaking my head. "Not at all. The baby just gave a real kick. I've felt some tiny stirrings before but nothing like this. Here.

Put your hand here." I took his hand and placed it on my tummy. The baby obliged by giving a well-aimed kick again. Darcy's eyes met mine. He looked awed in a way.

"Going to be a rugby player. I knew it," Darcy said, beaming now.

"Don't get your hopes up too high," I reminded him. "It might be an athletic girl."

"That would be fine too," he said. "I can't wait."

"Oh, I can. I want to enjoy Paris first."

"I hope you have a lovely time there," he said. "Make the most of it. It might be quite a while before we can travel again."

A whistle blew. The train gave a lurch and pulled out of the station.

"Darcy . . ." I began as the grimy backstreets of Calais moved past us. "This spot of business of yours. It's not going to be dangerous, is it?"

"Don't worry about it. It's all under control," he said.

It was not the answer I wanted, but it was the only one I was going to get.

"Do you want to go to the dining car for a late lunch?" Darcy asked. "Or was that sausage roll enough? I expect they'll come around with coffee and sandwiches."

"I'm still starving," I said. "Let's go and eat."

An hour later we returned to our compartment having enjoyed the miracles of French food—a fluffy shrimp omelet for me and a rare steak with frites for Darcy, followed by a chestnut meringue for me and cheese for him. I pictured happy days ahead, eating food that wasn't cooked by Queenie. I dozed for a while and when I awoke the sky had cleared. Sun was breaking through between cheerful white clouds. Flat French countryside stretched on either side, with a line of poplar trees running beside a road, a farmhouse with peeling brown shutters and fat cream-colored cows grazing in a field.

Then came the outer suburbs of Paris and then the city itself—the corner cafés, the shutters at windows, the strange signs painted on walls reminding me I was in another country. One wall proclaimed *Dubo Dubon Dubonnet* with a picture of a bottle. I was peering out of the window, hoping for a glimpse of the Eiffel Tower. I was rewarded as we went over a railway bridge and there it was, rising above the buildings in the distance. Suddenly I felt a rush of excitement. I was in Paris. I was going to stay with Belinda and we'd see all the sights and have lots of fun together, just like old times. Then we were slowing and entered the Gare du Nord, gliding smoothly to a halt. As the carriage door was opened there was a great flood of sound; the puffing and hiss of steam from the engines, whistles, shouts of porters. Darcy secured one for us; we were transferred to a taxicab and off we went into the streets of the city. It was five thirty and people were already sitting with a glass of wine at the outdoor cafés.

"It makes sense for you to stay with me tonight at the hotel," Darcy said. "You must be tired from traveling. And in the morning we can go to Belinda's. Is that all right?"

"Of course," I said. "And you're right. Belinda would no doubt whisk me off to a nightclub on my first evening."

We drove down a wide, straight boulevard lined with those typically Parisian buildings of soft yellow stone with wrought iron balconies and shutters framing the windows. Then we turned into a side street and came to a halt outside an unassuming building.

"Hôtel Saville, monsieur?" the taxi driver asked, sounding somewhat surprised.

"*Oui*," Darcy said. He helped me out.

I have to confess I too was a little surprised and disappointed, if you want the truth. I didn't expect we'd be staying at the Ritz, but I'd expected Darcy would want to stay at a proper hotel, not a pension, especially if someone else was footing the bill! This building was unassuming in the extreme. Only a glass door at the front with the name *Hôtel Saville* over it hinted that it might be some sort of pension. I stood on the sidewalk, taking in the smells—a slightly unpleasant odor of drains, a whiff of those herby French cigarettes, the more enticing scent of garlic cooking.

"This is it?" I tried not to sound disappointed.

"Come on. Let's go in," Darcy said and steered me up a couple of steps and in through a front door. Inside was a small reception area, quite clean but in no way fancy. Darcy went over to the counter and had a brief exchange with the woman in black behind it. Why do Frenchwomen always wear black? I wondered. It makes them look terrifying.

"*Et ma femme,*" I heard him say. And my wife. She looked at me and nodded.

"*Bonjour,* madame," she said. And then wished us a pleasant stay. I was now confused. Darcy had said I'd be staying with Belinda while he took care of a spot of business. Now he had made it sound as if I was to be staying here with him. He accepted a key, attached to a large block of wood, which I found funny, and then I followed him up a narrow stair to a room overlooking the street. Again it was simple but clean. Darcy tested the bedsprings, nodded and smiled. "It will do, I suppose. It has to do."

I sat on the bed. "Darcy, I'm going to Belinda's tomorrow, right?" I said. "From what you said to that woman you made it sound as if I'd be staying here."

"Ah well." He looked slightly sheepish. "It's better for all concerned that they think I've come here on a little holiday with my wife. I'll let the woman know that you'll be visiting your many friends in Paris while you're here."

"All right," I said, feeling slightly uneasy. I hate any kind of subterfuge.

"I'll take you over to Belinda in the morning."

"Oh, yes, of course," I said. "Is it far from here?"

"Not too far at all. If you followed that boulevard it would take you across the Seine, across the Île de la Cité, and her place should be not too far along the Quai. We'll take a taxi tomorrow but then there is always the Metro if you don't feel like walking." He paused, consulted his watch and then said, "Why don't you put your feet up for a while? I have to go out and find a telephone kiosk and make a phone call. Then we'll find somewhere for dinner and enjoy our first night in Paris, eh?"

I nodded, waited until he'd gone out and then lay down. The window was partly open and I could hear the sounds of the city outside—the honking of car horns, shouts, a burst of accordion music. It was too exciting for me to sleep. Instead I sat in the armchair by the window and started to write in my diary. Then I heard a voice I recognized. I went to the window and looked out. Darcy was standing on the pavement below, talking to another man. I couldn't see his face. He was wearing a trilby hat and he looked not unlike the man who had passed us on the train. In any case they were speaking English. Hidden behind the curtain I leaned out as far as I could. They were talking in low voices, making it hard to hear.

"Will she do it?" the other man asked.

"I haven't asked her. I'm not sure I want to get her involved," Darcy replied.

"It would simplify everything if she would. You can trust her, can't you? She's not likely to spill the beans to anyone?"

"Of course I can trust her. It's just that . . . well, we don't know, do we? They may be shadowing her. I wouldn't want to put her in danger."

"It is a matter of life and death, old chap," the other man said. "I thought we agreed on the plan."

A horse and cart went past with a clatter at the same time as a bus. I leaned even farther not to lose the conversation, lost my balance and only stopped myself from plunging to the street below by hanging on for dear life to the curtain. I heard an ominous ripping sound as I hauled myself back to safety. Luckily the curtain held firm. I think I must have given a little yelp, as Darcy looked up briefly. But I was back inside behind the curtain, my heart still pounding.

Anyway, my moment of drama had cost me the last few sentences of their conversation. I tuned in to hear the other man say, "So, what am I going to tell Berlin, then?"

"They are not arriving until next week, correct?" Darcy asked. "So we have a few days."

The other man muttered something I couldn't hear thanks to a motor van blaring its horn at a wayward pedestrian.

"Then let's get settled first and we'll make final plans."

"I can't stress to you the importance of this, old chap," the man said. "We'll meet on Monday. Usual place."

He tipped his hat and went on his way. Darcy lingered in the street, watching him, then turned and walked in the other direction. It was all rather disturbing. I didn't know who "she" was and why "they" might be shadowing her, who they were and why it was a matter of life and death. And Berlin? I felt a shiver of fear creeping through me. I had long ago come to the conclusion that my husband was a spy, but I always assumed it was for the British government. But what if he was a spy for the other side? What if he was being paid to help Hitler? I know Darcy felt he should be supporting his family better. What if he had offered his services to the highest bidder? I felt rather sick and sank down onto the bed. I wished I hadn't snooped and overheard. There was no way I could confront him. All this sort of stuff might be old hat for my husband, but it was upsetting to me to know he was involved in matters of life and death.

Chapter 4

SATURDAY, APRIL 18
AT THE HÔTEL SAVILLE.

Well, we are in Paris, staying at a funny little hotel on a backstreet. Tomorrow I go to stay with Belinda, leaving Darcy to get on with his "spot of business." Oh golly. I wish I hadn't overheard. I hate to think of him in danger. I hate to think what he might have got himself involved in.

Darcy didn't come back to the room for quite a while. When he did he seemed cheerful and relaxed, as if nothing had happened.

"Did you make your telephone call?" I asked innocently.

"I did. Had to walk a devil of a way to find a telephone kiosk where I could talk without too much interference," he said. "Did you have a nice rest?"

"I was too excited to rest," I said. "And now I'm getting hungry for dinner."

"You are turning into your mother." Darcy grinned. "Always hungry."

"I've got three months of puking to make up for," I said. "I actually lost weight at one stage, remember. The doctor was worried. Now I have to put it on again."

"All right," Darcy agreed. "But they dine late in Paris. Let's go out for an aperitif at one of the cafés and then we'll find somewhere for dinner. How does that sound?"

"Perfect," I said. We both spruced up and then headed toward the Seine. As we came upon the river I think I gasped. Ahead of us was the medieval stronghold of the Palais de Justice fronting the Île de la Cité. In the setting sunlight the river and the turrets glowed pink. I just stood, staring, entranced by the magical scene.

"If you are up to walking we'll go across to the other side," Darcy said, less inclined to have emotional responses to buildings. "It's the student quarter. More lively there and plenty of good little cafés."

"Oh, I'm definitely up to walking," I said. "When Belinda is working I plan to explore every inch of the city."

"Don't try to do too much." Darcy looked concerned. "Remember your condition."

"Darcy, I'm perfectly healthy now," I said. "I'm game for anything."

"That's good to know," he said, and immediately I found myself thinking about his conversation with the unknown man. Could I bring it up? Admit that I had overheard? Then I decided he'd tell me if he wanted to. Perhaps the less I knew, the better. There would be a good explanation, I told myself. He was my husband. I had to trust him.

We stopped for a Dubonnet at one of the outdoor cafés. It was a mild evening; the other tables were full of noisy groups of students, talking, gesticulating, arguing, laughing. It made me feel a pang of regret that I'd never had that stage in my life, when I'd been part of such a scene. My only outside education had been at a Swiss finishing school where we were reminded that as young ladies we should not mix with the ordinary folk. Of course Belinda ignored this instruction. She was known to climb out of our dorm window and go to join ski instructors at the local tavern. I had wished I could join her, but I didn't have the nerve.

When the sun went down a chilly breeze came off the river and we went to look for dinner. A small restaurant nearby was offering a prix fixe menu—three set courses at a reasonable price. The food was amazing: mussels in wine and herbs followed by duck breast, crispy on the outside and pink in the middle, and then a crème brûlée. The half carafe of wine went with it and we walked home feeling quite mellow. At this moment I was fully enjoying the sights and sounds of Paris, the dark waters of the Seine gliding under an old bridge. Lovers walking entwined around each other. This was the romantic Paris I had dreamed about.

"Tomorrow you'll be with Belinda," Darcy said as we undressed.

"How long do you think we'll be here?" I asked.

"My business should be concluded in a couple of weeks at the most," Darcy said. "I may have to leave in a hurry, but you can stay as long as you like and come home by yourself."

Again a shiver of worry passed through me. Leave in a hurry? I pictured him pursued, fleeing from danger. Going off to Berlin?

"When will I see you again?" I asked, and I heard a quiver in my voice.

"Oh, I'll be popping in from time to time, I expect," he said. "If you need me you can leave a message at the front desk of the hotel.

But I don't want you to worry about me. I want you to have a good time with Belinda. It's Paris in the spring. Enjoy it."

"I hope so," I said.

That night Darcy fell asleep immediately while I lay awake, wondering and worrying. He seemed quite at ease with what he had to do, but I wished I hadn't heard the word "Berlin." And that man in the trilby hat. Had his English been a little too perfect? Had I not detected the trace of a foreign accent? A German accent? I wondered what hold Berlin might have over my husband or what they might be paying him. Then I told myself that Darcy was absolutely true blue. He'd never do anything to harm his country or to harm me, however much he had been bribed. If he was going along with some kind of German intrigue, then he'd have a good ulterior motive. I just wished he could tell me about it. At last I drifted off to sleep, but my dreams were disturbed by men with guns in Nazi uniforms chasing us.

I was awoken by the sound of bells. Not the sort of bells one associates with England—the well-rehearsed, regimented peals, one bell following another. This was a cacophony: higher, lighter tones competing with the great bells of more important churches. And I realized that, of course, it was Sunday. Beside me Darcy muttered in his sleep, turned onto his back and opened his eyes. "What is that bloody row about?" he muttered.

"Church bells. It's Sunday," I said.

"Oh yes. Right." He looked at me then and smiled. "How did you sleep? The bed is quite comfy, isn't it?"

"The bed seems fine," I replied. "I have no idea what I might be sleeping on in Belinda's flat. She didn't mention whether she had a spare bedroom. I hope I'm not supposed to camp out on a couch."

"If it's too bad you can always come back here," he said. He stroked my shoulder. "I'll miss you."

"I'll miss you too. But as you said, we'll only be a few streets away."

"Yes," he agreed. "Quite close. But not as close as this." And he pulled me closer to him, nuzzling at my neck and making me laugh as it tickled. Then there was no more laughter for a while.

After we had washed and dressed we went downstairs, where a simple breakfast was laid out in a little dining room that looked onto the courtyard. Again nothing fancy, but it had pleasant checked tablecloths with vases of daffodils on them. I had looked forward to fresh rolls, croissants. But there were only stale baguettes with jam.

"It's Sunday," Darcy explained. "They don't bake on Sundays."

We drank our coffee and ate bread and jam. Then Darcy carried my suitcase downstairs and found a taxi. As we crossed the Seine again and passed through the Île de la Cité the sound of church bells became deafening. Crowds were flocking toward a building on our left. I followed them with my gaze and glimpsed Notre-Dame Cathedral, just as I'd always imagined it. That bubble of excitement rose inside me again. I was going to see all the places I'd dreamed of. I was going to have a good time, whatever my husband was doing.

We crossed the other half of the Seine by a pretty little ironwork bridge, then drove along the embankment until we turned into a side street and pulled up outside another typical Parisian building. It was built of that cream-colored stone, slightly dirty from the smoke of fires, of course, and every floor had wrought iron balconies and dark brown shutters. There was a bank of bells to one side of the front door. Now I was in a quandary as I didn't know which floor Belinda was on. I knew an American lived in the garret above her, so not the top one. I pressed four and hoped for the best. After a while I heard a buzzer sounding and then a click as the front door clicked open.

"In you go," Darcy said. "I won't come up, if you don't mind. I have things I should be doing."

"Oh, that's fine," I said. "You obviously don't want to listen to ladies' inane chatter for hours."

"Not that you two could be accused of inane chatter," he said hastily. "Go on. Up you go and have a good time. Please ask Belinda to come down to retrieve your suitcase for you. You shouldn't be lifting things." He came up the steps and slid my big suitcase into the foyer. Then he gave me a quick peck on the cheek and off he went with a cheery wave, as if he was meeting the boys for a drink and not doing something that involved Berlin.

Chapter 5

SUNDAY, APRIL 19
CHEZ BELINDA IN PARIS, ON THE LEFT BANK OF THE
SEINE.

I'm telling myself it's going to be fun with Belinda and exploring
Paris. I'm looking forward to both, but I wish I didn't have
those nagging worries about Darcy and what he'll be doing.

Darcy walked away, toward the Seine. I stared after him before I
stepped into the gloom of the foyer. The only light came from a
green skylight many floors above, making it feel that one was in an
aquarium. A marble staircase ascended around the atrium. The
floor was made of black-and-white marble squares like a checker-
board. In the center of the floor there was a wrought iron cage.
Rather alarming, actually. As I watched I heard a creaking and
groaning noise that grew louder and louder. I saw movement inside
the cage and realized that it was the lift. It descended slowly toward

me, then stopped with a clank and a shudder. An inner door slid across, then the outer one was pushed open.

I was already smiling, opening my arms and preparing to rush to Belinda's embrace. Instead a bearded man stepped out. He had tousled wet hair as if he'd just come from a bath, and he was wearing striped pajamas.

"Hi," he said, looking at me with interest.

"Oh," I said, taking a step backward. "I thought you were my friend. *Mon amie,*" I repeated, realizing I should be speaking French. I felt myself blushing. "I'm sorry. I was expecting to see Mademoiselle Belinda Warburton-Stoke. This is the right building, isn't it?"

"Oh sure," he said in American English. "Come on up. You must be Georgie?"

"Yes, that's right."

"Harry," the man said, holding out a hand. "Harry Barnstable. Belinda was taking a shower so she sent me down to get your bags. She should be out by now." He looked around. "You came alone?"

I wasn't quite sure about telling a strange man in pajamas that I was alone in a dark hallway. "My husband brought me, but he just left," I said.

"Right. Come on, then." He picked up my two pieces of luggage and ushered me toward the open door of the lift. It was a tiny cage, only big enough for two or three people. If I had been claustrophobic there was no way I'd have let him slide that door shut. As it was, my heart was still beating rapidly. After all, it's not every day that one steps into a cage with a strange man in pajamas, is it?

Harry must have seen the look of apprehension on my face. "Don't worry if this old contraption feels as if it's about to fall apart.

I am assured it has been this way since nineteen hundred and it's still going strong." The door closed with a clang. He pressed a button. There came a whirring noise and more creaking and grinding and we rose slowly.

I was still feeling highly embarrassed. Belinda's lifestyle in the past had been a little checkered, shall we say. Colorful. But I thought she had reformed of late. She had certainly been enamored of a Cornishman called Jago until recently. Would Harry Barnstable be sharing the flat with us? Would I have to face him in pajamas when I went to the bathroom? I was dying to ask for more information in a way that did not seem accusing or too inquisitive when he said, "Sorry about the outfit. I came down to Belinda to cadge a cigarette. I'd run out and I didn't want to have to get dressed to go down to the corner Tabac. I live on the top floor."

"You're the writer in the garret," I said. "Belinda mentioned you."

"Would-be writer," he said. "I keep trying and hoping, but I haven't sold anything of consequence yet. A few articles about Paris. A couple of obituaries. Hardly a great body of work to show for my years here. I've come to the conclusion that I'm no Hemingway or Fitzgerald. They were both here, you know. I met them both at Gertrude's. God, but that man thought a lot of himself—Hemingway, I mean. He acted as if we were expected to kiss the ring! And I gather he is coming back. Passing through on the way to Spain, so I hear. He's going to report on the civil war that's just breaking out. Loves danger, does our Ernest."

All the time he was talking we were rising slowly, giving me glimpses of one gloomy landing after another. The smells of French cigarettes, freshly ground coffee, baking. I caught snatches of music from a radio, a child's voice. We came to a shuddering halt and Harry slid open the inner door before pushing the outer one, holding it for me to exit.

"Door on your right," he said. "Go on in. It's open. She might still be getting dressed."

I turned the handle and walked through a small hallway. Light streamed in from an open door ahead and I stepped into a lovely bright room with French windows opening onto a balcony. The furniture looked both chic and comfortable—brocade-covered armchairs, a big sofa, low tables, a writing desk in a corner. An ormolu clock ticked loudly on the mantelpiece.

"Take a seat," Harry said. "I'll let her know you're here."

He disappeared. I heard an exchange of voices and he came back. "She'll be out in a minute," he said. "She's put the coffee on." He gave me a big, friendly grin and took a seat across from me. I was able to see him in the daylight for the first time: dark hair streaked with gray at the sides, bushy beard, also with hints of gray, in need of a trim. But not unattractive. It was hard to judge his age. Forties, maybe . . .

"You live upstairs, then," I said, uneasy in the silence and trying not to focus on the pajamas.

"It's not as grand as this place, I can tell you," he said. "Pretty basic, really, and freezing cold in winter, but it suits my needs. And a great view of the Seine if I lean way out of the window."

"Have you been in Paris long, Mr. Barnstable?" I asked.

"Harry, please. I'm a Yank. We don't stand on ceremony," he said. "And yes, I've been here for years now. I came after the Great War and I stayed."

"You were over here in the army then, I presume."

He nodded. "Oh yes. I was in the army, all right. And I don't wish to remember it. It was hell. Although hell might be better, as it's supposed to be hot. All I remember was freezing cold. Feet rotting in wet boots. Rats. Men dying in mud." And he shuddered as if he were there again.

"So what else do you do besides write?" I asked, rapidly changing the subject for him.

"Whatever I can get, really." He grinned again. "I've tutored spoiled French kids in English. I write the obituaries for the *New York Herald*. Sometimes I run a bookstall on the Quai for an old guy who doesn't like being out in the cold and damp. I get by. There is always something." He paused. "When all else fails I work as a bartender at Harry's."

"Harry's? What is that?"

He looked at me as if I were a creature from another planet. "Harry's New York Bar. It's world famous, honey. The first cocktail bar in Paris. Inventor of the Bloody Mary. Hemingway used to hang out there. He may show up this week, like I said. I should take you there."

"Oh, I'm not sure my husband would approve of me going to a bar with a strange man," I said.

"Nothing strange about me." Harry laughed. "I'm a regular good guy."

"Don't you miss America?" I asked. "Your family?"

"I'm no longer in touch with my family," he said, and his expression told me not to pursue that line of conversation. "But how about you? Belinda says you're high and mighty. Cousin of the king, right?"

"That's right," I said. "But I'm not far enough up the line of succession to get any benefits. No money or house or anything from them. Luckily I've a godfather who likes to go off climbing mountains and exploring places. He's never home and he has given me the use of his lovely country house, which is good as I'm newly married and we're having a baby this summer."

"Congratulations," he said. "Oh, am I supposed to call you 'Your Highness' or something?"

"If you're Harry, then I'm Georgie." I smiled at him.

"Great." He beamed at me. I realized if he had been in Paris since the Great War that he must be in his mid- to late thirties. There were frown lines showing up on his forehead, but when he smiled he looked younger with a boyish charm. I could see that Belinda might have fallen for him. As this thought was passing through my head she came into the room, wearing a black silk robe, trimmed with black feathers, her hair wrapped in a towel. She managed to make the outfit look impossibly glamorous.

"Georgie, darling!" she exclaimed. "I'm so sorry I wasn't there to greet you. I was at a bit of a party last night and didn't get home until the wee hours. And forgot to set my alarm clock. If dear Harry had not come down and banged on my door I might still be asleep. But here I am, and here you are!" She came across the room to me, arms open. I rose to give her a hug. She paused before she reached me and I saw her taking a good stare at me. "Look at you!" she exclaimed. "You're positively blooming." And she patted my middle. Why is it that everyone feels they need to pat a pregnant woman's stomach?

"I don't know about blooming," I said as I hugged her. "But I'm definitely spreading. None of my clothes fit me and this skirt is held with an enormous safety pin. When I get back I'll get the local seamstress to make me some tentlike garments."

"Darling, you can't go around in tentlike garments," Belinda said. "I'll design you some chic outfits that hide a multitude of sins." And she chuckled in her delightful throaty way. "I've never tried designing a maternity dress, so it will be a fun challenge. Not until after the new collection, of course. We'll be going crazy for the next week to have everything in order. I did tell you that Chanel is letting me include one of my designs. So exciting . . ."

When she stopped for breath Harry got up. "I should be going,

Belinda. I've probably shocked your friend enough by appearing in my pajamas, and I've got to watch the stall for ole Jacques today." He held out his hand to me. "Nice to meet you, Georgie. I'll see you around. I'm always stopping by, usually bumming a cigarette or some bread from Belinda. It was a godsend when she moved in here. Now I no longer have to worry about starving." He grinned as he said it. "See you around, ladies. Maybe Georgie would like to attend one of Gertrude's salons while she's here."

"I'm sure she would," Belinda said. "Such an interesting mix of people."

"Have fun, girls. Be good." Harry blew us a kiss and went.

Chapter 6

SUNDAY, APRIL 19
AT BELINDA'S FLAT, JUST OFF THE QUAI D'ORSAY, PARIS.

**After having been met by a man in his pajamas, things have become
more normal and pleasant. I'm going to have a good time with
Belinda, whatever happens.**

"He's such a dear," Belinda said after Harry had closed her front
door after him.

I gave her an inquisitive look. "And he feels comfortable coming
into your flat in pajamas?"

She laughed. "He is a little unorthodox, I agree. But that's how
the arty set behave in Paris. Very free and easy in all ways."

"Is Jago long forgotten?" We had met Jago last year and Belinda
had fallen for him in a big way.

"Oh, darling. Nothing like that with Harry," Belinda said. "I
do enjoy his company and he knows an interesting mix of people
here, but he simply wouldn't do as a lover. Too neurotic and ner-

vous. And penniless. That wouldn't do at all. I couldn't have a relationship in which I was the one with the money." She sank onto the sofa beside me. "As for Jago—I really don't know. I was really attracted, you know. And I think we got along so well. But then I sensed he was cooling off. Again it might have had to do with money. I have a lot of it. He doesn't. That's hardly the basis for a good relationship. And then there's the class thing. It shouldn't matter, but it does."

"I know," I said. "I go through it every time with my grandfather. He's just not easy when he stays with me because he doesn't know where he belongs. He's not comfortable in the sitting room being served tea, but he's not a servant either. It's quite stupid, but it's always there."

"It's not the same in Paris," Belinda said. "At least not among the bohemian types that Harry mixes with. I gather, by the way, that his family in America is quite high-powered, but he never speaks of them. Obviously a falling-out years ago. On the other hand, speaking of class, did I write to tell you about my French count?"

"You did mention him in your letter once. Is he still sending flowers?"

"Regularly. He may drop in today, so you'll be able to see him. Stunningly handsome, of course, and frightfully correct. Unmarried at thirty-five, which makes one wonder . . . but he has a dragon of a mother, I gather. Anyway, I'm taking it all as good clean fun." She laughed. "Speaking of dragons, did you encounter ours in the front hall?"

"Dragon?" I looked puzzled.

"The concierge, darling. She usually leaps out of her cubby when anyone comes past. And she's always mopping the floor so that it's slick as an ice rink."

"She wasn't there when I came in," I said.

"Oh, of course not. It's Sunday. She goes to mass and then has lunch with her sister on Sundays. You'll meet her and her cat tomorrow. Watch out for your ankles."

"Thank you for the warning," I said. "I presume I'll be amusing myself all week while you are working."

"This week, definitely," she said. "And next week is the unveiling of Chanel's fall collection."

I frowned. "Don't you mean spring collection?"

Belinda smiled. "Absolutely not, darling. It's to show buyers what everyone will be wearing in the autumn. Real fashion shows with a runway and press photographers. An absolute giggle. You must come to at least one of them. It's such fun to watch rich women fighting over the dresses they want. Chanel says it's a competition. None of them can wear the same dress, of course. And speaking of rich women . . ." She made a face. "What a pain they are. Trying to sneak a look at the collection ahead of time. You should see how Coco deals with them. Not at all intimidated by wealth or status in her own domain. She's brilliant. You wait till you meet her."

"Actually I have met her before," I said. "When I was staying with my mother in the South of France, Chanel was there with Vera Bate and I was forced to model in a fashion show. Utter disaster, naturally."

"Oh no, poor Georgie. What did you do?"

"I tripped in very high platform shoes and fell off the runway," I said, not adding that I had been wearing Queen Mary's necklace and in the melee afterward it was stolen. It was one of those embarrassing memories. I also remembered something about a handsome Frenchman. . . . I shut off that memory rapidly.

"So what do you want to do today?" Belinda asked. "It's lovely weather. We could take a picnic to Luxembourg. . . ."

"Luxembourg. Isn't that miles and miles away across Belgium?"

Belinda laughed. "Oh sorry. Silly of me. I meant the Jardin du Luxembourg. The nearby gardens. So pretty in the spring. Or we could picnic by the Seine, or go up to Montmartre."

"They all sound divine," I said. "But I'm dying to see the Eiffel Tower. I've come in and out of Paris several times and never really seen it."

"Then we'll picnic on the Champ de Mars," Belinda said.

I translated mentally. "The field of battle?"

She smiled. "It's what the park next to the Eiffel Tower is called. Very pretty view. I got in all sorts of provisions yesterday—half a cold chicken, pâté, cheeses and olives and rolls that should still be fresh."

"Goodness," I said. "What a feast."

"Well, it's not every day that my best friend comes to visit," Belinda said. "Come on. I'll show you to your room."

She led me through to a small bedroom off to one side. In contrast to the opulent feel of the sitting room, "spartan" was the word for it as this contained a single bed, a small wardrobe and a chest of drawers.

"I know it's rather dismal," she said, "but it's only supposed to be the box room for my bedroom. It's a one-person flat, apparently. But you'll only be sleeping in it and it is quite quiet, looking onto the courtyard, unless that infernal woman starts sweeping at eight o'clock in the morning." She stepped away again. "And the bathroom is right here. Lots of lovely hot water from the geyser, so have a bath anytime you feel like it."

She then showed me her bedroom and a small neat kitchen.

"I'm impressed, Belinda," I said. "You don't have your maid with you? Who cooks? Who looks after your clothes?"

She waved her hands. "Simple, darling. I take my main meal at Chanel. They eat their big meal in the middle of the day in France, apparently, and at night it's usually just a baguette and pâté or cheese, or something from the café around the corner. And I'm not often home. Harry is always dragging me off to a poetry reading or art show or something, and they always serve food and drink. It's a pleasant life, really."

"How long do you think you'll stay on here, then?" I asked. "Aren't you dying to open your own salon and produce your own clothes?"

"Actually, there is no rush. I'm learning all the time and getting better at designing. I don't need the money. And frankly, I don't really know whether I want to be dealing with clients. Coco says the rich ones are the worst. They never want to pay and you have to resort to blackmail to get the money out of them. But she's so good at things like that. I'm not sure I'm quite so ruthless."

"She's certainly a force of nature," I agreed. "She was the one who convinced me to model for her, in spite of my protests."

Belinda smiled. "But at least you'll be spared that now, unless she whips up a maternity collection."

"I'm looking forward to meeting her again, and seeing where you work too. Do you think you can bring me along one day?"

"Of course," she said. "Only don't be surprised if we are all rushing around crazily this week. But you can certainly come to one of the shows next weekend."

I unpacked as much as I could while Belinda dried her hair and dressed. Then we had some coffee (Belinda had an amazing machine that belched out steam and made coffee) and caught up on the time since we'd seen each other.

"So what's Darcy doing over here in Paris?" Belinda asked. "When you wrote to say you were coming I thought it might be a romantic trip for the two of you—a last escape à deux before the baby arrives."

I shook my head. "Oh no," I said. "You know Darcy. There is always something he has to do and can't talk about."

"Like turning up in Cornwall disguised as someone else when we were there."

"Like that," I agreed. "But I get the feeling this one is even more dangerous. In fact I'm not sure . . ." I wanted to tell her about the encounter and that ominous phrase, "What am I going to tell Berlin?" But I couldn't. He was my husband. A good man. He would never . . .

"You're not sure what?" Belinda asked.

"Oh, not sure he'd ever tell me if I pressed him," I finished. "He seems quite cheerful and relaxed, but you never know with Darcy."

"It's time that lad settled down and got a good steady job somewhere," Belinda said.

"That's what he said, but he'd hate a nine-to-five job, Belinda. I want him to be happy."

"And presumably stay alive," she added.

Golly. I wish she hadn't said that.

Chapter 7

SUNDAY, APRIL 19

**We're going to the Champ de Mars, next to the Eiffel Tower. And
we're taking a spectacular picnic. I'm excited. I think I'm going
to have a good time and try not to worry about Darcy.**

By lunchtime Belinda had packed a picnic basket, a rug and even a
parasol in case the sun was too bright, and we set off. As the lift
groaned and bumped to a halt on the ground floor we came out
into the sunshine to see someone about to press the doorbells.

"Louis-Philippe!" Belinda exclaimed. "What a lovely surprise."
She said the latter in French.

I could just see a man's dark hair and parts of a dark suit half
hidden behind a huge display of spring flowers. The scent of mimosa wafted toward me. He lowered them enough to look at her.
Enough for me to see that he was very handsome in a dark and
Gallic way, his hair smoothed into a perfect wave and with brown
eyes that flashed with pleasure at seeing Belinda.

"I came as soon as I could get away from my mother," he said. "We have been to mass together." His face fell. "But you are leaving? You are going out somewhere?"

"We're just going on a picnic," Belinda said. "This is my friend Georgie, newly arrived from England."

"Georgie?" He gave me a doubtful look.

Belinda sighed. "I suppose I'd better do this properly. Lady Georgiana Rannoch O'Mara, may I present Count Louis-Philippe de Montaigre. Georgie is a cousin of our king."

His expression changed. He extricated one hand from the bouquet and held it out to me. "*Enchanté*, my lady," he said. Then switched to English. "And welcome to my city. May you have a happy time here. Are you here on a visit?"

"Yes, I came with my husband, who has business here," I said.

"Business?" He looked puzzled. "He is not a fellow aristocrat?"

"He is, but he always undertakes certain assignments for the government."

"Ah. A diplomat. I see."

I thought it wise not to expand on this.

"So do you want to come on a picnic with us?" Belinda asked.

"Where do you go on this peek-neek?" he asked.

"Champ de Mars," Belinda said. "Georgie hasn't ever seen the Eiffel Tower properly."

"But it is Sunday. It will be crawling with people," he said. "Footballs and screaming children and dogs. Most unpleasant."

"I'm sure we'll find a corner somewhere," Belinda said. "Only come if you want to."

"I wish to spend time with you," he said. "So if necessary I will endure the peek-neek."

Belinda took the bouquet from him. "Thank you for the flowers. I'd better run up and put these in water first," she said. "They are lovely. And they smell divine. You are an angel."

He gazed at her adoringly now. Oh Belinda, I thought. Be careful. We waited, making the sort of small talk one does with a person one has only just met. Yes, the weather was fine. And yes, I did find Paris beautiful. I prayed for the lift to hurry up.

"My automobile awaits," Louis-Philippe said as Belinda returned. "Come."

"We could walk. It's a lovely day and it's along the Quai."

"*Non non*. Is too far," he said. "And the basket is heavy," and he picked up the picnic basket. Then he strode out for a large, dark maroon Citroën car parked nearby. He seated me with great civility in the backseat, tucking a rug around my knees before assisting Belinda into the front seat beside him. As we drove I was rather glad he had insisted on driving. It wasn't too far, but far enough, and I was not wearing my stout walking shoes. We passed a large ornate building on the quayside that Belinda said was a train station. It seemed a funny place for a train station, but who can understand the French? We rounded a bend in the river and there it was—the Eiffel Tower in all its majesty. It quite took my breath away. So incredibly tall and beautiful. I must have given a little gasp.

"It's rather impressive, I agree," Belinda said.

"Did you know they were going to pull it down?" Louis-Philippe said, turning back to me. "They built it for the great exhibition and it was the plan to pull it down afterward. Everyone thought it was an iron monstrosity. But it survived."

As we came closer I had to crane my neck to stare up at it. We parked the car and I kept on staring up at the impossibly tall structure. How could anyone have thought it a monstrosity?

We went up into the park.

"Where do you plan to sit?" Louis-Philippe asked.

"Here will do perfectly." Belinda went to spread out the rug.

"You plan to sit on the grass?" Louis-Philippe sounded horrified. "But it is damp. It will give you a chill."

"Nonsense. It hasn't rained for days," Belinda said. "And the rug is thick. Come on. Sit down."

"But I shall get grass stains on my trousers," he said. "And the creases will be ruined. And your dress—you will expose your knees, I think."

"Don't be such a fuddy-duddy," Belinda said.

"What is this? Fuddy-duddy?" he asked.

"A stick-in-the-mud."

"Where is this mud?" he asked, looking around nervously. "I do not have a stick with me."

When we both chuckled, he looked hurt and Belinda explained it was an English expression.

"Very silly, these English expressions," he commented.

To appease him Belinda suggested we move our picnic site across the park so that he could sit on a bench and thus not spoil his immaculate trousers while we spread the rug at his feet. I think he liked the idea of two adoring young women sitting at his feet and agreed to this. And so a pleasant picnic was had by all, and Louis-Philippe was delighted Belinda had brought a bottle of champagne that he had given her.

"Truly you are learning good taste," he said. "But I almost forgot the purpose of my mission—apart from seeing you, of course. My mother, the countess, would like to invite you to dine at her house on Wednesday."

"Gosh," Belinda said, sounding more like me than the sophisticated person I had always taken her for. "How lovely, Louis-Philippe. But I do have Lady Georgiana staying with me."

"My mother would be delighted to entertain a fellow aristocrat," he said. "You are most welcome, my lady. And I must tell you that my mother keeps a very fine table. You will not be disappointed."

"You're most kind," I said.

"And your husband? He will be with you? Please feel free to invite him also."

"I'm afraid he will probably be busy," I said. "But I will extend your generous invitation."

As we cleared up the remains of the picnic Louis-Philippe touched my arm. "Would you perhaps like to go up the tower? The view from the top is spectacular."

I gazed upward, dubiously. I was now carrying rather more weight than usual. "There must be an awful lot of stairs," I said.

"No, no, no." He shook his head. "There is an *ascenseur*. A leeft, you know."

"Oh," I said. "In that case I'd love to go up."

"You two go." Belinda waved her hand. "I'll stay here and guard our things."

"If you're sure?" He looked as if he was about to set off to Antarctica. "*À bientôt*, then, my darling." And he blew her a kiss.

It was such a dramatic parting that I tried not to smile. We went across to the tower, paid our money and joined the line for the lift. The first lift took us to a broad platform. We walked around, taking in the view from all sides. Louis-Philippe was a good tour guide. He pointed out the gardens and fountains of the Trocadéro on the other side of the river, the Arc de Triomphe looking quite small and insignificant from this height. He named gardens and parks, the impressive expanse of woodland that was the Bois de Boulogne, and on the far side of the city, high on a hill, a building with glistening white domes that even I knew was the Sacré-Coeur on Montmartre. It was all quite breathtaking and somehow gratifying to know that monuments I had dreamed about really did exist and that now I was among them.

My gaze moved down to the Seine below us, the river busy with pleasure boats on a Sunday afternoon. On the quayside I spotted a man with a bald head, poring over a large map. As I focused on him he approached a passing stranger, pointing at the map. The man stopped obligingly and pointed out a route. The first man nodded thanks, then set off. The other man watched him for a moment before turning away.

From this height it was impossible to see faces, but I could have sworn that the man who gave the directions was Darcy. I knew the way he walked, the way he tilted his head just a little when he was listening. Was he just being polite to a tourist, or was this more? I tried to recall exactly what I had seen. Had he just pointed at the map, or had something passed between them? A small piece of paper? As if in answer to my question, I saw two men who had been standing at the coffee kiosk on the quay move out of the shadow and set off after the man with the map.

$\mathcal{C}$hapter 8

This is such a strange experience for me. I go from being delighted
at being in Paris, enjoying being with Belinda, to reminding
myself that I'm worried about Darcy. I know that he does this
kind of thing from time to time, but surely he can't be involved
in any kind of intrigue with Germany. There must be a sensible
explanation. I just wish I hadn't seen it.

The vision of that brief encounter haunted me as Louis-Philippe
escorted me to the very top of the Eiffel Tower and we looked out
over the whole of Paris: the sparkling white domes of the Sacré-
Coeur basilica on top of Montmartre in one direction, the twin
towers of Notre-Dame in the other. He told me that no building in
Paris may be higher than the cathedral. How lovely. They still value
what's important.

I was probably rather quiet as we rode the lift down again, but

I expect Louis-Philippe put that down to being apprehensive about traveling in a little cage at quite a speed. I attempted to be sociable and bright as we returned to Belinda, put the picnic basket in the car and then walked along the bank of the Seine, enjoying the mild day and the view across the river to another park with spectacular fountains.

"I regret that I must now leave you," Louis-Philippe said as we drove to Belinda's flat. "My mother has invited the parish priest to dinner. I am expected to be present." He gave an embarrassed shrug. "One does not refuse the priest, you know. But I will see you on Wednesday, yes? We will have a splendid dinner. And every moment in between I shall be thinking of you, my little Belinda."

At the door he shook my hand and planted a chaste kiss on her cheek. The look in his eyes said he wished I wasn't there and the kiss would not be so chaste.

"I'm sorry if I was playing gooseberry," I remarked as we went into her building. "It was quite clear he wanted to be alone with you."

"Don't be silly," she said. "I'm not sure whether I want to encourage him or not. He is awfully rich and he's a count and all that, but I can see that his mother might be a problem, can't you?"

"Oh, absolutely," I said. "And he did make a fuss about the crease in his trousers."

She laughed at that. "Yes, he wouldn't do well at an English country house, would he? All of us mucking about in tweeds, going out shooting or fishing and coming back covered in mud."

"All of us stick-in-the-muds," I said and we laughed.

At the sound of our laughter a door to our left opened and a figure came surging out. In the gloom it was hard to see her features but she was a large lady, dressed in black.

"Oh, it's you, mademoiselle," she said, glaring at us. I could feel her eyes boring into me. "And this person is?"

"My friend visiting me from England," Belinda said. "An English my lady."

"Oh?" I saw this made an impression. "Milady? *Bonjour*, milady." I think she attempted a curtsy.

"*Bonjour*, madame," I replied.

"And she speaks French!" the woman exclaimed, as if this was an amazing feat.

"I do," I replied. "It is required that English aristocrats speak French. After all, it is the lingua franca of the world."

This pleased her, I could tell. She nodded. "Well, I wish you a happy stay in my city," she said and scurried back into her sanctuary.

Belinda was grinning as we rode up to her flat. "You made an impression," she said. "Usually she makes my visitors feel that doom will fall at any moment. If they once step out of line."

"She's only the caretaker, did you say?" I asked.

"She is. From the way she acts you'd think she owned the building." Belinda opened the front door and we went inside. "So what do you want to do now?"

"A little rest," I said. "We've done quite a bit of walking."

"I agree. Rest, then tea, then let's go out to dinner."

We spent a pleasant evening with another good meal that left me feeling relaxed and content. I slept well in the narrow little bed and awoke to see the sun streaming in on me. Belinda was up and dressed when I came out.

"I have to leave soon," she said. "Coco will not be pleased if I'm late. But take your time. Enjoy a bath. I've left croissants in the kitchen and the coffee is still warm in the saucepan. Come and visit me later and I'll show you around Chanel."

I thanked her and off she went. I sat in the window, eating my croissants and watching life on the street below. About eleven o'clock I took the guidebook Belinda had left out for me and set off to find the Rue Cambon. Having studied the map in the back of the book I crossed the Seine and saw the Place de la Concorde ahead of me. I recognized it instantly from postcards and walked around the edge of it, staying clear of the manic traffic, passing the edge of the gardens that had to be the Tuileries, until I came to the lovely colonnades of the Rue de Rivoli. I paused to stare at enticing shop windows and little cafés, then found the Rue Cambon leading away from the gardens. A very good address, I realized. Right in the heart of the most fashionable part of the city. But of course. Only the best for Coco Chanel.

I passed a hotel, banks, other shops until I came to the imposing front entrance of number thirty-one. In the windows were spare displays of a cardigan, a purse, a scarf, perfume. There were no prices. If you had to ask the price at Chanel, you couldn't afford it! Now I was here I felt my natural shyness returning. Should I really go in to say hello when they were so frightfully busy? Through the glass doors I could see the plush carpet, soft lighting and glass-fronted cases of the boutique on the ground floor. Quite intimidating for someone like me who had worn mainly castoffs all her life. I was sure they'd take one look at my dowdy outfit and indicate I was in the wrong place.

I decided this was one occasion to pull rank. I took a deep breath and went in through those glass doors.

"Madame?" An assistant headed toward me, her face expressionless.

Before she could say another word I said, in French I had rehearsed on the way over, "I am Lady Georgiana Rannoch, and I'm here to see Miss Belinda Warburton-Stoke and to renew my acquaintance with Madame Chanel."

Before she could reply there was a squeal of delight from across the boutique.

"Georgie, darling. What a lovely surprise!" And my dear friend Zou Zou, who was really Princess Zamanska, came flying toward me. "What are you doing here, dear girl?" she asked.

"I came over with Darcy," I said. "He has some business here. I had no idea you were in Paris. I thought you were supposed to be flying around the world."

Zou Zou made a face. "I was supposed to be doing that, but my mechanic warned me that the engine might not hold up in a sandstorm. But my little plane was dying to go somewhere. So I said to myself, 'What the heck. When in doubt go to Paris and do some shopping.' So here I am."

She was beaming at me, her luxuriant dark curls framing an ageless face. A small mink stole was draped around her neck. She looked, as always, impossibly elegant. I looked up to see the assistants watching us from a respectful distance.

"*Madame est une grande amie de moi*," Zou Zou said to them. She is a great friend. They nodded, smiling. One of them rushed to bring a chair over to me. Zou Zou's eyes traveled to the bulge inside my cardigan.

"But of course you should not be standing," she said. "Quite right."

"Oh, I'm perfectly fine. Never felt better," I said. "It's just that none of my clothes fit me."

I should not have said that. Instantly she replied, "Then we must find you something to wear immediately." And she started looking around her.

"No, I didn't mean that," I said hastily. "Absolutely not, Zou Zou. Please get on with your shopping and I must go up to see Belinda."

"Can we meet for dinner, then?" she asked. "Naturally I'm at the Ritz, just around the corner. Are you far away?"

"On the other bank, but not far."

"Splendid, then. Come to dinner at the Ritz. The food isn't bad."

I thought this might be an understatement and tried not to smile. I was about to say that I was staying with Belinda when she said, "Bring Darcy, naturally. I'm dying to see the dear boy again."

I felt my cheeks flushing. "Actually Darcy is rather busy so I'm staying with Belinda. She's working here, you know. With Chanel. Helping with the new collection. I popped in to see her." I could hear I was babbling.

Zou Zou frowned. "You had the chance for a romantic week with your husband in Paris and you are staying with Belinda? What is wrong with you two?" She paused. "Or is he treating you delicately because of the baby?"

"He's rather preoccupied, and having a wife around might complicate things," I said. "And of course I was dying to see Belinda again."

"Of course." She nodded as if she didn't agree. "Well, bring Belinda, then. By all means."

"That would be lovely," I said. "What time?"

"Shall we say eight? I'll look forward to it. We have lots of catching up to do. Did you ever find your chef? That agency I sent you to is so good."

"Long story," I said. "I'll tell you later. You need to get back to your shopping."

"I certainly do. The poor little thing has hung up all these garments waiting for me to try them on. Of course I won't buy too much now, knowing that the fall collection is coming out next week. I'm dying to see what is new. And between us, I'm also going to have a look at Schiaparelli. My dear, she is so adventurous these days. Almost outlandish. I do like making a splash, but not to shock. Do I dare wear an evening dress with a mermaid tail, I wonder?" And she giggled like a little girl.

We kissed on the cheek and I was escorted up a most impressive curved staircase, lined with mirrors. We came out to the salon, now already set up with the runway down the middle and gilt and white satin chairs positioned around the edges. It was unoccupied at the moment and the assistant peered upward. "Madame will probably be in the workshop," she said. "Do you wish me to announce you?"

"Oh no, thank you," I said. "I can make my own way."

I started up a second, equally grand stair. I caught sight of my reflection in the mirrors as I went up. Goodness but I looked frumpy—hair windblown, no makeup, shapeless skirt. I almost turned around and crept down again, but then I'd have to face Zou Zou and she'd only march me straight back up. I did find myself thinking how nice it would be to fly to Paris to take a look at the new collection and always be in fashion. But then my lifestyle with a baby in a country house did not exactly call for the latest in fashion.

I could hear sounds of activity before I reached the workshop level. The clatter of sewing machines, shouted commands, raised voices . . . I came into a large open space dotted with sewing machines, three-way mirrors at one end, bolts of cloth stacked everywhere and more cloth spread over cutting tables. Lots of dark heads with hair in neat buns hard at work. I paused at the threshold, not daring to halt this hive of activity. I looked around but could not see Belinda anywhere. I was still deciding which of the busy seamstresses I should approach when Chanel herself came into the room.

"Claudette. The sequins. They will work, won't they?" she called. Then she looked up and saw me.

"What are you doing here?" she demanded, striding across the length of the room toward me. "Out. Out. No outsiders of any sort. Who let you come up here? She will be fired instantly. Go away. Go away."

Chapter 9

MONDAY, APRIL 20

AT CHANEL, 31 RUE CAMBON.

I've just had a rather overwhelming morning: first Zou Zou and
    then an irate Chanel in full fury. Golly! My heart is still beating
    rapidly.

Madame Chanel bore down on me, flapping her arms as if shooing
away pigeons. Before I could turn to flee or try to explain my presence she stopped about three feet from me. I expected to be struck
or shoved or even strangled, but suddenly her expression changed.

"*Mon dieu!* It is the little Rannoch girl, Bertie's daughter.
Claire's daughter. Georgie, *n'est-ce pas?*"

"*Oui,*" I managed to get the word out.

"A thousand apologies," she said. "I thought you were an intruder, come to spy on my new collection before I reveal it to the
public next week. We have had many such, you know. Newspaper

people trying to get a scoop. Rich women wanting to snag the best pieces for themselves, or even spies from other designers wanting to see what items of genius I have created this time. Schiaparelli, you know. She will stop at nothing. And have you seen what she is doing this year? Only fit for the carnival." She paused for breath and then to my amazement she stepped forward, embraced me and kissed me on both cheeks.

"You forgive me, I hope?" she said. "Your little friend said that you might pay us a visit. Come. She is upstairs." She took my hand and dragged me up another flight of stairs, this one not so grand. Belinda was sitting at a table, poring over a chart of some sort. She looked up, smiling, when she saw me.

"Oh hello, Georgie. You found it all right, then?"

"Apart from being torn to pieces by the owner," Coco said in French, giving me her dazzling smile. She was simply dressed in a black cashmere jumper with her signature pearls at her neck, and really stunningly beautiful, although she was no longer young. "I regret that I mistook her for another of those intruders."

"Have we had another one today?" Belinda asked.

"Not so far. But the day is young," Coco said.

Belinda nodded. "You would not believe the cheek of some people. Respectable women. Rich women. You have to witness how madame scares them off." She glanced at her employer and chuckled. "Such fun to watch her in action."

"I can safely say that no woman has ever got the better of me," Coco said, with a small satisfied grin. "No man either, for that matter." She peered over Belinda's shoulder and I saw that she was working on a seating chart.

"A very important task," Chanel said. "We have the crowned heads of Europe coming to my fashion shows. It is important that enemies are not seated too close to each other, that one royal person is not given a better seat than another, or they will not buy my garments."

"And the ladies who intrude?" I asked.

Chanel gave a deep throaty chuckle. "We shall seat them at the back, next to the powder room—if there are any tickets still to be had."

On the far wall I spotted a rack of garments, half covered in tissue paper. Those must be the new designs for the show. I was dying to take a look but Chanel didn't offer and I didn't dare ask. Instead I pulled up a chair across from Belinda and waited patiently while she worked. Coco disappeared into her private apartment. Finally Belinda gave a sigh and looked up. "That is the best I can do," she said. "You'll be thrilled to know that your dear friend Mrs. Simpson is scheduled to attend the first showing."

"Oh no. How awful," I said. "Why can I never seem to escape from her for long?"

"Well, she is linked to your cousin, isn't she? She may well be his wife soon enough."

"Surely not," I exclaimed. "I don't see how that could ever happen. It would create a constitutional crisis. It might even bring down the monarchy."

Belinda nodded. "I foresee interesting times ahead. From what I've heard of the lady, she likes to get her own way and I think she intends to be queen."

I laughed. "Don't be ridiculous. Can you see the British public accepting a Queen Wallis? A twice-divorced Queen Wallis. It can never happen." The laughter faded. "Golly," I said, "I hope it doesn't happen. It would kill Queen Mary. She'd been dreading this for ages."

"Perhaps we can arrange to bump her off between us at the showing," Belinda said. "Stuff her in a bolt of cloth."

"Belinda, you are wicked," I said, laughing again now.

Coco Chanel came back into the room, now wearing a mannish tweed jacket over her black jumper and skirt. "Let's go and get some lunch, *mes petites.*"

"Oh, that's not necessary," I said. "I know how frightfully busy you are. I should go and leave you two to get on with your work."

"Nonsense," Chanel said. "One has to eat, even on the most frantic days. Come, Belinda, get your coat. I think we go to the Ritz."

Being invited to the Ritz twice in one day was not something that happened to me a lot. Never before, actually. I was now horribly conscious of how dowdy I looked compared to the two of them.

"But I'm not dressed for the Ritz," I said.

Chanel eyed me critically. "No, probably not. You are dressed to go tramping with dogs through the British countryside. But you are an eccentric aristocrat. They will overlook—" She paused. "You know what," she said. "Just a minute."

She disappeared then came back holding a white fox stole. This she draped around my shoulders. "Wear the right fur and you can get away with murder," she said, chuckling.

Conscious that I was wearing an expensive piece of incredibly soft white fur around my neck and was liable to spill soup on it, I wanted to decline. I had a mental tussle between wanting to refuse the offer and looking out of place. The latter won. I didn't want to embarrass the two chic women beside me. Chanel barked some last-minute orders as we passed through each level. We had reached the salon when we heard raised voices.

"Madame. You may not proceed. I have told you before." I heard a high French voice speaking English.

"Does this Chanel woman know who I am? I have money to

spend, you know." Definitely an American woman. "And I don't like to wait."

"You know who that is, don't you?" Chanel muttered. "The impossible Mrs. Rottenburger. She was here the other day, remember?"

Belinda nodded.

"Enough is enough," Chanel said. She smoothed down her jacket and descended the staircase. Belinda and I lurked, expectantly.

"How kind of you to visit us again, madame," Chanel's voice floated up. "But I thought we made it quite clear that nobody is allowed upstairs until the actual day of the showing. Absolutely nobody sees my collection before Sunday. Not even the crowned heads of Europe who will be there in force. Now, if one of my assistants could interest you in a handbag or scarf while you wait."

"This is ridiculous," came the angry American voice. "Do you French people not actually want good American money?"

"Madame, you have obviously not been in Europe long enough to know that money cannot buy everything," Chanel said. "*Bonjour*. We will no doubt see you at one of my showings."

We came down the stairs to see a large figure storming out like a ship under full sail. She was wearing a dark mink and an extravagant-looking hat with lots of feathers. The two did not go together. And in her wake was a smaller person dressed in a humble raincoat and carrying a large umbrella. A daughter? I wondered. A maid, probably.

"Another battle won," Chanel said, turning to us. "Now I think we need a little champagne to fortify ourselves."

We set off down the Rue Cambon. It seemed that everybody knew her. There were polite bows and murmured *bonjours* as we made our way to the magnificent butter-yellow building occupying the whole of one side of the Place Vendôme. Chanel stalked in as if she owned the place. We followed in her wake.

The doorman and other employees also greeted her by name as we made our way through to the dining room.

"I do love this place," she said as we were seated at a delightful table next to a giant display of flowers. "So civilized. So welcoming. I'm thinking of taking a suite here rather than living above the shop. That is so bourgeois, don't you think?"

Having heard the story of her humble beginnings I was amused by this. In many ways she reminded me of my mother, who had come from equally humble origins but now expected to be treated as a dowager duchess everywhere she went. The two had a lot in common, including relationships with many men ranging from dukes to polo players. And they were both ultimate survivors. Needless to say, they were also friends.

"How is your dear Mama?" Chanel asked me as if she could read my thoughts. "I look forward to seeing her again. It's been too long."

"I haven't seen her since Christmas," I said. "I expect she'll show up when the baby arrives. She's dying to be a grandmother, which is amusing as she was never dying to be a mother."

"We all soften with age," Chanel said. "But now I see why this skirt fits you so poorly. My dear, you are with child. How exciting. But this outfit does not become you."

"I'm having some maternity things made at home," I said, "but I thought it was a little early to walk around in a flowing tent."

Chanel shook her head, despairing of me. "My dear child, one must never walk around in a flowing tent. Even pregnant women have a shape. I'll design something for you." She paused, then waved an excited hand. "Better yet, I'll run something up in time for the collection. You shall model it. What a coup that will be. A young woman blossoming in the season of blossoms."

"Madame, no!" I tried to interrupt. "Remember the last time you made me model for you? Utter disaster."

"But it was not your fault," she said. "Someone tripped you on the runway so that they could steal your necklace. This time there will be no necklace to steal and you will be quite safe. So—I will not take no for an answer. I will design you a divine gown and you can keep it after you have modeled it. Perfect, *non?*"

Oh golly. What a decision. I'd dearly love a Chanel gown rather than anything Mrs. Tubbs in the village could run up from a paper pattern, but the thought of walking that runway in front of the crowned heads of Europe plus Mrs. Simpson sent shivers down my spine.

"Only if you don't make me take part in the first show," I said. "That's when all the important people will be there. Later in the week, perhaps?"

"But you do not realize it will be a feather in my cap, no? That Schiaparelli, she will gnash her teeth that I have a royal person as my model."

"Not exactly royal. Only a relative."

"You are the king's cousin, no?"

"Well, yes."

"There you are, then. You will not want to disappoint Coco and rob her of a chance to outscore her rival, will you?"

"Coco, I'm a terrible model. I'm clumsy. I'll land in someone's lap again."

"We'll have a handsome young man to escort you," she said. "You can hold his arm."

She gave me a challenging smile. "I'll design it and we shall see. Now"—she picked up a menu—"to more important matters."

Like my mother she had a prodigious appetite. We had a creamed turnip soup followed by a terrine that was composed of delightful layers of goodness knows what. Then a poached fillet of sole with pommes dauphine and finally a baba au rhum and coffee. All this was accompanied by a crisp white wine, and I was frankly ready for a nap when we returned to the Rue Cambon. Once there, Coco insisted that Belinda take my measurements while she held various fabrics up against me. I found this highly embarrassing, if a little exciting, as some of the fabrics were divine. Having made a quick sketch she breezed out again, leaving Belinda to show me around, including the outfit she had designed.

"Come in later in the week for a fitting," Chanel called as I tried to slink out unnoticed. "And if you have time to spare you can help Belinda with the last-minute details."

"I'll be happy to help," I said. "Not so happy about modeling."

"You must not lack courage, my child," she said. "Where would I be if I had no courage? I'd still be in the gutter."

She went back to work and I made my way back across the Seine to the flat, where I have to confess I lay down and fell asleep. I woke refreshed and went for a walk, following the Quai to the Île de la Cité to Notre-Dame, where I gazed in awe at the sunlight streaming in through the glorious windows. I arrived home at the same time as Belinda and realized I hadn't passed along the invitation from Zou Zou. Belinda shook her head. "Thank you, darling, but I'm going to refuse. I've been running all day and I don't think I could face another dose of the Ritz. After that lunch I'll have a simple baguette and cheese, I think, and a glass of wine with Harry if he's home." She looked up with a cheeky smile. "I have to use my charms to persuade him to help out at the showings. At least at the first one, which is the one that matters when the press will be there."

"Harry as a model?" I had to grin. He was not what you'd call suave, I was sure.

"No, I don't think so. Chanel needs young men to serve champagne, usher guests to their seats, move chairs around, and she doesn't have enough yet."

Belinda helped to dress me for the Ritz, skillfully pinning one of her long skirts and then adding a velvet opera cape over it. I felt quite chic and took the liberty of hailing a taxicab. I must say it felt rather good to say "the Ritz" as if it was the sort of place I visited often. An added thrill was when the doorman recognized me from earlier in the day.

"*Bonsoir*, milady," he said.

I sailed in, did not trip over the carpet and felt quite proud of myself until a bejeweled dowager chose that moment to rise from her seat, hailing a friend who had come in at the same moment as me, and stepped out into my path. Needless to say, we collided. There was a lot of her. It was like bumping into a feather bed. She reeled, almost sat down again, and had to grasp the back of her chair.

"*Mon dieu!*" she exclaimed, eyeing me with displeasure.

I apologized, sure that everyone was now watching. One person who was watching was Zou Zou, who came over to me. "There you are, my sweet," she said. "Come, let us go through to the bar." And she whisked me away.

"I feel terrible," I whispered. "I almost knocked over that woman."

"It was entirely her fault," Zou Zou said, her arm now comfortingly through mine. "I saw the whole thing. She was not watching you at all. She saw someone she knew, stood up to greet him and got into your path."

"You're sweet," I said, giving her a smile.

"We'll have a wonderful dinner and you can catch me up on everything since I saw you last." She whisked me into the dining room, where an attendant murmured, "Your table awaits you, Your

Royal Highness. And the bottle of Dom Pérignon that you re-
quested."

"How kind," she replied, making the young man blush. Zou
Zou did have that effect on people, especially men.

We sat. Dom Pérignon was poured. Smoked salmon topped
with caviar arrived.

"So tell all to Auntie Zou Zou," she said. "How is little Archibald?"

"Who?"

She pointed at my front.

"Anything but Archibald," I said. "Kicking away. Definitely a boy,
I'd say. But we haven't discussed names yet. Not Thaddy after Darcy's
father, I hope. Alexander is a family name. So is Hugh. And ours are
awful: Murdoch, Hamish, Lachlan on the Scottish side, and you
know the royal ones: Albert, Edward, George, Leopold."

"After all that it will turn out to be another Victoria," Zou Zou
said. "I must say you are looking positively blooming right now."

We attacked our food, sipped our champagne while she told me
about her latest exploits. I only know a couple of people whose day-
to-day activities count as exploits. Zou Zou is one of them. When
the lobster with herbed butter was served she looked up again. "And
darling Darcy? How is he? Frightfully busy, one hears."

I wanted to tell her what was worrying me. I was just trying to
phrase things correctly when she said, "You know I could swear I
saw him in Paris yesterday. I was strolling on the Faubourg Saint-
Honoré and there he was, hurrying down the other side of the road.
I called out to him, waved. He didn't glance once in my direction.
Something on his mind, it must be."

"Oh dear," I said. "Yes, I'm afraid he does have something on
his mind. He's on some frightfully hush-hush assignment and that's

probably why he couldn't acknowledge you. He was most likely being followed."

"My dear, doesn't he lead a wonderfully exciting life," Zou Zou said.

"Too exciting," I said. "I worry about him. I'm afraid he's mixing with the wrong people."

"Oh, I wouldn't worry about Darcy, my darling," she said. "If anyone can take care of himself, it's Darcy." The way she smiled reminded me that when I first met her I suspected she and Darcy had been more than friends.

"I'd be quite tempted to do that sort of thing myself," she said, as if toying with the idea, "but I'm afraid I know too many people. And I do rather stand out in a crowd."

"You could be a seductive temptress, luring state secrets out of men," I said, making her burst out laughing. "I would rather enjoy that," she confessed.

We moved on to lamb cutlets so tender you could cut them with a spoon, then to ice cream, cheese and fruit, plus a glass of cognac.

"What are you doing tomorrow?" she asked as we sat there, replete and content.

"I hadn't planned yet. I have to go sightseeing. I've only done the Eiffel Tower and Notre-Dame so far. I have to visit the Louvre and see Montmartre. . . ."

"Not tomorrow morning," she said. "I only have a short time here. I promised a dear friend that I would join him for dinner in Antibes tomorrow night. He does so hate dining alone, so I thought I'd pop down in my little plane to join him. So that only leaves tomorrow morning for me to take you shopping."

"Zou Zou," I protested. "I don't need to be taken shopping. . . ."

"Nonsense. We can't have you going around Paris looking like someone who was dressed by the Salvation Army. I'll pick you up around ten?"

It was no use arguing with Zou Zou. I had to agree. Besides, I enjoyed her company. But after she had sent me home in a taxi, the worries returned. Why didn't I have the nerve to tell her that I worried that Darcy might be doing something that involved Germany. Of course, Germany wasn't officially the enemy at this moment, but Hitler had made it clear that he aimed to dominate Europe one day. Surely Darcy couldn't want to do anything that helped that odious little man?

Chapter 10

**Such a day of contrasts: I'm feeling quite out of breath when all I
want is a chance to explore Paris on my own. . . .**

Belinda was sitting in her pajamas on her bed, drinking hot choco-
late with Harry (luckily not in pajamas this time), when I arrived
back at her flat. They looked awfully cozy together and I found
myself wondering whether . . . No. I would not allow myself to
speculate.

"Hello." She looked up with a bright smile. "Had a good
dinner?"

"Fabulous," I said.

"Tell me all about it," Harry said. "In exquisite detail. Do not
omit one morsel or crumb of bread."

"Oh, I'm sure you don't really want . . ." I began, but he waved
his hands in encouragement. "But I do want. How can I ever write

convincingly about food if my own diet is limited to bread, cheese and coffee?"

"Well," I began and started to describe the meal. He interrupted me frequently. "And the caviar, how was it arranged on the smoked salmon? Were there capers? And the lobster—we used to catch the most amazing lobsters when we spent summers in Maine."

"You grew up in Maine?" Belinda asked.

He shook his head. "Pennsylvania. But we had a summer house there. On the coast. Small fishing village. We had clambakes on the beach." For a moment his face had changed and I could see the excited boy he used to be.

"But you don't want to go home again?" I asked.

"No. I'm done with my family and with America," he said. "Now, to get back to the meal . . ."

I watched him, wondering what terrible rift had happened in his family that he now felt he'd never eat another Maine lobster. How would I feel if I could never see Eynsleigh again? Or even Castle Rannoch?

"So what have you seen so far?" he asked, changing the subject. When I told him, he shook his head. "Tourist traps, all of them. I'll make it my mission to educate you on the real Paris tomorrow, and maybe let you see how the other half of Paris lives. Dinner with my friends, huh? Can you join us, beautiful Belinda?"

"Darlings, I'd love to," Belinda said, "but I fear it will be a long day of drudgery ahead. We have the first runway rehearsal tomorrow afternoon and I expect it to stretch into the night. Also Georgie is to blame for heaping more work on me."

"Me? What did I do?" I looked to see if she was joking. She wasn't.

"Remember Chanel said she'd have to design you an outfit? Well, she did. She sketched it and then threw it onto my desk and told me to create it. Do you know how long it takes someone like me to turn a Chanel design into a garment that someone can wear?"

"I'd rather you didn't make it," I said. "Madame Chanel had a crazy idea about my modeling it at the showing. Can you imagine it? So sew slowly."

Belinda shook her head. "You don't know Chanel. When she wants something she wants it now or there is hell to pay."

"But you're not actually an employee, are you? Aren't you more like an apprentice, learning her skills?"

"An apprentice does what the master tells her," she said. "Anyway, I've cut out the garment and one of the seamstresses has started sewing it. You'd better come in for a fitting. Not tomorrow, because of the rehearsal. The place will be teeming with mannequins. Fitting on Thursday and you simply can't refuse or I'll turn you out of the flat tonight and send you back to Darcy."

"All right," I said. "I certainly don't want to get you into Chanel's bad books."

"Right. Well, that's settled then. All right, everyone. Bugger off. I need my beauty sleep."

Harry and I crept out, Harry promising to take me out at three o'clock the next day.

※

I awoke to the sound of rain on the windows and wondered if that meant the afternoon's sightseeing was off. At least shopping with Zou Zou was suitably under cover. Belinda had gone at first light again, leaving pain au chocolat for me. I showered, ate breakfast and tried to make myself look as chic as possible with the clothing at my disposal. Then, of course, I had to top it with my mack. Zou Zou actually shuddered when she saw it. "Darling, what a frightful garment," she said. "Why do the British think that a mackintosh should be worn outside of farms and stalking deer? Come quickly. We must remedy this immediately."

She had the taxi drop us on a fashionable boulevard and whisked me into Galeries Lafayette, where the first thing she bought was a long navy blue woolen cape, lined with pale blue silk. She actually made me take off the mackintosh and replace it with the cape, before finding a pale blue umbrella and navy cloche hat to accompany it.

"Now at least you look civilized enough not to be tossed out of the Galeries," she said and bustled me up to the dress department, where she challenged the assistants to find me items suitable for hiding bulges. She settled on a straight gray woolen skirt (large enough not to need a safety pin), a long embroidered tunic and over it a three-quarter-length jacket that hung loosely. The result was rather stunning and the assistant muttered that madame had the height to carry off such an ensemble.

We had coffee together and then she dropped me home on her way to the airport, hoping the weather would improve as she flew south. Golly, what an exhausting life she led! I had a light lunch and was ready when Harry called for me. I thought he might have been impressed with my outfit but he looked horrified. "You can't meet my friends dressed like that," he said. "They are all struggling artists or communists. I thought you looked just right when I first met you."

So I was forced to change back into the old Georgie before we went out on the town. The rain had slowed to a drizzle so we started with the most important parts of the Louvre, then crossed the Seine. "I planned to show you the Sainte-Chapelle," he said, "but there is no point if the sun isn't shining." Instead he showed me the Hôtel de Ville, then led me across to the university. My feet were beginning to ache when we came to rest at a café on the Boulevard

Saint-Germain. *Café au Flores* was the name painted outside. It had stopped raining and a waiter was busy drying off the outside chairs and tables, but we went inside, where a group of men were already seated at a table.

"Harry's finally got a date," one of them shouted, bursting out laughing. "There is hope after all."

"I'm afraid to disillusion you," Harry said, "but my date is actually an English titled lady, staying with Belinda. A married English lady."

"As if that matters in France," another of the men said, and they all laughed again. "Here. Take a pew. And watch your language, you guys."

A chair was pulled out for me. A glass of red wine was poured for me, while Harry introduced the other members around the table. Two Americans, a Swedish painter and two Frenchmen. These latter were smoking those pungent French cigarettes and my previous nausea returned. I hoped I wouldn't have to make a speedy exit.

"I wanted her to see the real Paris," Harry said. "Where none of us has a sou but we all seem to enjoy life pretty well."

"Speak for yourself," said the Swedish painter. "I am miserable most of the time."

"But then you're Swedish," another American replied. "All Swedes are miserable. It's the dark winters. And you couldn't paint if you were happy. You said so."

"True." The Swede nodded. "And Pierre, he is also miserable, *n'est-ce pas?*"

To my amusement the waiter pulled up a chair and joined us. "One must suffer to write good poetry," he said. He nodded politely to me.

"So you're a poet as well as a waiter?" I asked. He was rather handsome.

"I have the soul of a poet, the desire of a man and the skill of a chef," he said, as if this was a normal way of talking. "Me, I train as a chef but alas Paris is full of good chefs so I wait, as a waiter, you see, and write my sad and eloquent poems."

He gave me a dazzling smile, making me wish for a second that I wasn't married.

"And I should add that I am also a communist." He shrugged in that most Gallic way.

"Until some rich lady invites you to come and cook for her," another of the Frenchmen said.

"I am a practical communist," Pierre said. "One must eat. And I do not approve of the way Russia is handling its communism. Quite against the spirit of the whole thing. So uncivilized. My brand of communism is enough. Good food and good wine for all." He got up again and headed back to the kitchen.

"Are you a writer or a painter?" I asked the lanky American who was sitting beside me, who had been introduced as Arnie. His face was quite young but his hair was already graying. Like Harry's.

He shook his head. "Writer," he said. "Like Harry. Would-be novelist. Several novels in a drawer but none in the bookshops. But I keep hoping."

"What do you write about?"

"The war," he said. "Always the war."

"It's a long time ago now. Do you think that people want to go on being reminded of it?"

An angry spasm crossed his face. "But I have to remind them. They must never forget. How many of us never went home, or went home deeply scarred? Gassed or blinded or missing limbs. It must never be allowed to happen again."

"I suppose you and Harry were lucky, then," I said. "You came through unscathed."

The anger was still in his eyes. "Physically, maybe, but mentally? I'd imagine we don't have too many nights without nightmares. You can't unsee what we saw. Going over the top with the bright flashes all around us and the friend beside us blown to pieces, never knowing when it's going to be our turn." He put a hand on my arm. "I went home after the war, and back there they were celebrating the glorious victory. My family actually treating me like a hero when all I did was try to stay alive. We're a big military family, you know. My father went to West Point. Just like Harry's family. Glorifying war. It's no wonder we both came here instead."

"Don't depress the poor girl," Harry said. "Talk about something uplifting. I'll tell you something amusing: Belinda tried to draft me into helping out at a fashion show at Chanel."

"You? A male model?" There was raucous laughter.

"God no. More like a flunky. Help to seat people. Move the chairs. Pass around champagne. That kind of thing."

"So are you going to do it?"

"Hell no. She said I have to look presentable. As if I can do that. I'd have to trim my beard, for one thing. And iron my shirt."

"Hey, does this pay?" Arnie asked.

"Sure," Harry said. "Quite well, I think. But not well enough for me."

"I'd do it," Arnie said. "I'd do anything for money right now. Serving champagne and moving chairs sounds a lot better than starving."

"How many men do they need?" the Swede asked.

Harry shrugged. "She didn't say that, but I can find out for you if you like. All she said is you have to wear a dark suit and look presentable."

"That counts me out," the Swede said. "I look like the artist I am."

"*Moi aussi*," the poet-waiter-chef Pierre said with a grand flourish as he deposited a plate of pâté and bread on the table. "Why would I wish to assist in such a bourgeois activity—aiding the rich in buying clothes that cost as much as a family's food for a year?"

"I agree, *mon vieux*," Harry said. "I feel the same way."

"But one has to eat, and she's paying," Arnie said. "Tell your friend Belinda I'll get my one suit out of mothballs," Arnie said. "Who knows—one of the rich dames may take a fancy to me. Set me up in an apartment." He raised an eyebrow, making the others at the table shout out insults again.

"Only if the fashion show is for blind women. For desperate old crones . . ."

"Hey, you know what? I've just had a thought. This may lead to something," Arnie shouted over them. "Perhaps I can bring my camera and get some candid shots to sell to magazines. Do you reckon, Harry?"

"You'd probably have to be sneaky about it," Harry replied. "The official press will be there in force."

"Then I'll be part of the press, representing, let's see—the *Oklahoma Tornado*?" He grinned.

"Arnie is a terrific photographer," Harry muttered to me. "You should see the pictures he takes. Quite as good as Man Ray. I keep telling him he's got more chance of making it with his pictures than his writing."

"I do still own a suit," one of the Frenchmen said. "As you say, it can't hurt to meet rich women. And speaking of rich people, you cannot guess who is in town."

"Who?"

"Hemingway. I swear I saw him."

"That's right. He's on his way to Spain to cover the civil war." Arnie turned to me. "Now that's a guy who actually does revel in bloody battles. Do you think he'll go to Gertrude's if he's here?"

"Sure he will," Harry said. "You know that Gertrude adores him, and he does love to be adored."

"Then we have to show up at her soiree this week," Arnie said. "Besides, she has food and drink. I can always slip some portable and not-too-squishy items into my pockets. If it weren't for Gertrude I'd have starved years ago."

I studied them carefully. They were not young, certainly mid-thirties if they had fought in the Great War. And yet they were clearly living from hand to mouth. Is that what people were willing to do to be writers and artists, hoping to sell something they had created one day? The phrase "the Lost Generation" came into my head. I was now meeting them in person.

Chapter 11

We're having dinner with the count and his mother tonight. I'm
quite curious to see how he lives. I wonder if Belinda is being
vetted for approval?

Belinda went off to work, but it was again pouring rain so I decided
to put my sightseeing on hold. Actually I was becoming anxious
about Darcy. I had expected him to contact me by now—just paying a quick visit to see how I was, at the very least. But I'd seen or
heard nothing from him. All I knew was that Zou Zou had spotted
him and he had ignored her. It was all quite worrying and I was
tempted to go to the Hôtel Saville just to make sure he was all right.
But I knew I shouldn't interfere when he was on a job. I'd just have
to pretend I was having a fabulous time—which I was, in many
ways. I had a new outfit. The promise of another one, although it

came with the threat of having to model it. I was determined to refuse that. It had been bad enough walking in front of people when I was still slim and with no tummy bump. Now my balance wasn't always steady. Oh golly.

Because the rain didn't look like it was easing up anytime soon, I took my new blue umbrella and headed for the Louvre Museum, to see what I had missed with Harry. After I had completed about five galleries I had had enough. The Flemish school with their dead hares and fruit could wait for another day! And the *Mona Lisa*—what was so special about one tiny painting? Perhaps I needed more art education.

I came out to find the clouds had broken. I stopped for a baguette with Brie, then walked to the bottom of the Champs-Élysées, admiring the outdoor cafés and the Arc de Triomphe at the top of the hill. Then I decided I needed a rest if we were to go out to a special dinner. I turned around and headed back over the Seine.

Belinda arrived home just as it was getting dark, sinking down onto the nearest chair.

"Utterly exhausted, darling," she muttered. "I really don't want to go out tonight, but I can't refuse Louis-Philippe, can I? Besides, I'm dying to see his house. Ornate in the extreme, don't you think?"

I dressed in the outfit Belinda had concocted for me on Monday, held together with many pins and topped with a fringed silk shawl. I looked a little like a fortune-teller, but it would have to do. Belinda, I noticed, looked positively stunning in a straight emerald-green gown that hugged her body like a second skin.

"I see you're pulling out all the stops," I commented.

She gave a little grin. "Maybe."

We set off in a taxicab to the address between the Seine and the Champs-Élysées—clearly the best neighborhood in the city—and pulled up outside a grand front entrance with boxwood topiaries on either side. A footman in black velvet livery ushered us inside, then escorted us up a flight of marble stairs. From the salon ahead of us came the sound of low voices and I suddenly felt that moment of fear realizing I'd have to be speaking French all evening—and not spill anything. Louis-Philippe, looking incredibly handsome in evening dress, came toward us, arms outstretched, and kissed first my hand, then Belinda's. The room was, as Belinda had predicted, incredibly ornate. Gilt furniture, hanging tapestries, giant vases of silk flowers, prancing horse statues. Too many items waiting to be knocked over by one wrong move. I began to wish I hadn't come.

Louis-Philippe took our arms and led us toward an elderly woman, wearing purple velvet and decorated with many diamonds, seated like a queen on her throne. A priest stood at her side. I, who had visited a real queen many times in my life, still felt overawed.

"Maman, may I present our two visitors from England," he said in French. "Lady Georgiana and Miss Warburton-Stoke."

"*Enchanté.*" She nodded her head slightly. "You are most welcome. My son has spoken highly of you. And this is Father Dominique. I take it you do speak our language."

"We do, Countess," I said. "We were both educated at school in Switzerland."

She gave a little shrug. "Well, the French they speak there is a little rustic, shall we say, but at least we shall be able to converse. That is good. Let us go in to dinner."

There was no sherry, no aperitifs or nibbles. We were ushered straight to a magnificent dining room. Candlesticks and silverware sparkled on a polished table. We took our seats.

"Where is our other guest?" the countess demanded. "Has he not arrived yet?"

"Here he is, Mother," Louis-Philippe said.

I looked up, half expecting to see one of my royal cousins, or even Darcy, as had happened to me before. But instead it was another man I knew.

I think Belinda gave a little gasp as Count Paolo di Martini came into the room.

"May I present a good friend from our school days," Louis-Philippe said, gesturing to Belinda and me. "The Count di Martini. And this is—"

"I already know both these charming ladies," Paolo said. "How are you, my dear Georgiana? And you, Belinda?"

"We are both well, thank you, Paolo." Belinda's voice was shaky. She had shared a long, passionate affair with him and now shared a secret.

"How is Camilla?" I asked as he was seated beside Belinda. Bad move, I thought.

"Well, thank you. She is visiting her parents in England. Our son is with her." His eyes went to Belinda, who looked away.

"And your son?" Belinda asked.

"A fine boy. Strong and intelligent, as you would expect."

You could cut the tension in the air with a knife. I was glad when soup was placed in front of us. It was a creamy shrimp bisque, followed by scallops on their shells, and then a dish of small crispy items. The footman put one on my plate, then one on Belinda's.

"What are these?" she asked, looking at Louis-Philippe, then taking a tentative bite.

"They are *alouettes*," he said. "Do you not know them? *Alouette, gentille alouette?* Little birds that fly high and sing. 'Larks,' is that the word?"

Belinda shot me a horrified look. "We're eating little birds," she whispered.

"Don't be afraid," the countess said. "You just crunch them, bones and all."

I gave Belinda a despairing look. I didn't think I could crunch little bird bones even when not pregnant. Now my stomach reeled. I pretended to take a bite with a smile of delight on my face. Beneath the table my left hand was opening my evening bag. I waited until Louis-Philippe said something amusing to Paolo. His mother looked away, and I whisked the bird onto my lap.

"I hear you will be attending Chanel's collection this weekend," the countess said to Belinda. "My son tells me you actually work for this woman?" She spoke the word "work" as if it was somehow sinful.

"I have been studying design with her," Belinda said. "But yes, I have been assisting with this important show. Will you be attending yourself?"

"But naturally. I always do."

She turned to me. "You will also attend?"

"Yes, I've promised to help Belinda."

"So you will not be shopping for clothes yourself?"

I shook my head with a rueful smile. "I'm afraid I can't afford Chanel's prices. Besides, we expect a baby, so this is not the time for new clothes."

"I congratulate," she said. "An heir is so important. Let us pray it will be a boy."

I hadn't thought of it like that before. Was it important that Darcy had an heir to the title? I supposed it was. "Will you be looking for a special outfit?" I asked.

She shrugged. "For me? Oh no. I am always fascinated to know what new horrors she will produce this year. Men's jackets with silk pajamas? What next? The world has gone mad. But Jacqueline likes to go, and I find it amusing."

"Jacqueline is your daughter?" I asked.

She smiled. "No. The fiancée of my son."

"You have another son?"

"No. Just the one," she said.

Belinda was talking with the two men across the table. She hadn't heard. I didn't ask any more questions. I couldn't wait to tell Belinda. The meal continued, course after rich course. Veal in creamy mushroom sauce, then a gâteau piled with layers of cream and glacé fruit. I began to feel quite sick and longed to go home. When we finally left the men to their brandy, I went to powder my nose. Belinda followed me. "What was all that about?" she asked. "I saw you looking at me in a funny way."

"Did Louis-Philippe ever mention to you that he had a fiancée?" I asked.

"Louis-Philippe? Of course not. He doesn't." A horrified look crossed her face. "Does he?"

"Oh yes, he does. Her name is Jacqueline and she is apparently a model of fashion and of virtue. His mother told me. She goes to mass every morning and does good things for the poor."

Belinda had gone awfully pale. "The rat," she said. "How did he conveniently forget to mention this?"

"What should we do? Sneak out now?"

"Absolutely not. I need to have a little talk with him."

"I don't think you should make a scene, Belinda."

"I won't make a scene. I shall be terribly civilized."

We joined the others. Belinda started chatting with Paolo. I saw Louis-Philippe looking anxiously in her direction. "The Count di Martini is an old friend of Belinda?" he asked.

"A very good friend," I said, giving it all the meaning I could.

He frowned. Then he got up and went over to them. He took Belinda's arm and they went out onto the balcony, his mother watching his every move. When they returned I could see that Belinda was furious, in spite of the sweet smile on her face.

"I'm sorry, Countess, but we should go now," she said. "I have to get up for work tomorrow. We working girls need our sleep."

I took our leave politely. It was all done in a most civilized manner. I admired Belinda for her restraint, but I noticed she gave Paolo a long, lingering handshake and I saw the look that passed between them. We didn't speak until we got into the cab that the footman had hailed for us.

"Bloody cheek!" Belinda finally exploded. "Did you see how she talked down to me? Patronizing. Who does she think she is? My father has a title. A proper British title, not some pretend, made-up continental one. And as for her slimy son—I confronted him about his fiancée. And do you know what he said?"

"He denied it?"

"Not at all. He said they had been promised to each other since birth. He would marry her one day, but he had no romantic interest in her. Merely a convenient arrangement between two old families." She took a deep breath. "Then he suggested he would buy me a nice apartment in a good quarter of the city and he would come and visit me. I would have a very pleasant life and want for nothing, he said. A kept woman! Me! Can you imagine?"

I wanted to laugh but tried not to. "Oh, Belinda. I'm so sorry."

"Why am I always the one they don't want to marry?" she demanded. "Do I have *spoiled goods* tattooed on my forehead? I haven't even slept with the man yet."

"You can't compete with a saintly fiancée who goes to mass every morning," I said. "Frenchmen take it for granted that they have mistresses, don't they? So do many Englishmen."

"Well, I don't intend to be one of them. I set him very straight. I told him I was an heiress in my own right, and I didn't need his flat or anything else from him." She stared out of the cab window as we crossed the Seine. Lights sparkled in the water. A couple strolled over the bridge, their arms wrapped around each other.

"He wasn't right for you anyway," I said at last. "Far too prissy and correct."

She laughed. "He did go on about the crease in his trousers, didn't he? And who would want a mother-in-law like her?"

"Plus the priest," I reminded her. "Don't forget the priest."

She grabbed my hand, giving a nervous laugh now. "Oh, Georgie," she said. "I'm so glad you're here. Why are men such a problem?"

"I wish I knew," I replied.

"And Paolo appearing like that out of the blue," she said. "What were the odds that he and Louis-Philippe should know each other? I nearly died when he walked into the room, darling."

"So did I. I nearly choked on my wine."

"Oh, Georgie. To know that Paolo is in Paris, without Camilla. How much tension is a girl supposed to take?"

"You do lead an interesting life, I must say." I had to smile now.

"I'm tired of an interesting life," she said. "Maybe I want your life now. A nice safe home with a husband who adores you and a baby on the way. You know where you stand. You can look forward to a lovely smooth future."

I sincerely hoped she was right and that I wasn't married to a man who was playing with fire.

Chapter 12

THURSDAY, APRIL 23
AT CHANEL, RUE CAMBON.

Still no word from Darcy! I hope he's all right. Should I telephone
the hotel? I just wish I knew what was going on. It is so
frustrating to worry that he might be doing something
dangerous. I thought this would be a relaxing holiday, but it is
getting more complicated by the minute.

Belinda had gone by the time I awoke the next morning, leaving a
note reminding me to come in for a fitting of my new outfit. I
dressed in the items Zou Zou had bought for me, then set off for
the Rue Cambon, walking today as the weather was bright and
breezy. White clouds scudded across a blue sky and the whole of
Paris seemed to be clean, fresh and glowing. I entered the Chanel
boutique with more confidence than the last time I was there and
was pleased that the assistants nodded with approval of the way I
was dressed.

"*Bonjour*, milady, please to go up," one of them said. "You are expected."

"How come she can go up but I can't?" proclaimed a rich voice from a dressing room. What's more, it was a voice that sounded horribly familiar.

"Is that the Dowager Duchess of Rannoch?" I whispered to the assistant.

"I am not permitted to disclose . . ." she began, but I had crossed to the dressing rooms. "Mummy, is that you?" I asked.

The door opened and a blond head peered around it. "Good God, Georgie, what on earth are you doing here?"

I found her shocked expression strangely satisfying. "What else does one do at Chanel but try on clothes?" I asked.

"But darling, you can't afford Chanel—not unless you've become a rich man's mistress, which in your current condition is highly unlikely. Just a minute. Let me put some clothes on." She shut the door and in a remarkably short space of time she reopened it, fully clothed and looking gorgeous as usual. (For those of you who don't know, my mother was a famous actress before becoming a duchess.) "Now, you can give your aged mother a hug." We embraced, kissing a few inches from each other's cheeks. "Now, tell me what you are doing. Are you on some kind of assignment? Hush-hush? For the royals?"

"Not at all," I replied. "Darcy brought me to Paris with him. I'm staying with Belinda and she is working for Chanel. And today I'm here for a fitting of an outfit Chanel has designed for me." I didn't add that I wasn't paying for it! "What are you doing here? Have you escaped from Max and boring Berlin?"

"Not at all, darling. I'm here with Max. He's part of a German trade delegation. Very high-level stuff. Trying to persuade the French to stop buying Peugeots and Citroëns and start buying German motorcars. Göring brought his wife with him, and some of her friends, so I was invited to tag along. We're all planning to attend the fall collection on Sunday, but I thought I'd get a jump start on the others and pick up a few pieces now. Also to pump the assistants for what delicious pieces might be in the collection. I gather there is a stunning gold lamé dress. Form-hugging. I'd look divine in it. And Max is so frightfully generous now he's making oodles of money."

She sounded so bright and cheerful, but I sensed that she was putting on an act. "Is everything all right?" I asked.

"Of course. Why shouldn't it be?" Again a defensive bristle.

"I just wondered if you're still enjoying life in Germany with Max."

"Never been happier," she said. "We're planning to get married later this year. You must come and be bridesmaid—or is it matron of honor when you're married?"

"You have to come and be grandma first."

"Grandma. Doesn't that sound so frightfully old?" she said with a little laugh. She examined me critically. "You're looking awfully well. And your dress sense has certainly improved."

"Thanks to Zou Zou, who dragged me to Galeries Lafayette yesterday," I admitted.

"Oh, I never buy clothes off the rack," she said. "They are made for average figures, not mine. But then you're also having something made here, so you say?"

"Yes, Madame Chanel was kind enough to design me an outfit for my current shape. I should go up for my fitting," I said. "Can we meet for a cup of coffee later?"

"Of course, darling. I'll try to fit it in," she said. "I'd invite you to dinner but it seems to be one trade banquet after another. All so deadly dull and boring with long speeches in French and German. You know that my linguistic skills are limited, don't you? But I will make time. Where are you staying?"

I gave her Belinda's address. She wrote it in a little notebook.

"How long have you been here?" I asked, suddenly thinking of Darcy.

"Only a couple of days. We arrived on Monday."

"You haven't seen anything of Darcy, have you?"

"Darcy? Why should I?"

"No reason at all. It's just that he's out and about in Paris and I thought you might have bumped into him."

"I haven't exactly been out and about myself. We seem to be on a frightfully organized schedule. . . ."

At that moment another dressing room door opened and a decidedly stern-looking woman came out. She was middle-aged, broad and wore her light brown hair coiled around her head. What's more, her fashion sense left a lot to be desired. "You are ready, Duchess?" she asked in clipped English, with a heavy German accent.

"Yes, I think so," Mummy said. She turned to the assistant. "I don't think I want any of these now. I'll wait until I see the collection on Sunday. On second thought, I will have the long blue one. Have it sent over to the hotel, will you?"

"Of course, Duchess," the assistant replied.

"Must hurry, darling." Mummy kissed my cheek, actually making contact this time. "Another luncheon to attend. Coming, Frau Bruhler."

I watched her leave with a sinking feeling in my stomach. My mother had a minder, I was sure. My mind was still racing as I went up the stairs. Too many strange associations with Germany. Darcy's conversation when the man said, "What am I going to tell Berlin?" And the man with the map on the quayside, and now Mummy coming over with a trade group including highest-level Nazis. Somehow these things had to be tied together, didn't they?

I took a deep breath and went to find Belinda.

"You're going to love this, darling," Belinda said as she stood up to greet me. "I think it's almost the most adventurous thing that Chanel has designed this season." She leaned closer. "Between ourselves, her new collection is rather staid, compared to what we hear Schiaparelli is doing this year. Classic, of course, but nothing startling like this."

The outfit was not what I had expected. I associated Chanel with perfectly cut suits, almost mannish in their simplicity, or little black dresses with her signature pearls. But this was a long, flowing garment, more like a Japanese kimono than a dress, in a gorgeous embroidered fabric. I had to say it was perfect for hiding my stomach bulge, but the skirt was tight, with a slit up to the knee, making walking a little hard.

"Can we make the slit higher?" I asked Belinda, who was busy with pins as she adjusted my shoulders.

"Then you'd be showing your knees, darling. That wouldn't be right."

So I must learn to take very tiny steps—not easy for one like me who has been used to striding out over moorland all her life.

"I'm positively not wearing this on a runway," I said. "There will be too many important laps I could fall into."

"We'll see," Belinda said, easing the garment off over my head.

"By the way, speaking of important ladies," I said, "I just bumped into my mother downstairs. She's here with a German trade delegation, or rather Max is here and she's tagged along."

"We've heard all about it," Belinda said. "Mrs. Göring, no less. They're all coming on Sunday. Chanel was annoyed she hadn't found out earlier. She said she would have designed some fashionable dirndls." Belinda chuckled. "They seem to encourage good healthy females in Germany right now, who are not the right shape for Chanel garments."

"The one with my mother certainly wasn't," I said. "I hope she's all right, Belinda. I sensed she was putting on an act for me— acting as if everything was wonderful, when it really wasn't."

"It's her choice to stay with Max, isn't it?" Belinda said. "She could leave him if she didn't like his money so much."

"I hope she could. I don't like what we're hearing about the Nazis and those who get in their way."

"Your mother is the ultimate survivor. She's probably charmed Hitler by now," Belinda said. "Now since you're here you can help me with the place cards for the seats."

I worked with her for the next hour until she was called downstairs. She came up again, her face flushed and her eyes rather bright.

"You'll never guess who that was," she said. "Paolo. He's taking me to dinner tonight. At Maxim's."

"Oh, Belinda, do be careful," I said. "I don't want you to make any more mistakes."

"I'll be at a restaurant," she said. "I can hardly make any big mistakes there, can I?"

"But I saw the way he looked at you. And Camilla is hardly the warmest of women, is she?"

"I'll be the soul of decorum," she said. "Actually I want to see pictures of my son. I've been thinking about him a lot lately. I suppose it's because you are pregnant and you'll be able to watch a lovely child growing up."

I suppose by now you've guessed that Belinda had a baby who was then adopted by the childless Paolo and Camilla. I put my hand on her shoulder. "Belinda, you will meet the right man and have a family of your own one day. I really thought that you and Jago . . ."

"So did I," she said. "I suppose I have come to accept he's not the sort of man who wants to feel inadequate."

"Surely he's not inadequate?" I raised an eyebrow.

She chuckled. "Not in that way. Not at all. I meant that I'm rich and he can't provide for me in the way I'm used to."

"If you love him, for heaven's sake go and find him and tell him. Don't let his stupid pride stand in your way."

She shrugged. "Perhaps I will. If I ever get through this next week."

It's funny how prophetic those words were. Belinda came home quite early that evening.

"Did you have a good time?" I asked, politely.

"Very good meal," she said.

"And did you see pictures of the boy?" I was careful not to say the words "your son."

She nodded. "And he's beautiful. I know that's not the right word for a boy, but he's a beautiful child."

"I would expect nothing less," I said. "You are quite a beauty yourself."

She said nothing for a while.

"You must be pleased that it all worked out so well," I said. "He's having the best life."

"Yes."

Again she was silent.

"You said yourself that you weren't the maternal type," I reminded her.

"I know. And probably I'm not. Nor am I in any position to raise a child alone. But when I look at you, I'm reminded of what I've lost."

"Well, I'm glad you've seen pictures of him," I said, feeling awkward now. "And that the meeting with Paolo didn't turn into anything more."

"He wanted it to," she said. "He suggested that we go back to his hotel."

"Belinda. That's awful. What did you say?"

"I declined. Which was hard for me. You know he was the love of my life, don't you? And he said he always felt the same way about me. Just that he had to marry a suitable Catholic girl."

"What's wrong with these men? Agreeing to marry someone suitable they don't love? I'm glad I put my foot down when it came to Prince Siegfried and married Darcy instead."

"Much more fun, I should think," Belinda said. "Imagine being kissed by Fishface!"

And with that we both laughed, the tension of the evening dispelled.

Chapter 13

FRIDAY, APRIL 24
AT BELINDA'S FLAT.

Things are beginning to make sense now, but I rather wish I didn't know. Crikey, this is scary stuff.

Belinda left on Friday morning, saying they would be involved in rehearsals and final adjustments all day, probably late into the evening, so would I mind fending for myself. She didn't mention my participation in any rehearsals, for which I was heartily glad. I spent a delightful morning up on Montmartre, visiting the basilica and enjoying the breathtaking views over the city. I stopped for lunch at a little café and had a bowl of vegetable soup, which tasted much better than it sounds.

I returned to the flat in midafternoon to be greeted by the dragon lady.

"A man came looking for you," she said. "Dark hair. Very handsome. Tall."

"Did he say his name?"

She shrugged. "I told him you were not home and I did not know when you would return."

"So what did he say?"

"You know this man, do you think? I do not allow gentleman callers."

"I expect it was my husband, who is also in Paris," I said. "He's here on business."

"Huh." She shrugged again and folded her arms across her chest.

"Did he leave a message?"

"He said he would be in the Jardin du Luxembourg."

"How long ago was this?" I was fighting back my annoyance. Darcy had come to find me and I wasn't home, and this annoying woman had not let him wait for me.

"An hour, perhaps."

"I'll go and find him." I turned away, then had another thought. "If he returns here, ask him to wait for me. His name is Mr. O'Mara."

"Mr. O'Mara? But you are a lady, *non*? A royal lady?"

"And married to the son of a lord. He is the honorable Mr. O'Mara."

"Ah. Very well. I tell him."

I hurried out of the door, map in hand, down the Boulevard Saint-Germain. I was still fuming that I might have missed seeing Darcy, thanks to an interfering caretaker. But I supposed I could see her point. She had no way of knowing which male visitors might be welcome at a young lady's apartment. And perhaps there was a reason Darcy could not tell her who he was.

The garden was a huge park with walkways leading to a round pond in the middle, where a small boy was sailing a miniature yacht. On one side of the pond was a stately, elegant building that looked like a palace. There were spring flowers in the beds, and trees full of blossom, but I hardly took in any of the beauty as I scanned the park for a glimpse of my husband. Then I approached a park bench. A man was sitting on it, his face hidden behind a newspaper. The newspaper was lowered and Darcy stood up, a big smile on his face.

"There you are, my darling," he said, planting a kiss on my cheek. "Had a good day sightseeing? I expect you're tired. Let's go straight back to the hotel so you get a rest before we meet your friends for dinner tonight."

He took my hand, ushered me from the park at great speed and bundled me into a waiting taxicab.

"What's all this?" I asked. "How can we go back to the hotel when all my clothes are at Belinda's?"

"We're not going to the hotel," he said as the taxicab set off. "We're going to drive around a bit until we've had a talk. So that anyone who happened to be following me loses us. I don't want them to know where you are staying."

"You think someone might be following you?"

"It's possible."

"Darcy, can't you please tell me what's going on?" I tried to sound calmer than I felt. I looked up at the back of the driver's head. "Is it safe to talk here?"

"Don't worry, I made sure I hired a cab driver who speaks no English." He gave me a reassuring little smile. "You're right. One can't be too careful."

"Are you in danger?"

"No more than usual," he said.

"You're not doing anything . . . wrong, are you? Something I wouldn't approve of?"

"Wrong? In what way?" He frowned. "You have some idea of what I do, Georgie. Not always aboveboard. Not always quite legal."

"Then can you tell me what's going on? What are you doing here? Why are you keeping me in the dark?"

"I'm afraid it's a very delicate matter," he said. "I wanted to keep you out of it, let you have a nice stay with Belinda. But the situation has become rather urgent." He took my hand in his. "I know I can trust you," he said. "This time I have to trust you because we need your help. I wouldn't have asked if there had been another way." He turned to me then. "Whatever I tell you must not be repeated to a single soul ever. Do I have your word?"

"Yes, I suppose so." I stammered out the words. Suddenly it was all very real. And very scary.

"There is a German delegation just arrived in Paris," he said.

"I know. My mother is part of it. I met her at Chanel."

"Oh, of course. That makes sense. Her boyfriend should make a lot of money if the motorcar deal goes through." He paused, glancing out of the taxi window as we came to a stop in the Place de la Concorde and motorcars pulled up beside us. Apparently satisfied, he continued. "Your mother is here because top-level Nazis have brought their wives on a shopping spree. One of those wives is called Frau Goldberg."

"And?" I waited.

"You might have picked up that Goldberg is a Jewish name."

"I didn't know," I said. "Oh. I see. A Jewish person as part of a Nazi outing?"

"She's not Jewish, actually. She's a German aristocrat and childhood friend of Mrs. Göring, which is why she's here. She's also heavily guarded."

"In case she runs away?"

He shook his head. "Her husband, Professor Wilhelm Goldberg, is a distinguished scientist. However, he's no longer permitted to work in his lab because he is a Jew. He has invented something we want. A system to detect small amounts of gas in the air. Since so many men were gassed in the last war, this warning system would be vital in the future. He wants to share this discovery with Britain. However, he too is heavily guarded. In all likelihood he will be taken to one of their new prison camps soon—where they shut away anyone who is an enemy of the state."

I shuddered. I was sitting in a cab with my husband, having this conversation about life and death, and it seemed unreal.

"As you can imagine," he went on, "Mrs. Goldberg is getting a great deal of pressure to leave her Jewish husband and resume life as a friend of the Nazis."

"How horrible. She won't do it, will she?"

"She is giving the outward appearance of being willing to do so. That gives her time and maybe a chance to find a way to spirit him out of the country. But for now the only thing they can get to safety is his formula and notes. She has brought them with her. As I said, she is heavily guarded."

"So you've been assigned to receive them from her and bring them back to England?"

"Exactly," he said. "However, I've come up with a better idea. I'd like you to get them from her."

"Me?" The word came out as a squeak. A picture of myself as a secret agent, slinking through a back alley, climbing a drainpipe, flashed through my mind. It seemed so absurd I had a desire to giggle.

"You're in a perfect position to do so," he said. "Chanel's fashion show. I take it you'll be attending with Belinda?"

"I will."

"So will Frau Goldberg and her German pals. We're going to arrange that Frau Goldberg is not seated close to the others. Obviously Mrs. Göring will get the front row. A general's wife and a senior aide's wife will sit on either side of her. But Mrs. Goldberg will be put in the back row—out of the spotlight, so to speak. It's quite dark up there, so I'm told, when the lights are on the runway. You will go up to her and say, 'I'm sorry, madame, but you were given the wrong program by mistake. You've got tomorrow's. Here, let me give you the correct one.'

"And you will exchange programs with her. Of course, his notes will be inside the one she gives you. She will shake your hand in German fashion and say, 'Thank you.' And in doing so she will pass you a canister of microfilm—which is the most important part because it also contains photos of the secret research facility he was working in. You will then walk away and go about your business, as if nothing has happened. Disappear into a back room."

"And then?" I asked.

"As soon as possible you will go out into the street, where we will have someone waiting to take them."

I shook my head. "That won't work. The salon is up a flight of very grand steps where models will be making their entrances and exits. I'll be trapped until the show is over."

Darcy frowned. "Of course. We need to think of a way to conceal both items until you can carry them out. It's just possible you'll be observed. They manage to have their spies everywhere. Can you wear something with a pocket?"

I shook my head. "I'm wearing an outfit designed by Chanel for the occasion."

He looked horrified. "You're not going to have to model it, are you?"

"Golly, I hope not. I've told her I'm not going to."

"If necessary say you feel faint. Say you need to sit by a window. You are pregnant. That's a great excuse."

"The windows in the salon will be closed and the drapes drawn during the show," I said. "So if I say I feel faint they might whisk me upstairs, away from the action," I said. "But what about the canister of film and the notes? What am I to do with them until I can get outside?"

"I'll have someone scope out the place and see what would be best. The one thing we don't want is to draw any attention to you. Can you sketch me a plan of the setup?"

"All right." I heard my voice wobble again.

"There may be a convenient potted palm or flower arrangement. Or even a simple carrier bag with innocuous items—a scarf, the sort of things that might be needed for the show."

"Yes, I suppose so."

He put his hand on mine. "Don't worry. I promise you won't be in danger. We just need you to pass along the items as quickly as possible. Once they are gone the Nazis will have no interest in you."

Somehow this did not sound too reassuring. When I didn't answer he said, "I'm only asking you this because it seems like the simplest solution. If you say no, we'll have to arrange for someone to gain access to her room at night or set up a rendezvous at a restaurant—both much more risky for all involved. She appears to be watched at all times."

A thought just struck me. "How will I know what she looks like?" I asked.

Darcy reached into his pocket and produced a small snapshot. It showed three women walking together, arm in arm, all dressed in German peasant fashion—with dirndls and coils of hair around their heads. "The one in the middle is Frau Göring," he said. "The one on the left is Gerda Goldberg. That picture is from several years ago. Having caught a glimpse of her as they emerged from the train station I'd say she's rather more stocky now. Her hair has been cut and permed, still quite blond, and she will be wearing a green cape with a Tyrolean-style hat—you know, with feathers on one side. That should be easy enough to identify her, shouldn't it?"

I nodded, still not quite able to talk. I knew by now that my husband was involved in clandestine operations, but it had never occurred to me that I might be part of them one day. And yet I wanted to help. If my action could save men from being gassed in any future war—and it looked as if Hitler had designs on expanding his borders—then I'd be doing a good thing.

"So will you do it?" Darcy asked. "I'm not going to pressure you in any way. If you say no, we'll never mention it again. All I can tell you is that we will have someone on hand, nearby, to step in if needed. I can't tell you who. But you'll be safe."

I just wished I could believe him.

$Chapter$ 14

SATURDAY, APRIL 25

Tomorrow is the fashion show. Today we have a final rehearsal.

Darcy wants me to rehearse exactly how, when and where I'll be able to take a valuable canister of microfilm and hide it safely. It feels all too silly and unreal, as if I've suddenly found myself as part of a film. I just wish this whole crazy business was over. I wish I'd never come to Paris. . . . No, I don't. I love it here.

I woke feeling nauseated, and it had nothing to do with the baby I was carrying. Ahead of me was a day of rehearsal at Chanel, during which I had to scope out the ideal place to hide a secret microfilm and notes. And then, to complicate matters even more, Harry had insisted that we accompany him to the home of someone called Gertrude that evening. He seemed shocked that I hadn't heard of her. Apparently she was a big patron of the arts and collector of artwork, and her walls were covered with paintings of the most famous artists of the century. What's more, he said, it was quite probable that Hemingway might show up. And one couldn't turn down a chance to meet him. I could have, but Belinda agreed that we should go.

"It's something one has to do when in Paris, darling," she said, squeezing my hand. "Anybody who is anybody in the art world goes to her soirees. You never know who you might meet there. And you'll be seeing how the other half lives."

How could I say that at this moment a good night's sleep would be more beneficial than meeting artists and writers? I would need all my wits about me the next day. So we had a full day ahead of us. At ten o'clock we took a taxi to Chanel. Belinda insisted we do this, as she didn't want me to be too tired to go to Gertrude's. I wished she had been equally thoughtful about turning down the evening invitation. It wasn't as if we'd be wanted or welcomed there—we'd be inquisitive outsiders, neither part of the art world nor rich enough to be potential collectors. But Belinda was my hostess and I could hardly refuse.

The House of Chanel was buzzing with activity when we arrived, fraught-looking assistants rushing up and down, seamstresses with pins sticking from their mouths making last-minute adjustments. To my dismay I was also required to try on the new outfit. I tried not to show my horror at the garment. The fabric was still gorgeous, but it was like a large vase, ballooning out at the waist and then becoming very narrow again by the time it reached my knees. I could only take tiny steps in it, and as for going up or down stairs—almost impossible.

"Belinda, I can't wear this," I whispered. "I can't even walk."

"You'll be fine, darling," she said. "And it looks stunning. You know why she did it, don't you? She heard that Schiaparelli had designed something like this for a Hollywood star who is pregnant and she wanted to outdo her."

"Then let someone else wear it," I protested. "Someone who actually knows how to walk in it."

My protestations were cut short by the arrival of Chanel herself. "*Magnifique*," she exclaimed as she saw me. "The shape, it is perfect. And nobody would know that a baby lurks inside." She eyed me critically. "You are happy, no?"

"I would be if I could walk in it," I said. "I'm terrified of falling over."

"Don't worry, *ma petite*. I will not force you to make the grand entrance down the stairs. You shall be in the small back room until the show is over. When I give my final speech you shall appear and I will present my latest design to the world—as a little extra treat for the spectators, *non*? You can go along with that, yes?"

"I suppose so," I said. "As long as no stairs or runways are involved."

She laughed. "You must learn to have courage, my child. You are an important lady. People are excited to meet you. You must act as if you are doing them a favor. Besides, there will be certain people in the audience that I need you to charm. Mrs. Simpson, for example. I know that you are acquainted with her. She is coming to the viewing, but I hear that she has already asked Schiaparelli to make her summer outfits. This is not good. You will work on her for me. And several royal persons—Princess Maria of Bulgaria? You know her?"

"Matty? Oh yes. I know her quite well," I said.

"Oh, and your mother. She has impeccable taste. She will buy from me, but she brings with her a group of Nazi wives and you know they have no idea. Do you speak German?"

"I'm afraid not," I said.

"No matter. You and your mother must flatter them into making big purchases. I'm counting on you, my sweet."

"I'll do my best," I said.

"Voilà. What an asset you will be to me." She patted my arm and rushed off again, leaving me rather breathless, the way one always was when encountering Chanel.

The rehearsal went as all final rehearsals go—full of minor disasters that would never be repeated on the actual day. The most spectacular of these was me almost falling down the stairs in my new dress and grabbing onto the model in front of me, who then grabbed onto the person in front of her, and so on like a pack of cards. Luckily there were no broken bones—only a few headdresses out of place and one torn shoulder, easily repaired.

"You see," I said to Belinda as she helped me down the last of the stairs. "I am a walking disaster area, even more so when I can only take six-inch steps and those stairs are nine inches high."

"You'll be safely in the back room before the thing starts, so don't worry," Belinda said.

"But if I have to mingle? How can I even mingle?"

"The place will be crowded. Nobody will be able to move much."

My mind raced to the crowded floor with a microfilm hidden somewhere in the back room and me with no way to make it down the final flight of stairs and out to safety. Compared to the collapse on the stairs during the rehearsal, this was a major disaster waiting to happen.

Our rehearsal ended at five. We came home exhausted and sank into armchairs with cups of tea.

"Really, do we have to go tonight?" I asked.

"Oh yes. Harry has already told Gertrude we are coming." She leaned across and patted my knee. "Good for us, darling. Loads of culture and intellect. And I have to confess I am a little curious to meet Hemingway."

"You've read his books?"

"Of course. Hasn't everyone?"

I hadn't taken my friend for a big reader—more a social but-terfly. Now I had another way to feel inadequate. I realized my own reading was limited to writers like Agatha Christie. Well, there was a fine library at Eynsleigh. Perhaps I could become an educated woman before my child was born!

We ate a snack before setting off. Belinda felt that food might not be served until very late. Harry arrived, looking only slightly less scruffy than usual. He was wearing a dark blue fisherman's jersey and light blue trousers. The outfit suited him, however. He couldn't have tried harder to present himself as a struggling writer if he had had the word tattooed over his brow. But I realized that for once I would not feel underdressed in my long cardigan and straight wool skirt.

"Should we find a cab?" Belinda asked.

"It's not far. It's a nice night and we can walk. It's right next to the Jardin du Luxembourg. Rue de Fleurus."

We walked. It was a fine night and the Left Bank was teeming with activity. Loud students outside cafés, music spilling from open windows, couples locked in embraces right there on the pavement, not seeming to care who saw them. This was Paris, I thought. A city that was fully alive, and I realized how cut off from everything I had been for most of my life. How I would enjoy all of this if it weren't for that small nagging whisper that reminded me of what I had to do tomorrow. I tried to dismiss it and enjoy the moment.

Halfway down the Jardin du Luxembourg we came to the Rue de Fleurus. Harry led us through to one of those little courtyards that seem to be a feature of many Parisian buildings. Inside, a door was open. Two men were standing on the gravel of the courtyard arguing passionately. It looked, from the hand-waving, as if they were ready for a fight. As we came closer I heard one saying, in

French, "But of course if you think that Picasso's latest is not the greatest thing he has ever done, then you are a blind fool."

Harry squeezed past them and led us up a flight of stairs. We stepped into a large room, the walls of which were covered in paintings, mostly of the Impressionist school. Large paintings, small paintings both traditional and modern, reaching up to the high ceiling. It took me a moment to notice that people were sitting on sofas around the walls, all engaged in intimate conversations. A tight knot of people stood together in the middle of the room and from the midst of that knot came a loud and deep voice. "It's only at that moment when you are facing death that you know you are truly alive!" said the voice.

Harry nudged us. "Hemingway. He's here!" he whispered with awe.

Before we could reach the group of people, a stout middle-aged woman with a very short haircut, wearing a long skirt and a cardigan rather like mine, came up to us. "Harry, dear boy. I'm so glad you came," she said. "And these are your new friends?"

"Hi, Gertrude," he said. "Yes, this is Belinda and this is Georgie. This is our hostess, Gertrude Stein."

"Welcome, welcome," Gertrude said. "Grab yourselves a drink. You're artists, I take it. Do you paint? Write?"

"Neither, I'm afraid," Belinda said. "But I design clothes."

"Ah. Also a creator then," Gertrude said. "Never had that much interest in clothes myself. Never had the figure for it, I suppose. Alice has always despaired of me."

She didn't say who Alice was and left us to welcome another newcomer. We wandered over to a table where cocktails and wine were being served. Harry immediately made a beeline back to the group around Hemingway. I just got a glimpse of a mop of dark hair and noticed he was taller than the rest of the crowd around him. Belinda gave me an indication that we should go over to join them. I followed, reluctantly. Harry pushed into the group and I saw that Arnie was already there, his gaze fixed on Hemingway.

"So do you think I could take a photograph of you, Mr. Hemingway?" he was asking as we approached.

"Sure. Why not? Who knows, when I go to Spain I may get too much into the thick of the fighting and not return. Always a risk, but I wouldn't have it any other way. So yes, dear boy. You may be taking the last picture of Hemingway."

He struck up a pose—chin jutted out, manly stance. I found it all a bit theatrical, as if Hemingway were playing himself in a film.

"Harry, quick. Hold my flash equipment," Arnie called. Harry picked up the big flash attachment and obliged. The flash made us all blink.

"Come on," Hemingway boomed out the words. "All join in. Let's commemorate the occasion, shall we?"

As the group gathered around him, he noticed us.

"And who are these delectable creatures?" he said, his eyes traveling over Belinda's body. "They are not your usual types, Gertie. Models?"

"We're British aristocrats," Belinda said. "Come to enjoy the delights of Paris."

"Splendid. Paris is the one place in the world where you feel truly alive."

I didn't point out that a minute earlier he said that only when you were facing death did you feel truly alive.

"I'm a great admirer of your work," Belinda said.

"Really? A gorgeous beauty who reads books? Amazing. Which is your favorite?"

"I'm afraid it's *A Farewell to Arms*," Belinda said. "I cried buckets at the end."

"Me too," he said, "but it had to end that way. No happy endings after that war. It's a pity I'm leaving again in the morning. Going down to Spain, you know. I'm reporting on the civil war that has broken out. Nasty business. I'd love to have shown you around my favorite haunts." And the way he looked at her indicated that he was interested in getting to know her better. Belinda had that effect on men. "But you two must stay and take in all the delights of Paris. Have you been to Harry's bar yet?"

"Not yet," I said, because he was looking at me.

"Probably better not," he said. "Full of Americans. You want the real Parisian haunts. Americans can be deadly dull, which is why I escaped in the first place."

"You're so right," Arnie said. "That's why we all escaped."

"One of the reasons," Harry added.

Hemingway looked at him with understanding. "The war. I get it. We were all damaged. None of us would ever be the same afterward. That's why I write—" Then a wicked smile crossed his face. "That and the fact that they pay me large amounts of money."

"Come on, you guys," Arnie interrupted. "Harry and I are standing here, waiting to take a photograph. Bunch together now with Mr. Hemingway in the middle."

We did as we were told. I noticed Belinda managed to position herself beside him and he put his arm around her. Again the flash went off.

"Don't stand there not drinking, children," Gertrude interrupted. "And there is food in the kitchen. Grab it." She broke off as she stared at the doorway. "Now who could this be? Someone I don't recognize."

We followed her gaze. The woman in the doorway stood out in that she was dressed quite differently from the rest of us. A blue velvet evening cape was draped around her shoulders. Under it she was wearing cerise silk with lots of necklaces and a cheeky feathered hat on her head—she looked more suited to a garden party than an artist's soiree. "Hi," she said. "Am I in the right place? Gertrude Stein? Someone at the Plaza Athénée where we are staying said that you had the best collection of Impressionist art in Paris. I adore Impressionist art. Just adore it. So . . . peaceful. Tranquil. I have to have some."

"And you are?" Gertrude walked toward her.

"Mrs. Rottenburger. Elsie Rottenburger of the Philadelphia Rottenburgers."

Chapter 15

What an evening of strange encounters. After my dull and peaceful life in England, to meet Hemingway, a rude millionairess and a lady art collector in one evening is all a bit much. But at least it took my mind off what I have to do tomorrow.

Belinda gave a little gasp. "Rottenburger," she whispered. "She's the awful woman who kept pushing her way into Chanel, trying to buy pieces from the collection before the fashion show."

"How do you do?" Gertrude said politely. "You are most welcome. Any friend of the Impressionists is a friend of mine. I knew them all, you know. They used to come here. Renoir, Manet. And then the Expressionists, Cubists. Picasso, of course. He's been a regular." She held out her hand.

The other woman extended a pudgy hand full of rings to grasp it. "Thrilled to be here. Absolutely thrilled. One of the highlights of my Paris trip. My husband has kept bugging me to go to Europe. Go and enjoy yourself, Elsie, he keeps saying. He can't get away, of course. Much too busy. In steel. Made a fortune." She realized she was still pumping Gertrude Stein's hand, and dropped it. "Here, take my cape and gloves, dear." She turned to a girl who had been almost invisible in the shadows behind her. A small, dowdy creature with frightened eyes, looking nervously around the room. "I always find capes are so useful, don't you? Hide a multitude of sins." And she laughed at her own joke.

"And who is this?" Gertrude asked kindly. "Your daughter?"

"God no," Mrs. Rottenburger said. "I only have one child. My beloved son Richie. This is my niece and companion, Madge. I take her everywhere with me. Invaluable when it comes to hailing cabs and carrying things. Here you go then, Madge. Find somewhere to put them where they won't get damaged."

Madge took the items she was given and Gertrude indicated where she should put them.

"I can't tell you how relieved I am that we're speaking English here," Mrs. Rottenburger went on. "My French is limited to *bonjour* and 'where is the toilet.'" Again she laughed loudly. "Are most of your guests American, then?"

"About half and half," Gertrude said. "It's always a good mixture of nationalities."

"Don't tell me those bearded young men are American," she said. "They must be French, not nice, clean-cut American boys."

"Oh, I think you'll find that American boys are never clean-cut once they are over here," Gertrude said with a wink at Harry and Arnie.

"Well, I suppose this is the realm of artists, isn't it? The Left Bank? I've seen *La Bohème*. I know how artists suffer. That's what makes great art, isn't it? Suffering?"

"Harry, get the lady a drink, for heaven's sake." Gertrude looked around. Harry was standing against the far wall, a look of horror on his face at the new arrival.

"Just a minute," he said. "I just need to take care of this." He didn't mention what "this" was and I suspected it was escaping to the kitchen.

"Oh, I'll do it myself," Gertrude said. "Come on, honey. Over here."

"That was a fellow American, was it? The one who walked out so rudely?"

"That's right. Harry Barnstable. I expect he's gone to stock up on food. They don't come to me for the art and culture, you know. They come for the free food. Starving artists, all of them. Not that I mind. I enjoy their company."

"Barnstable? He looked familiar," Mrs. Rottenburger said, then gave a little shriek of delight. "I'm sure . . . Wait. Now there is a face I recognize!"

"Oh, you mean Mr. Hemingway," Gertrude said. "Yes, we are old and dear friends. I encouraged his first writing attempts, you know."

"Fancy that," Mrs. Rottenburger said. "Well, I just have to meet him so I can tell the ladies at the Junior League back home that I mingled with celebrities. Hey, Mr. Hemingway." She pushed through his crowd of admirers. "Delighted to meet you. Elsie Rottenburger from Philadelphia. I think we may know some of the same people. You know Joe Kennedy, of course? His wife, lovely woman. Such good fashion sense."

I could see from Hemingway's face that he was half amused, half appalled.

"I don't think we move in the same circles, Mrs. Rottweiler," he said, making some of the group turn a chuckle into a cough.

"It's Rottenburger," she corrected. "And I'm a great patron of the arts at home, you know. My son would have done brilliantly in the arts if it had not been for the war. He showed great promise as a writer and painter. He is probably about the same age as you, poor boy. He came home from France badly damaged. He had breathed in mustard gas that ruined his lungs, but it was his poor mind that suffered most. He saw his best friend blown to pieces beside him, you know. Absolutely blown to pieces. There was no body to recover." She stopped, staring out past the group as if she were seeing something from long ago and far away.

"I'm sorry to hear that." Hemingway gave an embarrassed cough. "The war was hell for a lot of people. Some of the things I saw still give me nightmares. But if you'll excuse me, I have other places to go tonight. I just stopped by to see old friends."

He extricated himself from his admirers and went over to give Gertrude a kiss on the cheek. "Sorry, old girl," I overheard him saying in a low voice, "but you know what I think about people like her. Another moment and I'd have strangled her with my bare hands. Why on earth did you invite her?"

"I didn't. She arrived. Out of the blue," Gertrude said. "I could hardly throw her out, could I?"

"I would," he said. "But I have to go."

He turned to wave to the assembled group. "Good to see that Paris is still thriving. Must go. Enjoy life, kids." And he went down the stairs.

"What a pity," Mrs. Rottenburger said. "Just when we were getting to know each other better. But I suppose famous men like him are much in demand. But now to get down to business—let me see which of these magnificent paintings I'd like to buy from you."

There was a small gasp around the room.

"I'm afraid they are not for sale," Gertrude said politely. "This is my personal collection."

"Nonsense." Mrs. Rottenburger laughed. "You don't need all these. My decorator always says one painting per wall for the best effect. They just cancel each other out when they are stacked like this. So which can you most bear to part with? I'll pay good money."

"I told you, they are not for sale," Gertrude said. "You don't walk into someone's private residence and try to buy their paintings. At least you don't in my world."

Mrs. Rottenburger's face was now bright red, but I couldn't tell whether it was from anger or embarrassment. "Well, that is a disappointment," she said. "I'd set my heart on going home with at least a Monet."

"Here, have a drink," Gertrude said. "At least you shall enjoy my hospitality for free."

She led the woman over to the bar.

"And how do you know Hemingway?" she asked.

"I've known him since he first came here as not more than a boy," Gertrude said. "I taught him to write, you know. He won't admit it but I did. You should have seen his first attempts. Pitiful. But we have remained dear friends. He comes to visit any time he's in Paris. They all do. Fitzgerald, Picasso, Matisse. They think of this as their home away from home, don't they, Alice?" She looked across the room to a slim, dark-haired woman, who smiled and nodded.

Mrs. Rottenburger was looking around as Gertrude was speaking. "Oh, you have a camera, young man. Let's take a picture to commemorate the occasion. Do you work for one of the newspapers? I'd sure love to see my photo in a newspaper."

"I'm freelance right now," Arnie said. I could see he felt uncomfortable.

Mrs. Rottenburger frowned, staring at him. "You look familiar too. Of course, it's hard to judge under all those whiskers. What's your name?"

"Arnold," he said. "Arnold Franzen."

"See—I knew it. The Franzens. The Pittsburgh Franzens, right? Your brother was at West Point, wasn't he? I never forget a face even though it's been years. So what are you doing here? Not going into the family business?"

"I'm escaping," Arnie said. "And not going into the family business."

"Do take a picture and I'll give you my address to send me a copy back home."

Arnie grudgingly raised his camera. "Harry, where's the flash?" he called.

Harry did not appear, but the flash attachment was sitting on a nearby table. "Where's he gone now?" Arnie said angrily. "Here, Pierre. Hold the attachment, will you?" I noticed then that the handsome waiter was also in the room, looking tonight like the suffering poet.

The photo was taken. An odd silence followed as if the photo had frozen the moment. I moved over to the companion, Madge, who was standing awkwardly by the doorway. "Come and have a drink," I said. "I'm Georgie."

"Oh, I don't think I should drink, thank you. Aunt Elsie likes me to be alert for hailing cabs and the like."

"I'm sure one drink won't make you less alert." I gave her an encouraging smile. "Here. A glass of wine can't hurt."

She gave me a grateful smile. "And I gather they've some really good food in the kitchen. Come on." I led her through to a magnificent spread of cheeses, cold meats, pâtés, terrines. We both helped ourselves, then I led her back into the salon and invited her to sit beside me on a vacant sofa.

"Do you enjoy traveling with her?" I asked.

I saw a spasm of annoyance cross her face before she answered,

"I get to see places I never would otherwise. My branch of the family lost all its money in the crash of '29, you see. We were destitute. So Aunt Elsie took me in, partly to be a companion for Richie."

"He's not at all well, I understand?"

She nodded. "The poor thing was wounded in the war. His lungs, his eyesight and also really bad shell shock. He gets nightmares, you know—over what he saw. It's enough to snap anyone's mind. And he can't seem to settle to anything. I shouldn't say this, but his mother does baby him too much. I think he'd improve if he had something to keep him occupied, not sitting around staring at the wall all day."

"Oh dear. That does sound horrible," I agreed.

"I tried to get him to put the horrors behind him and move on, and I think I was making progress, but Aunt Elsie stopped me."

"Madge, don't sit there gossiping!" came the commanding voice. "Get my cape again. It's time we were going, since there seems to be no point in staying on." She looked at Arnie. "And you, young man. You should stop by the hotel tomorrow. Oh, wait, not tomorrow. Tomorrow is the Chanel fashion show. I have my eye on a couple of outfits I simply have to have. But maybe Monday? I'll treat you to lunch. We'll have a chat about old times. I can report back to your family. I don't suppose they've seen you in a long while. You look to me as if you could use a decent meal, and a haircut."

"I'm quite happy the way things are, thank you," Arnie said. "But you are welcome to give my family my best wishes."

"And the other young man . . ." She looked around the room. "The other American man?"

"Harry?" Arnie said.

"Is that his name? He looks familiar too, but also in need of a good haircut. Where did he get to?"

"I think he went off with some fellows down to the café."

"Pity," she said. "I was quite prepared to report back to families at home. I know everyone who is anyone, you know. Never mind. I'll catch him another time." She wagged a finger. "I know. I should have a little reception for my fellow Americans at the hotel. Make them cook hamburgers and serve Coca-Cola. Give you all a taste of home. Wouldn't that be a riot?" She turned to Madge, who now held her outer garments. "Make a note of that, Madge, and see if you can set it up with the management tomorrow. Give me your addresses, will you, and I'll be in touch." She turned to Gertrude. "I may be back. I won't give up on my painting. I'll wear you down, you know. I usually get what I want in the end."

"Over my dead body," Gertrude muttered.

"But I tell you what—just to show there are no hard feelings, I'll invite you to my American party too."

"Not wishing to be rude," Gertrude said, "but the last thing in the world that I would want is to eat hamburgers and drink Coke in a room full of your American friends, and I expect my guests feel the same way."

"Well, really. That's gratitude for you." Mrs. Rottenburger snatched the cape, swung it over her shoulders like a bullfighter and stalked from the room.

Chapter 16

The big day. They are not butterflies in my stomach—they are giant
moths wearing army boots and dancing around. I wish it was
over. I wish I could go back to Darcy and just be a tourist in
Paris. Actually I wish I could go home. . . .

It was quite late when Harry came back. I had been wondering if
we could leave without him. He apologized, saying he'd promised
to critique a friend's poetry, but I suspect it was more to avoid the
dreadful Mrs. Rottenburger. She quite spoiled the party and left
everybody on edge.

"Now I know why you left America," Belinda said as we walked
home. "People like her must be awful."

"She is new money," Harry said. "Tries to buy her way into
society."

"She tried to buy her way into Chanel." Belinda chuckled. "But she didn't get the better of Madame. I doubt anybody can. So can't I persuade you to come and help out tomorrow?"

"I don't look the type for Chanel," Harry said. "And I'm not trimming my beard. It's taken me ages to grow it this full."

"Probably a good idea to stay away," Belinda said. "Mrs. Rottenburger will be in attendance, trying to outbuy half the royal families of Europe, I don't doubt."

"That I'd like to see." He chuckled. "She's tried to worm her way into New York society, I bet." He paused. "With little luck."

"I just hope she doesn't cause a scene," Belinda said.

One more thing for me to worry about.

THE NEXT MORNING Belinda boiled eggs for breakfast. "There won't be any time to eat all day," she said. "We'll need our energy."

At noon we changed and took a taxi across the Seine. It is amazing how easily one slips into the habit of taking cabs when one is with rich people. At home I've always counted the pennies and walked. I rather hoped there would be another message from Darcy, preferably saying that the whole business had been called off. But there was not a peep from him. So I presumed it was going ahead as planned. I took a big carrier bag with me, stuffed with odd pieces of clothing and suitable for the rapid hiding of a microfilm.

As we entered the boutique all was ready. There were enormous vases of flowers on either side of the staircase and the air was full of rather sickly perfume. The seating chart was at a front table in the boutique and the plan was that the ladies would check in down there, and be escorted up the staircase on the arm of a handsome young man. There were several of these, dressed in evening suits and looking extremely dashing. My American friends were not among them. The young men would take the ladies to their assigned place, so there could be no last-minute fighting over the best seat. I took a glance at the back row on the far side and saw Frau Goldberg's name about halfway along. I would be in the anteroom at the rear of the salon, watching from the shadows, hoping I wouldn't trip over anything when I made a swift sortie to exchange programs. Oh golly! I wish it were over.

We passed through the salon, now looking very grand with two rows of gilt and brocade chairs facing a central runway, which was draped and swathed with gray satin on either side. The blinds had been lowered over the tall windows and chandeliers sparkled, making it feel as if it were the middle of the night and not midafternoon. The beautiful young men were putting programs on chairs. I was glad to notice a pile of extra programs on a chair just beside the back room and helped myself to one before they all disappeared. I'd be needing it later.

As we entered the back room a table was now almost blocking the entrance, concealed behind the heavy velvet drapes, and on the table were trays of glasses and ice buckets with champagne, waiting to be opened. In the corner of the room a curtain had been drawn back to reveal another staircase—a small wrought iron affair that led up to the workshop.

"I'll never get back down those stairs again in this," I complained once we'd reached our destination.

"Just hitch it up, darling," Belinda said testily. "Nobody will see in the darkness of that room."

Chaos was reigning up in the workroom, with half-clad models standing patiently while seamstresses made last-minute adjustments. Belinda ushered me over to a far corner and helped me into the dreaded dress. It seemed even tighter and narrower around my legs than before and fear gripped at my stomach. She then proceeded to arrange my hair and make up my face. I looked like a strange doll when I saw myself in the mirror. I've never been one for much makeup, having grown up in the wilds of Scotland, but I had to admit the result was fetching. I hitched the skirt up to above my knees and was making my way down the back stairs, very cautiously, one step at a time, and hanging on to the central pole, when I heard a wolf whistle.

"Nice legs," said a man's voice, and it was Arnie. Harry was standing beside him, both watching as I exposed my legs to the world.

I blushed furiously. "What are you doing here? I thought you hadn't passed muster."

"We didn't pass muster as escorts," Arnie said. "Not pretty enough, obviously, but she needed extra guys for the heavy stuff. We put out the chairs and we have to clear away right after the show so that the guests can walk around and mingle."

"I thought this wasn't your thing," Belinda said to Harry.

He shrugged. "She pays good money. I have to eat. And I don't mind being invisible."

I noticed they were both wearing suits. Arnie had his camera with him.

"So will Chanel let you take pictures?"

"I'm going to take first and ask permission afterward," Arnie said. "I gather there are press photographers downstairs, watching the arrivals. I'll try to catch the ladies as they enter here." He peered out into the still empty salon. "Trouble is the light is bad in there. They'll turn on the spotlights for the runway but the rest will be impossibly dark. And I don't know if I dare use flash. We'll just have to play it by ear."

"Maybe you'll have to wait for the reception afterward," I said. "Everyone will be milling around then and the lights will be turned on again."

"But that's when Harry and I will be toting chairs." He glanced at the staircase, which I now noticed also descended from this room, winding down in darkness to the ground floor. "I suppose I could go down and try my luck with the big boys as the celebs arrive."

"Why don't you?" I said.

"You're darned right. I will. I like your style, Georgie." He glanced at Harry. "Coming?"

"Not me," Harry said. "I don't mingle well with celebrities. I'll stay and keep Georgie company."

Actually I didn't want company, but I could hardly tell him to go with Arnie. I looked around the room we were in. Behind the table with glasses there were extra chairs stacked against the walls. Various garments hung from a rail. I couldn't tell if they would be used during the show or were not needed. I placed my carrier bag on the floor in the corner, out of sight. If Harry was going to hang around here throughout the whole show, that might make it awkward.

We heard voices coming up the stairs. Chanel appeared with one of her assistants. She spotted me standing in the doorway. "Out of sight, *ma petite*. The guests arrive. The curtains, Minette."

And the assistant crossed the room to where we were standing, releasing the drapes across the doorway so that we were now hidden. That was annoying. I had expected to be able to watch everyone arrive. I stood to one side, pulling back the curtain enough so that I could look out through a crack. The lights were dimmed so that the salon now felt like a fish tank with a soft, greenish glow. Voices were heard coming up the stairs.

"Let me show you to your seat, Your Royal Highness."

Curiosity got the better of me. I peeked out and saw the crown princess of Bulgaria, alias my former school chum Matty, being led by one of the dashing gentlemen. Another woman followed behind, a lady-in-waiting, I presumed. Matty was seated in the middle of the front row. The other woman was given a seat against the wall. It was going to be fun to surprise Matty after the show, I thought, but then I remembered, after the show I would have to escape as soon as possible. I was to make my way out to the street, where Darcy, or someone sent by him, would collect what I had brought with me. He'd bump into me, say, "Excuse me, madame," and take my carrier bag. It seemed simple enough. But now Chanel expected me to stay and mingle. When would I be able to get away? And what if the Nazis had sent a spy with them—one who noticed the exchange with Frau Goldberg? And what if he or she came into the back room and produced a gun and demanded . . . ? I felt a cold sweat come over me. Golly, I wished this was over.

More voices on the stairs. A ring of laughter that I recognized and Zou Zou appeared. It must have been a flying visit to Antibes! It was all I could do not to rush into her arms. Behind her was Mummy. I don't ever remember rushing into her arms. She wasn't the hugging type, at least not with other females, but she would have been a comfort to me. Actually it was a comfort to know those two were nearby. The room began to fill. There were elegantly dressed Frenchwomen, probably aristocrats, who were seated in the front row. Then I heard the assistant say, "Your seat, Frau Göring." I peered out, trying to get a good look at her. Frau Göring and another German woman were put at one end of the front row—not deemed as important as a princess, then. I tried to see where the rest of the German party was being put but couldn't. I thought I made out the feathers in Frau Goldberg's hat. I had to dart back as one side of the curtains was opened and one of the young ushers came in to open more champagne.

"Do you want help with those?" Harry asked. "I work at Harry's bar. No, I'm not that Harry." He laughed, took a cloth and deftly opened the champagne bottle. The waiter accepted the bottle with a smile and began to pour. Some glasses on the table had tipped over. I righted them and held them out to be filled. Harry opened the other bottles until the glasses on the tray were filled and then carried out into the audience by the usher. Harry opened another bottle with a satisfying pop and started to fill the last tray of glasses on the table. "Here, hand me those," he said. "It's kind of hard to fill without spilling."

I obliged, holding out glasses while he poured.

At that moment I heard a voice I thought I recognized. "But I was supposed to sit at the front. There are no more seats. Can't you move one of these people?" So Mrs. Rottenburger had arrived.

I didn't hear the reply, but I would guess it was no.

Then I heard, "Oh wait. Here's a spare seat. I'll take this one."

This time I did hear an urgent "No, no, madame. This is for a very important lady. She is a little late but she will be here."

"Important lady? What important lady?"

"Ah, here she is now," said the voice that I now realized was Chanel herself. "Welcome to Chanel, dear Mrs. Simpson."

I pulled the drape aside to see that familiar boyish figure, wearing a suit with military-style black jacket and silver buttons, with a fox fur draped over her shoulders. She took her place at the end of the front row closest to where I was standing and looked around to see who had noticed her. My mother was sitting across from her on the other side.

"Well, look who's here," she called across to Mummy, although most of the women were chatting in hushed voices. "So they let you out of Germany, huh, honey?"

"Hello, Wallis," Mummy replied. "Fancy seeing you here."

"So you have finally left what's-his-name and are getting ready to go back into circulation?"

"No, I'm not intending to. In fact we're planning a wedding,"

Mummy said. "What about you? Are *you* planning to be back in circulation?"

There were a couple of shocked faces from those who overheard this. Mrs. Simpson might still be unknown to the British public, thanks to the newspapers' agreement not to mention her, but on the Continent she was fair game and had been photographed with the Prince of Wales for years.

Mrs. Simpson gave her a cat-with-the-cream smile. "Not in a million years, honey. In fact you might have to start practicing your curtsy next time you meet me."

I stared at her with shock. So she really did plan to go ahead and marry the new king. It seemed impossible, but if anyone was used to getting her own way it was Wallis Simpson.

The ushers were now carrying out trays of champagne and serving them to the seated ladies. Harry obliged by helping out and opening more bottles with a skilled ease I found impressive. The buzz of conversation rose higher as the champagne was consumed. I noticed Arnie had come back up the stairs following a bevy of press photographers who were ushered to the far side of the room. He gave me a thumbs-up sign and moved close to where I was standing.

"I got a couple of great shots," he said. "One of Mrs. Simpson. Now if I can . . ." He didn't finish the sentence because one of the official photographers noticed his camera.

"No, no," he said in French. "Who are you? It's forbidden." And he tried to take Arnie's camera.

"Hey, get your hands off," Arnie said in English. Harry darted out to help him, taking his camera to safety, and confronted with two tall Americans the photographer backed down. I don't know what might have happened next, but suddenly the lights were dimmed completely, the room now in semidarkness. An expectant hush fell upon the attendees. A lone spotlight shone onto the stairs. Chanel made her entrance down the mirrored staircase, looking stunning in a high-necked black gown with three rows of pearls. She welcomed everyone in French, English and German. I stood alert, program in my hand, wondering if this would be a good moment to complete my task. All eyes were on Chanel. But then I didn't want to risk her seeing me when she had told me to stay hidden until the show was over. She welcomed their royal highnesses, old friends and new friends, and told them they were in for a treat. Her collection comprised classic elegance, the Chanel they knew and loved, with daringly modern pieces sure to make a sensation if you chose to wear them at home.

Her speech finished to a round of polite applause. Again the room was plunged into darkness. I saw Arnie slip into the back of the salon, camera in hand. It would have been a good moment for me except that I now could not see where I was going and risked blundering into something or someone. A spotlight danced over the staircase and music was playing in the background.

"For my first creation I present Danielle," Chanel said. "Wearing an updated version of my classic suit. The perfect outfit for crisp autumn weather."

A tall model came slowly down the stairs. She was wearing a soft pink and mauve tweed with the familiar braid-trimmed jacket. Flashbulbs went off from the photographers who stood around the walls. I wondered if Arnie was one of them. The model strode the length of the runway, paused at the end close to me and removed her jacket, revealing a silk blouse and mannish tie. She trailed the jacket as she walked back toward the staircase, turned, paused, posed, then made her way down the stairs to the floor below to more polite applause. Clearly this outfit had not excited the audience. It was classic Chanel but nothing new.

More models followed, each outfit a little more daring than the last. The applause level rose with each one.

"I'm going out for a smoke," Harry whispered to me. "They won't need me for a while."

"You're not interested in high fashion?" I asked.

He chuckled. "What do you think? I'll be back."

I was relieved he was going. Then I wouldn't have to explain my darting out with a program in my hand.

Immediately the spotlight focused on the top of the staircase again. Another model. Another outfit. I decided this would be the perfect moment to do what I had to. I knew that the gold lamé dress was coming—the most gorgeous thing in the collection. All eyes would be on it the moment it appeared. I waited, holding my breath. The music grew louder.

"And now the piece you have all been waiting for," Chanel said. "My most daring design of the season. Who will have the nerve to wear this, eh?"

And the model in the gold dress appeared at the top of the stairs. The crowd broke into gasps and applause. The long gold lamé dress came with a hood and completely clung to the figure of the model, almost looking as if she had been dipped in gold. You could see every small curve. She was definitely not wearing a brassiere, or panties as far as I could tell. But I couldn't wait another second to watch her. Clutching my program I crept behind the seated figures. The spotlights made the darkness here almost complete. But I picked out the feathers sticking from Frau Goldberg's Tyrolean hat, saw her cape and tapped her on the shoulder.

"Excuse me, madame, but you were given the wrong program," I whispered in her ear, in French, as instructed. "Here is the correct one."

She did not look up or hand me her program as I had expected.

She did nothing. Perhaps she was so focused on the model now descending the stairs, or the music that had now risen in volume and intensity, that she had not heard me whispering to her. I tapped her shoulder. "Madame? Your program?" But clearly she hadn't felt it through the thick cape she was wearing. I touched her shoulder again, a little more forcefully. My heart was beating so loudly that I was sure those around me must hear it. The model was close to the bottom of the stairs by now. Was the lady so engrossed that she forgot why she was there? I touched her hand. "Frau Goldberg?" I whispered. Then I recoiled. Her hand was cold. I shook her. Her head lolled to one side and to my horror she pitched forward, out of her seat.

The ladies sitting on either side of her gasped.

"She has fainted, poor thing," one said in French. "Get her out to the fresh air." She beckoned to one of the young men who was standing behind us. "Quick. This lady has fainted. Remove her to fresh air immediately."

Arnie was also standing nearby. He put down his camera and rushed to carry the woman out to the back room. Harry had returned and came out to help too.

"What happened?" he whispered to me. "Did she faint? Should we get a doctor?"

I was already kneeling in the darkness of the back room, trying to take her pulse. She had several bracelets on her wrist and it was hard to find the right place, but from the coolness of her skin I feared the worst. Someone had managed to kill Mrs. Goldberg. She no longer held a program. Her killer must have stolen it.

I turned to the usher who had carried her. "Can you go downstairs and telephone for a doctor? This lady has—" I couldn't come up with the French word for "fainted." What had the woman beside her said? "She is sick," I added.

"Should we carry her down to fresh air?" the man asked.

"I don't think you'd manage to get her down that little stair-case," I said. "And we can't move her from here until the show is over."

"I cannot leave. Madame will want me . . ." he said.

"I'll go," Harry said.

"I'm sorry, but I must try to get a good shot of that dress. I just missed the best angle. Harry, can you bring the flash?" But Harry had already run down the stairs to find a doctor. Arnie sighed and went out alone.

I peered out again through the slit in the closed curtains. Those sitting around Frau Goldberg seemed to have already forgotten her and everyone was staring at the runway as the gold-clad model moved forward, taking tiny steps in that narrow, form-hugging dress. My heart was still beating fast. There was nothing I could do before the show was over. No way to let Chanel know. If someone had already stolen the program, I had no way of retrieving it. And the microfilm? That was supposed to be in her hand. She was sup-posed to slip it to me when we shook hands. Had it rolled off her lap and onto the floor when she pitched forward, or had somebody taken it from her? I'd have to wait until the chairs were cleared away before I had a chance to look, and then it would be hard with so many women milling around. And someone else, her killer, maybe, would also be looking, trying to beat me to it.

Then I realized that her handbag must still be beside her chair. There was a slight chance the film was still in it—a chance worth taking. I risked slinking out again. The model in gold was now standing on the steps giving a final pose to loud applause. I crept forward, as swiftly as the stupid skirt would allow, and bent to re-trieve her bag.

"Is the lady all right?" the Frenchwoman beside her asked.

"She will be, but she needs her purse," I said.

"Naturally." She nodded.

I picked up the bag and carried it to the back room. The woman lay where we had put her on the floor. Feeling rather sick I opened the large handbag. I fished around inside it. Lipstick, powder compact, coin purse, wallet, handkerchief, comb, but no canister of film. I was too late, then, unless it had rolled across the floor. I'd have to be alert as soon as the show ended, because my adversary might also be seeking it. I was putting the items back when I saw her passport. I took it out. There was a letter tucked inside it. It was too dark to read in the gloom of that back room, so I carried the passport to the doorway, where the spotlights shone on the runway. Then I frowned. Weren't German passports green? I stared at it. The passport said "United States of America." I opened it and found myself staring at the letter tucked inside it. I was so shocked I almost dropped it in surprise.

Mrs. Elsie Rottenburger, C/O Hôtel Plaza Athénée, Paris.

Chapter 17

Oh golly, what an awful mess I'm in now. Why do these things
always seem to happen to me? I just wish at this moment I
could go home to my big safe house and my naughty puppies.
At least I know what I'm doing there.

My hand was trembling as I put the passport back into her purse. I
took a good look at her for the first time. In the twilight of the
room it was hard to see properly, but her eyes were open, almost as
if she were staring at me, and her face looked rather flushed. I also
thought I detected a faint smell coming from the body. Quite horrid, actually. I looked away. If Mrs. Rottenburger hadn't died of
natural causes there had been a terrible error. Someone had mistaken her for Frau Goldberg. It was easy enough to do. They were
of the same build, same light hair. She had worn a hat, which, although not Tyrolean, had feathers sticking up on one side, and she

also wore what seemed to be a small green cape. I couldn't tell the exact color as we were in darkness, but she had also been sitting in Frau Goldberg's seat or really close to where Frau Goldberg should have been.

Harry came up behind me. "What are you doing?" he whispered.

What could I tell him? Thoughts were whirring around in my mind, a mile a minute.

"I wanted to see who she was so we can notify the rest of her party," I said. "You'll never guess who it is. It's Mrs. Rottenburger."

"Who?" he asked.

"Do you remember the awful American woman who came to Gertrude's? She wanted to buy Gertrude's pictures."

"Oh, I do remember," he said. "She was one of the reasons I was persuaded to make a fast break for it and go to hear Simon's poetry. And she tried to buy Gertrude's pictures, didn't she?"

"She did."

"I bet Gertrude was furious. She never parts with her artwork."

"You weren't there when Mrs. Rottenburger left? She threatened to come back and said she always got what she wanted in the end."

"I suppose I'm not allowed to say, 'If anyone deserved it she did,'" Harry quipped, but then shook his head. "That wasn't nice, was it? Be tactful, Harry. The poor woman obviously got too excited and had a heart attack. She was a real high-energy type, wasn't she? That type comes with heart problems."

"Yes. I suppose you are right." I truly hoped that he was. "I'm not sure what we should be doing," I said.

"There's not much we can do at the moment. They've gone for a doctor. He'll sign a death certificate. Do you know if she was with anybody here?"

"She had a companion," I said. "A poor relation whom she bullied . . ." I stopped in mid-sentence. Who might have finally had enough of being bossed around and humiliated and taken her chance to kill the bully. But I couldn't see any kind of wound on Mrs. Rottenburger. She was lying there quite peacefully, almost as if she were asleep. I found myself hoping that I'd gotten it wrong and she had only had a fainting fit. Any minute now she'd stir, sit up and start making a fuss again.

But she didn't. More evening dresses floated down the runway to rounds of applause. Then saucy evening pajamas. I paced, trying to breathe, trying to think what to do. "I can't get to Chanel without causing an awful scene, so I suppose we'll just have to wait," I said. "And knowing Chanel, she would hate me to cause a scene and put anybody off their buying sprees, but she'll have to know. I'm not allowed to come out until she fetches me. Maybe I can tell her then."

"Don't get yourself in a state," Harry said. "It's not your problem if some woman keels over. Who knows, perhaps she took stimulants. Cocaine or something. I hear they are really popular among the rich these days."

If only it were that simple. I prayed the doctor would arrive and take over. Maybe I was overreacting and she had died of natural causes, but it seemed too much of a coincidence that Mrs. Rottenburger had died in the exact location where I had expected to find a German woman about to hand over a secret formula.

"You don't think you should go and get the police, do you?" I whispered.

"The police? What on earth for?" He frowned.

And then I heard Chanel saying, "So that is my fall collection, highnesses and ladies. Who wants to make a fashion splash this autumn? Some of these will be offered as exclusives and others will be more readily available. But rest assured none of them will be offered to the masses. You will never see any of them on the peg in the high street.

"Lights, please, Jacques. Let us call back your models, ready to give you a closer look at those dresses you desire. And before we all stand and the young men put away our chairs, I have one more small surprise for you. I am not in the habit of designing clothing for expectant mothers, but this young woman is special. How could I resist when she is a cousin of the king of England? And so I made her a dress that no other pregnant woman will have, one that makes her look tall and elegant and she can wear throughout her pregnancy."

The voice stopped and before I could do anything sensible, the curtain was wrenched back and Chanel grabbed my hand.

"Mesdames, may I present Lady Georgiana Rannoch in my latest creation."

"Wait," I whispered to her. "There has been an emergency. We should do something. There is a dead woman on the floor. A doctor is coming. She collapsed."

Chanel looked past me to eye the corpse. "Who is it? Anyone of note?"

"It's an American lady. Mrs. Rottenburger. I checked her passport."

"Oh, her," Chanel said and gave a very Gallic shrug. "So the excitement was too much for her. All that shouting and blustering. But if she is dead she can wait awhile."

"But shouldn't we call the police?" I asked.

"The police? What for?"

"In case there was foul play."

"Foul play? Are you mad? Half the important women of Europe are in that audience. I cannot afford any scandal."

We could hear the crowd getting restless. The scraping of chairs.

"Leave her. Come. You are needed." And she dragged me out, blinking, into the bright light. There was another round of applause as I tried to waddle forward with tiny steps as Chanel led me down the room, in front of the audience. I was conscious of their eyes on me, the nods of polite approval. I tried to spot Zou Zou or Mummy—any friendly face. For one terrible moment I thought Chanel might try to take me up onto the stage, but instead she led me toward Princess Maria—my school friend Matty.

"I think you two ladies need no introduction," she said.

"Georgie!" Matty embraced me and kissed me on both cheeks. "What a lovely surprise. I had no idea you were in Paris, or that you were expecting. We wanted to come to your wedding last year, but as you know, I had a baby myself. He's adorable. Nicolas is besotted with him."

"Congratulations," I said. "Darcy is certainly looking forward to our little one. So did he come with you to Paris? Official visit?"

She laughed. "Not at all. It was his gift to me for presenting him with a son and heir. When I got my figure back he told me to go to Paris and choose new clothes. Wasn't that sweet of him?"

Here we were making small talk about babies and shopping while someone lay dead on the floor a few feet away. And possibly there was a murderer in the room. And a valuable canister of film waiting to be handed over. I just wished I knew what to do. I wished I were the sort of person with more natural authority who would have clapped her hands and demanded that everyone remain where they were because there had been a suspicious death. A few minutes later they would all be gone and it would be too late to question them.

I tried to keep my face relaxed and smiling while my eyes scanned the room. The women on the other side of the runway had now been asked to stand while Harry and the ushers moved the chairs back to the walls. Arnie, I noticed, was not helping with chairs, but was still taking pictures. I tried to see if I could spot Mrs. Goldberg, but there were plenty of hats, feathered and otherwise. Would I perhaps have a chance for a brief chat with her? Could I improvise? Shake her hand? Did my mother perhaps know her, and could I get them talking?

I had to get away from this conversation before it was too late. The men were going back and forth with chairs. The runway was in my way. Was this an occasion when I could be rude to a princess? Years of training had drummed into me that one only spoke when spoken to and that she would be the one to end the conversation.

But this was a matter of some urgency. "Would you excuse me, Your Highness?" I said, reverting to formality. "But I'd love a word with my mother before she leaves. I haven't seen her for ages."

"Oh, of course, your mother is here. You must go to her. I'm staying at the embassy. Perhaps you'd like to come to luncheon before I go home? We have quite a good chef." She saw my worried face. "And don't worry. I promise my brother won't be there." She gave a merry laugh. "Aren't you glad that you didn't marry him?"

I tried to laugh too. There had been an attempt to hook me up with her brother, Prince Siegfried of Romania, whom Belinda and I called Fishface and who was one of the more repulsive individuals I had met. Added to which he had a distinct preference for other men and told me if I gave him a son he'd never bother me again. Luckily these were no longer the days of forced marriage.

"I'd love to, if I can," I said. "A lot depends on when Darcy wants to return to England."

"Of course. Let me know your plans."

We kissed on the cheeks again and I began to make my way around the runway to the side where Mrs. Rottenburger and Mrs. Goldberg had been sitting. My progress was impeded by women who came up to me, examined my dress, asked me to turn around, congratulated me on my impending arrival. I felt as if I would scream at any moment. My eyes scanned for Zou Zou. If anyone would know what to do, it would be her. But she was involved in animated conversation on the other side of the runway. Belinda had now appeared and was standing beside a model wearing the black silk evening pajamas that I remembered she had designed. Frankly I thought they looked better than Chanel's, but of course I'd never say that.

Then I saw Madge, Mrs. Rottenburger's companion. She was standing against the wall, looking lost and puzzled. I went over to her.

"Did something happen to my aunt?" she asked, her forehead creased in a worried frown. "I was watching that lady in the gold dress come down the stairs and when I looked back her seat was empty. I can't get through that crush of people to try to find a restroom in case she's fainted. Aunt Elsie wouldn't leave without me—besides, how could she get out when the models were on the stairs?"

I put my hand gently on her arm. "I'm afraid your aunt was taken ill," I said. I took a deep breath. "In fact it's worse than that. She's dead."

"Dead?" Madge's mouth dropped open. "Are you sure?"

I nodded. "Maybe it was a heart attack. Did she have a weak heart, do you know?"

"Aunt Elsie? She was as strong as an ox. Never sick. Where is she?"

"They carried her through to the anteroom behind the curtains," I said. "Would you like me to take you to her?"

"Oh yes," she said. "I must go to her. What am I to do now, do you think? I'll have to arrange to have her body taken home, won't I? Oh gee, I didn't expect anything like this."

"If I were you I'd cable your uncle," I said. "Let him arrange everything from America. You'll probably have to deal with the French police, which won't be easy, but let him make the decisions."

"Police? Why would we have to deal with police?" She sounded dangerously close to hysteria.

"Before they will release the body to be shipped overseas," I said quickly. "You know French bureaucracy. So much formality."

"Oh, I see," she said. "I'd much rather my uncle handled it. My French is poor at the best of times. And I have no experience in dealing with customs and things."

"Don't worry too much. It will all sort itself out, I'm sure." I put a comforting hand on her arm.

"Yes. Thank you, Georgiana," she said. "You're most kind."

As we talked we eased our way through the crowd toward the curtains. A thought struck me. "Your aunt wasn't supposed to be sitting in that seat, was she?"

"No." Madge shook her head. "She wasn't. But they had put her back against the wall in the corner with people like me and she was furious. She took an empty chair and when the real occupant showed up Auntie told her to get lost. There was nothing the poor woman could do without causing a scene. And the show was about to start." She gave an awkward shrug. "You saw how my aunt was. She wanted her own way all the time, and she usually got it."

This confirmed my suspicion. It was a case of mistaken identity. I opened the curtains to show Madge her aunt's body, just as a man was coming up the stairs, breathing heavily after the climb. The French usher was with him. "Here is the doctor," he said.

He was a slim dark man sporting a goatee and he was all business. "Out of my way, please. Are you a relative of the deceased?"

"This lady is," I said, pointing to Madge.

"And you?" He looked at Harry, then at me.

"Not related," Harry said.

"Then please leave us. Go."

I would like to have said something—that she was in the wrong seat, that I suspected she had not died of natural causes. I gave a reluctant look back and reentered the salon. The ladies were now standing around the runway, fingering the fabric and chatting about the models as if they were mannequins and not real people at all. Finally I spotted the Tyrolean hat at the far end of the room. And the green cape, exactly as I had been told. Our eyes met. I was sure she knew who I was and why I was there. I inched my way toward her. Before I could reach her, Frau Göring summoned Chanel.

"I'm afraid we must be leaving, madame," she said in remarkably good French. "One of my party is not feeling well. But thank you for the opportunity. I'm sure we shall return to purchase some of these lovely creations before we go back to Germany."

"Thank you so much for coming, madame," Chanel said. "Such an honor."

Frau Göring gave a gracious nod as if she was quite aware of the honor. And before I could reach Frau Goldberg, one of the other German women took her arm and they started down the stairs. I wondered if Darcy was out in the street, or if someone else was waiting out there for me. I wondered what they would think or what they could possibly do. Nothing, I suspected. A taxi would be summoned and off they would go with the plans and the film still in Frau Goldberg's purse.

As I turned to go back to the room where the doctor would now be examining Mrs. Rottenburger, I overheard a voice I recognized only too well.

"I'm not letting you have it, Claire honey. Besides, it wouldn't suit you. You don't have the height to carry it off."

My mother and Mrs. Simpson were standing in front of the model wearing the gold evening dress. Both had determined looks on their faces.

"I'm about the same height as you, Wallis," my mother replied, "and it would go so much better with my coloring. With your dark hair you should stick to silver, I think."

"But I have the figure for it," Mrs. Simpson said. "Any little curve or bump would spoil the silhouette."

"You need some shape to carry it off," Mummy said. "You are straight up and down. You'd look like a gold drainpipe."

"You're rather bold, aren't you? I should warn you that I may well go ahead of you in the next procession we find ourselves in. You might have been a duchess once, but I believe the king's consort trumps duchess, doesn't it?"

"You really think that Parliament will let him marry you? You're living in a dream world, my dear," Mummy said.

"He's the king, isn't he? He'll change the law. You'll see. We've got it all planned. And that dress might just be part of my trousseau."

"I was thinking it might be part of mine," Mummy said. "But no matter. I leave it to you. It's rather too garish for German society. And probably a little too garish for English high society too, especially royal circles. But I'm sure it will go down well in Baltimore." She gave Mrs. Simpson a little smile, a little pat on the shoulder and walked away.

"Darling, that dress," Mummy said, eyeing me critically. "It makes you look like an elongated Humpty Dumpty."

"Thank you for the vote of confidence," I said. "Between ourselves I'm not too keen on it either."

"The moment you get it home have your dressmaker remove the bottom two feet. It won't be too bad as a short, flowing sort of dress."

"You're right," I said.

"We should get together and see if I can find you something more appealing to wear before I leave Paris," Mummy said. "Now that the trade delegation has done its bit they'll all be heading home. Max and I thought we'd stay for a few days on our own.

Romantic Paris, you know. It's been so long since we've had a romantic getaway." She gave a little sigh.

"They are all heading home?" I asked.

"Oh yes. All the official bigwigs. Göring and his mob. Frightful people, between ourselves, but one has to be polite to them because they hold so much power these days."

"Did you ever meet Frau Goldberg?" I asked.

Mummy frowned. "Goldberg? Is she Mrs. Göring's friend? Yes, I expect I said a few words to her. You know what my German is like—not too wonderful. Besides, I tried to keep myself apart from her little clique. Too much risk of saying the wrong thing. You know how it is in Germany these days. One has to be so careful what one says, and I'm not always the most tactful." She paused, considering this. "Why, do you know her?"

"Not personally," I said. "I had expected to meet her today, but they beat a hasty retreat."

"Why? What's the connection?"

"Oh, just a friend of a friend," I said.

Mummy glanced at her watch, looked around the room, then said, "Darling, I have to get back to clothes buying or these odious women will snap up my favorites. I'll be in touch. We'll go shopping." She kissed my cheek and fled, the way she had done so many times during my life, leaving me breathless and a little sad.

I was about to waddle my way around to Zou Zou when a stern male voice said, "Ladies, may I have your attention. There has been a suspicious death and I'm afraid nobody is to leave this building until the police arrive."

Chapter 18

SUNDAY, APRIL 26

AT AND AROUND THE HOUSE OF CHANEL.

Oh no. It looks as if things are going from bad to worse.

There was an uproar among the assembled guests.

"Ridiculous! What suspicious death? Who has died?" The words rang out in various languages.

"You can't keep us here against our will," one woman was shouting in English. "I'll call the ambassador."

Mrs. Simpson pushed past me. "Well, I'm certainly not staying," she said. "David can't afford any scandal connected with me right now. Chanel will understand."

As she headed for the staircase other women were coming up. "We can't get out. The front door is locked," one of them wailed.

"I'm sorry, madame." Chanel had walked over to the microphone. "I was told that nobody may leave for the moment. I ask for your patience. When an inspector arrives from the Sûreté I am sure you'll all be allowed to go."

Mrs. Simpson looked absolutely furious. "You'll be hearing about this," she said. "We will complain to the highest levels."

"Dear Mrs. Simpson, do not distress yourself." Chanel tried to placate. "Once the inspector knows who you are, of course you'll be allowed to go. Now please have a second glass of champagne. . . ."

I felt I had to step in. "I don't think anyone should touch the champagne," I said. "It might have been how this lady was killed."

"She was poisoned?" Chanel asked. "Are you sure?"

"I have no idea," I said, "but I saw no wound on her, so she wasn't stabbed. If the doctor thinks the death was suspicious enough to call the police it had to be something she swallowed, and that points to the glass of champagne."

"You think someone could have poisoned more of the glasses?"

"I don't know," I said. "But we should err on the side of safety."

"Oh là là." She shook her head. She turned to one of the ushers standing beside her. "Pierre, remove the trays of champagne before anyone takes another glass."

I suspected some women had already done so, but since none of them had keeled over yet it seemed logical that only one glass contained whatever it was that killed Mrs. Rottenburger. From the speed with which she died it was probably cyanide. That is known to act in seconds. I glanced across the room. "And we should try to find out which glass Mrs. Rottenburger drank from. The police will want to know. Do you have the seating plan?"

"Somewhere. But I'm not sure where la Rottenburger sat. My assistant said she put her against the back wall because she was being difficult."

"She changed places with another lady—Madame Goldberg," I replied. "One of the Germans."

"She did? Tiresome woman. How she ever got in, I'll never know. And if I had any idea how much she would upset everyone I would have moved body and soul to keep her out."

The usher was hovering nearby, obviously listening in to our conversation with interest. "Shall I wash the glasses and pour fresh champagne?" the usher asked.

"I think you should leave them as they are," I said, addressing him. "They might be evidence of a crime."

He shot me a look of alarm, then turned to Chanel for confirmation. She nodded. "Bring out new glasses," she said. "And open new bottles. We'll need to keep these women happy."

I didn't think the champagne was going to do much to lighten the mood. Now that I had a moment to consider I realized that the stable door had been closed after the horse had bolted. The party of German women had already left. If my suspicions were true and the poisoned champagne had been intended for Frau Goldberg, then her killer could have been a member of that party—perhaps the minder who was with my mother when I last met her at Chanel. I had heard whispers of secret police. Did they employ women? I realized that I felt sick and scared. I went over to one of the chairs and sat down.

Chanel's voice came on the loudspeaker again. "Do not distress yourselves, my dear friends. Take this as an opportunity to make your clothing selections in peace. See, the models are still here. And Marie-Claire, downstairs at the desk, will take your orders."

Just like Chanel, I thought. Business before anything. It hadn't fazed her at all that a woman had been killed on her premises, now that she knew it was a woman of no importance. The music was put on again. The noise level remained high.

Belinda came over to me. "I know who I'd like to murder," she said, taking a seat beside me. "Louis-Philippe's mother. She's here. Have you seen her yet? And she beckoned me over and treated me as if I was a shopgirl. When I looked askance she said, 'But you do work here, don't you, my dear? I'm sure my son told me.' Bloody cheek."

I gave a commiserating smile. "You're better off without him. Think what life would have been like if she was your mother-in-law."

"Oh goodness, imagine." She shook her head, then she frowned as she looked at me. "Are you all right?" she asked. "You look awfully white."

"It's all been a bit of a shock," I said.

"Do you know what happened? Any idea who died?"

"Mrs. Rottenburger, actually."

Belinda put her hand to her mouth in surprise, then gave a little chuckle. "I can think of a dozen people who would have liked to murder her, can't you?" Then she shrugged. "Oh dear. I shouldn't have said that, but it's true, isn't it? She was the sort of woman who made enemies wherever she went."

"She was," I agreed. "But . . ."

"But what?"

I realized then that I couldn't tell her what I knew—that she was almost definitely killed because she was in the wrong place. That the person that champagne glass was aimed for (if it was indeed the champagne) was a German spy, smuggling out a secret. I couldn't tell anyone, because there was a small chance that the microfilm could still be handed over.

"But it's horrible to think of anybody being killed, isn't it?" I finished lamely. "Someone will miss her at home. Her husband and her son loved her."

"You're becoming sentimental since you started expecting." Belinda chuckled again. "I must say, I'm not looking forward to being grilled by French police, are you? They are always so heavy-handed, I've found. Not that I have anything to worry about. I was upstairs, preparing the models to make their entrances. Perfect alibi."

Mummy came over to join us. "Isn't this too, too tiresome?" she asked, taking a seat beside me. "I expect we'll be stuck here for hours and now they've removed the champagne, which was the only thing that would have made it bearable."

"Spending time with your only child should make it bearable," I said, making her give a little shrug and a smile. "And besides, they've ordered more champagne. So why aren't you buying any clothes?"

"I didn't see anything that was really me," she said. "Except for those divine black evening pajamas. And someone else has already snapped them up. I simply couldn't wear the same outfit as anyone else."

"I designed those." Belinda looked delighted.

"Did you, my dear? How frightfully clever. I've just had a thought, then. Maybe you'd like to come over to my room at the Ritz to take my measurements and you could design me my own collection for my trousseau. Something nobody else has?"

"Golly. I'd love to." Belinda's face went pink, reminding me that for all her sophistication she was still young and vulnerable, just like me. "It would be an honor, Your Grace."

Mummy loved being called "Your Grace," in spite of not loving the reality of being a duchess since she and Daddy divorced. Of course, now that my brother was the duke, she could claim to be the Dowager Duchess of Rannoch, which she did.

"My own collection. How delightful," Mummy said. "I can't wait to wear it on a special occasion."

"Your wedding?" Belinda asked.

"In front of Mrs. Simpson," Mummy said and gave a throaty chuckle.

The place was beginning to calm down, the women having accepted their fate. The models had gone back up to the workroom. Some of the guests were now downstairs in the boutique, shelling out a lot of money on orders for some of the outfits. Champagne was being served again. Zou Zou came over to us.

"Well, this is exciting, isn't it? Somebody died? Who was it?"

"An American lady," I said.

"How strange. And they think her death was suspicious? What on earth happened? I didn't see any kind of altercation, did you? Do you think one of the women stabbed another over a dress she wanted?"

"I believe the lady was poisoned," I said. "Although I'm not sure."

"Poisoned? How strange. I could understand an anarchist using the occasion to kill a royal person. It happened to my own dear husband, after all. Not at a fashion show, of course, but after we were leaving a ball. But poison? Who would think it was a good idea to kill someone at an event like this? Much easier to do it where there weren't a finite number of people in the room. It seems quite improbable at a place like this, doesn't it?"

"Bizarre," Mummy agreed. "Surely there is no way an outsider could have sneaked in. Which means it's either an employee of Chanel or one of us."

"Well, I'm dying to see what happens next," Zou Zou said. "Do you think the police will question us all and one of the women will break down and confess? Or one of the servants will turn out to be an illegitimate child, cut out of the inheritance? That happens all the time at home in Poland too. Let's have a wager over who might have done it."

"Zou Zou!" I said. "It's not a game. It's a murder."

"I know," she said. "And I feel sorry for the poor woman, but it's not every day that one is at the scene of a suspicious death."

"Unless you are Georgie," Mummy said dryly. "She seems to attract it."

"I certainly don't," I said. "I hate it, if you want to know. I just seem to have witnessed more than my share."

"You certainly have," Mummy said. "What about that time in Devon when all those people died over Christmas?"

"That was awful."

"And last Christmas at Sandringham when that poor man was knocked off his horse and someone shot the poor major?"

"That was awful too," I said. "Really sad and frightening."

"Although that major had it coming," Mummy commented. "He had the nerve to suggest we pop into my bedroom for a quick one. I mean, darling, as if I could fancy someone like him after all the men I've known."

"He did the same to me," I said, laughing now.

"What is wrong with these middle-aged men that makes them think they are irresistible?"

We were all laughing together, as one does at moments of great tension, when there was the tread of heavy steps up the stairs and the police arrived, several men in uniform and two plainclothes detectives.

"The police have arrived," the older detective said. "Remain in your seats. Nobody is to move."

Chapter 19

Still at the House of Chanel. We may be here forever . . . if we are
    not taken off to jail. Oh dear. I don't know what I can tell them
    when they question me. I wish Darcy were here. He'd know.
    But it's his fault I am involved in this whole charade!

It was a dramatic entry, almost a stage entry, and it shocked the
complaining women into momentary silence. The older of the two
police detectives sported a black mustache and hair that I guessed
had been dyed black, because the face beneath it was pale and old
and tired. He looked around the room, recoiling at the sight of so
many well-dressed women.

"Who is in charge here?" he asked.

"It is I, naturally, since this is the House of Chanel." She stepped
out to meet him. "And your name is?"

"Chief Inspector Mauville," he said. "And this is Sergeant
Lapin."

Since *lapin* was the French word for rabbit and he looked kind of rabbity with big front teeth, I tried not to grin.

"I'm glad you have come, Chief Inspector," Chanel said. "And I trust that you will clear up this little unfortunate occurrence as quickly and smoothly as possible. These are important women. Some are members of the great royal houses of Europe. They are naturally desiring to leave as soon as possible."

"Believe me, madame, I would also hope that this can be concluded as quickly as possible. For me it is Sunday afternoon. And my men had hoped to watch the Saint-Denis football game." He glanced back at his officers, one of whom grinned. "However, duty comes first for us at the Sûreté. These women will be allowed to leave when our investigation is complete and not before, madame." He paused, then wagged a finger at her. "I may remind you that France discarded its aristocracy a hundred and fifty years ago. In the eyes of the law all are treated equally—rich man or beggar."

"All the same, these are important women whose husbands can create a big fuss if they are not treated properly."

Chief Inspector Mauville eyed the women now sitting around the walls with a suspicious gaze, probably wondering which ones had husbands who could make life difficult for him. Then he spotted press cameras. Not all the pressmen had left after the show.

"You. Out. Leave immediately. Go." He pointed to the stairs. "There is to be no reporting of this until you are given permission, is that clear?"

The newspaper reporters were escorted reluctantly down the stairs. Arnie, I noticed, had put away his camera and stayed.

"Now," the detective addressed Chanel. "Madame? Can you tell me what this is about? I see no body. Where is the body? This had better not be a joke at the expense of the police, because I must warn you we have no sense of humor in such matters."

"It is no joke," Chanel said. "One of my guests apparently expired during the showing. She was carried to the anteroom. Allow me to escort you to the poor woman's corpse. The doctor awaits you."

The inspector clapped his hands. "Ladies, may I remind you this is now a crime scene, pending my investigation of the body. Nobody is to leave until I say so, is that clear? My men will take down the particulars from each of you. Your name. Your address and where you are staying in Paris, if you are visitors." He looked across to the two uniformed officers standing near the stairs. "Granger. Dior. Nobody is to leave under any circumstance. I don't care who they are. If you have any trouble, come to me."

The two young policemen looked highly uncomfortable, picturing themselves having to grapple with powerful women. Chanel disappeared into the back room with the detectives. We sat waiting. Conversation had dropped to a hushed whisper.

"What exactly did they say?" Mummy whispered. "You know my French isn't as good as yours, since I didn't go to an expensive finishing school in Switzerland."

"Nobody is to leave. That's about it. Now we wait."

Mummy drew out her powder compact, examined herself in the mirrored lid and dabbed powder onto her nose. "One must look one's best if we are to be grilled," she said. Then a worried look crossed her face. "Oh dear. I hope Max isn't cross with me if this gets into the newspapers. They are so keen on creating a good and wholesome image in Germany—you know, the one country where family and healthy activities matter."

"And yet you and Max have lived in sin for several years now."

"Which is why we have to get married quietly, somewhere else," she whispered back. "At our little lakefront home in Lugano, Switzerland."

"And I notice the Germans aren't so wholesome about their treatment of the Jews."

A spasm of annoyance—or was it regret?—crossed her face. "Max doesn't agree with that, of course. But one can't say anything. In fact one has to be so careful what one says because . . ." She broke off as a young policeman approached.

"Your name, madame," he said.

"The Dowager Duchess of Rannoch," Mummy replied smoothly. "That is Rannoch." She spelled it out. It was clear that it wasn't the word "Rannoch" that was bothering him but the word "dowager."

"The former duchess?" he asked.

"Not exactly," Mummy replied. "I am the mother of the current duke."

This was not exactly true. She was his stepmother, but Mummy had always been good at bending the truth to suit her. The policeman looked suitably impressed and deferential. He gave a little bow. "I am sorry to disturb you, Duchess. But where do you stay?"

"At the Ritz. Where else?" Mummy replied.

He gave another bow and almost backed away from her presence. When he came to me I told him that I was her daughter, Lady Georgiana Rannoch. I didn't mention that I was now Mrs. O'Mara or, God forbid, he might have wanted to interview my husband. I gave him Belinda's address and he went away, seeming quite satisfied. I turned to Mummy. "I notice you preferred to be the Duchess of Rannoch, rather than the future Mrs. Max von Strohheim. That will be rather a comedown in the world, won't it?"

She gave a delightful shrug. "Darling, I have had many identities. I was married to the polo player, and the race driver, remember? And your adorable godfather Hubert. But once a duchess, always a duchess, in my book. Besides . . ." She broke off as the curtains were pulled back and the inspector came out. A hush fell on the assembly. It was like the opening of a play, waiting for the first line to be delivered.

"I regret to inform you that the distinguished doctor has made a thorough examination of the deceased woman and expresses the opinion that this woman was killed by ingesting the chemical cyanide. This, of course, will have to be verified by a postmortem examination, but he seems fairly sure of his diagnosis."

"Cyanide," I thought. So I was right. That was the smell I had noticed—the faint scent of bitter almonds on her. And her face had looked flushed.

There was a collective gasp. Some of the women fanned themselves with their programs, as if they might be about to faint. Seeing the programs made me wonder what had happened to Frau Goldberg's. Did she take it back with her to the hotel? Was there any chance that she took the initiative and left it for me to find? I wondered if I'd have a chance to check. Or perhaps she saw what happened to the person in her seat and lost her nerve. So what would happen to her now, if an attempt had already been made on her life? Would the assassin find her in her hotel room? I felt sick again. This was all so out of my league.

"My men are in the process of taking a statement from each of you," the inspector said. "So. Madame Chanel. All the details, please. The name of this woman?"

"A Mrs. Rottenburger."

"An American?"

"That is correct."

"This happened exactly when?"

"I can't tell you that," Chanel said. "When the showing was over I was informed that a lady had died. She had certainly been alive and well an hour before."

"And she was seated where?" he asked.

"She was supposed to be seated against the wall, over there to the right," Chanel said, pointing in the direction I was now sitting.

"No, that is not correct." An elegantly dressed Frenchwoman, her graying hair in a perfect coil, raised her hand. "She was seated beside me."

"So she sat beside you, madame?" The police detective moved toward her.

"She did."

"Where was this?"

"About the middle of the second row."

"The second row?" He looked puzzled.

"The chairs are not as you see them now," Chanel said. "They were in two rows on either side of the runway. Then a third row against the wall on each side for the . . . less important visitors."

"So you were on one side of her, madame?" the chief inspector asked. "And who sat on the other side of her?"

"I believe I did." An older woman with the distinguished air of an aristocrat replied.

"And did either of you ladies notice anything untoward? Anything strange?"

"I can't say I paid her any attention," the older aristocrat said. "One comes here to see the fashions." She shrugged. "All I can tell you was she was alive when the lights were dimmed because she annoyed me by moving her chair around to get a better view."

"So may I ask who came with the victim to this event?"

There was silence. I looked around the room, trying to locate Madge, but couldn't. I presumed she was still in the back room with her aunt's body, but then wouldn't the inspector have seen her? I waited for her to emerge, but she didn't.

"Nobody admits to coming with this woman? To knowing this

woman? This is foolish. Nobody can leave and it is my job to find out everything. We can all stay here all day if necessary. Now, let me ask again. Is there anyone else who was with her? Anyone else who knew her?"

There was silence again. I shifted uncomfortably in my seat. Should I say something? But I really didn't want to.

"So this woman was a complete unknown to all of you. Is this not unusual? It is my experience that women do not like going places alone, *non*?" He nodded. "Very well. Madame Chanel, you know your clients, perhaps you can shed some light on her?"

"Of course," Chanel said. "But I can tell you little, I'm afraid. She was not one of my regular clients like most of these ladies. She appeared last week and managed to secure a ticket to today's event. I'm not sure how she did that since the first day of the collection is usually by invitation only. She was not, as far as we could see, a very agreeable woman. Rich, definitely, but the type that thinks her money can buy anything, which, as we know, is not the case in Europe."

"You say she was not an agreeable woman. She annoyed somebody? Did she cross swords with anyone while she was here, to your knowledge?"

"Not to my knowledge, but I was fully occupied putting the final touches together for the show," Chanel said.

"Did anyone here notice any unpleasantness with this woman before the show started?"

He looked around the room.

The elegantly dressed woman tentatively raised a hand. "I believe she was not supposed to be sitting in the place she took beside me."

The inspector pivoted in her direction. "And your name, madame?"

"I am Lucille de Moret, Chief Inspector."

"Then please tell me what you know, madame." He took several steps in her direction.

She looked around, uncomfortable at being the center of attention. "This woman sat herself beside me. She did not say *bonjour* or greet me in any way, which I felt was strange. Just as the lights dimmed another lady came up and tapped her on the shoulder. She seemed surprised, and words were whispered, but the American lady spoke no French, or pretended not to understand French. The lady who claimed it was her seat then spoke in English, but I'm afraid the American lady ignored her. So in the end the other lady had no choice but to find another seat. The show was about to start. She gave up and went away. She looked quite upset, and the American lady looked satisfied."

"Ah. Now we are getting somewhere," the inspector said. "And who was this other lady? Which of you exchanged words with the murdered woman?"

Of course nobody answered. I knew I should speak up, but I wasn't sure what to say. I was grateful then when Madame de Moret, who had volunteered the information, said, "I believe she was with the party of Germans. She was wearing a rather Germanic hat."

"A party of Germans? Which of you ladies are German?" He looked around the room.

"I'm sorry, but they already left," Chanel said.

"You let them leave? With a murder on the premises?"

Chanel gave one of those Gallic shrugs. "At that stage we only knew that one of the ladies had regrettably died. We assumed it was a heart attack. That there was anything suspicious or criminal did not enter our heads until the doctor informed us."

"Who were these Germans? And where would we find them?"

"They are the wives of a trade delegation," Chanel said. "Staying at the Ritz, I believe—is that not right, Duchess?" And she looked across to Mummy.

Mummy's face flushed. "Oh God. Now she's got me involved, stupid woman," she whispered.

Chief Inspector Mauville stalked across to her. "You are a duchess? From Germany?"

"No. I'm an English dowager duchess," she said in her horribly English-sounding French. "The Dowager Duchess of Rannoch. But my fiancé is German and I came with him to be part of the trade delegation, and to buy some clothes."

She gave him a sweet smile. The smile had had a melting effect on many men on most continents. The inspector was no exception. "I am sorry to trouble you, Madame la Duchess," he said, "but can you tell me which of your party was denied her seat by this woman?"

"I'm afraid I can't, Chief Inspector," she said. "I was not really associated with their party. The women were all friends of Frau Göring."

That name had an effect, all right. "Göring? Not that Göring? Hitler's right-hand man?"

"Yes. That Göring," Mummy said.

"*Merde*," he muttered loud enough for us to hear. "That is going to make it tricky. Diplomatic relations and all that. They can presumably refuse to answer any questions if they don't want to."

"Inspector, just because her seat was taken does not make her a suspect," Mummy said. At least her French said that we should not think the woman had bad ideas.

"Of course. All we have been told is that the dead woman took the seat of another lady—a German lady." Chanel came over to stand beside him. "The German lady being wellborn and of good manners went to find a place elsewhere. I don't think we have any reason to suspect that she carried cyanide with her and dropped it into the dead woman's glass. What normal person carries cyanide? And what normal person would kill if their seat at a fashion show was taken from them? Does the lady who saw the original exchange remember the German lady coming back to Mrs. Rottenburger?"

They turned to focus on the elegant Frenchwoman who had volunteered that information. Now she looked uncomfortable. "No, I can't say that I do," she said. "The only person I noticed approaching the dead woman during the entire show was the young English lady who modeled the last outfit."

And all eyes turned to me.

Chapter 20

Things are getting worse by the minute. How on earth am I going to get out of this?

"And who is this English lady?" the inspector asked.

It was as if the world stood still, the actors in this play frozen in time. My brain was racing as I tried to think what I was going to say. What excuse on earth could I give for going up to someone in the middle of the show and then finding that woman dead? Golly. It made me look very suspicious, didn't it? And yet there was no way I could tell him the real reason. It would certainly put Frau Goldberg in even more danger, and possibly create a diplomatic incident. And it would involve my husband—something I could never do.

I raised my hand. "I am Lady Georgiana Rannoch," I said, in my best imperious tones.

"You were the one who approached the dead woman during the presentation?"

"Yes," I said.

He came toward me. I wasn't sure whether to stand up so that we were of similar height. I felt at a disadvantage sitting down. But if I stood up it might look as if I was uneasy, or ready to make a break for it. Before I could decide, he was standing over me.

"Madame, why did you go to this woman? Was she a friend of yours?"

"Not at all," I said. "I didn't know her. I had only seen her once, at the salon of Mademoiselle Gertrude Stein, but I was never introduced to her and did not speak to her."

"Then why did you choose to do so in the middle of an important fashion show?"

"Ah, well," I said, my brain still trying to come up with a plausible excuse, "I did not expect the American lady to be sitting in that seat. As you have been told, it was supposed to be occupied by a German lady called Madame Goldberg. And before the show started someone said she had asked for an extra program because champagne had been spilled on hers. So while I was waiting to make my entrance in the back room I noticed some extra programs and thought I'd take her one. So I crept out and went up to her and said, 'Your program, madame.' And that was when I realized that she was dead."

I stopped. I realized I was babbling, talking rather too fast. It wasn't a brilliant excuse, but it was the best I could come up with at short notice. The inspector was still looking at me, frowning. "I think you had better accompany me to somewhere a little more private, where we can continue this without being overheard."

He turned to Chanel. "Do you have a room where I can interview this lady? It is not right that such an interview should be conducted for all to hear."

"You could go upstairs to the workroom, or my private quarters are on the floor above that," Chanel said.

Oh golly, another complication. I could not climb any stairs without having to hitch up my skirt.

"Not necessary, I think," he said. "We shall move to the anteroom where the deceased woman is lying. Come. Follow me, please."

I shot Mummy and Zou Zou a despairing glance as I got up and set off after him, trying to keep up with my ridiculously small steps. We entered the room, in which a standard lamp now shone an anemic light onto the woman on the floor. The doctor was sitting on one side of her. Harry was no longer there. Neither was Madge. The inspector closed the curtains.

"Now, madame," he said. "We can talk more easily if we speak in low tones." He indicated one of the seats around the wall for me to sit. I obliged and he pulled up a chair to sit facing me. The word "grilling" that Mummy had used came to my mind. "Please repeat what you had just told me."

What had I told him? My mind was now a blank. Something about taking a new program to a lady because someone had spilled champagne on hers. I stammered through it again. It didn't sound particularly convincing, even to me. The inspector sat staring at me.

"You knew this German lady?"

"No. I'd never met her. That's why I wasn't aware that the wrong person was sitting in the seat." I paused, trying to harness the thought still whirring around my brain. Was this even sounding plausible? "But she had been pointed out to me right before the program started. A lady with a feather in her hat, I was told. So

naturally I assumed . . ." I broke off, spreading my hands in a ges-
ture of confusion.

"You are one of the guests at this event?" he asked. "You are an
English milady, *non?*"

"I am an English milady. That is correct."

"Then why are you the one in charge of programs?"

"I'm not. I was just trying to do a good turn." I didn't quite
know how to say this in French and I'm not sure it came out the
right way. Did I just say that I spun around well?

He was still eyeing me suspiciously.

"And what was this entrance you mentioned? Why were you
waiting to make your entrance? You were one of the models?"

"Not exactly," I said. "Madame Chanel is a friend, you see. And
she designed a special dress for me because I am . . ." Gosh, what
was the word for pregnant? "I await a baby." I put my hand to my
front to demonstrate.

This seemed to appease him. A pregnant Englishwoman wasn't
likely to have killed a woman she didn't know.

"Madame Chanel was proud of this dress she made for me," I
said, "so she begged me to show it to her guests. That's why I had
to stay in the back room until she summoned me. She wanted it to
be a surprise at the end of the show."

"But you came out to deliver a program when you could have
asked one of the young men to do it for you?"

Oh dear. This was getting tricky. I could feel sweat trickling
down the back of my neck. Yes. I know a lady never sweats, only
glistens, but something was trickling down the back of my neck. I
felt hot and clammy as if I might pass out.

"Chief Inspector, it seemed such a simple thing to do. I noticed
the programs. I remembered that a lady needed one and I tiptoed

out when everyone was watching a lovely gold gown, sure that nobody would notice me."

"Nobody would notice you. Convenient, yes? I am sure the murderer expected that nobody would notice her, or him, when all eyes were on the runway."

"Are you suggesting that I—an English lady from a noble family, related to the king—would want to kill a woman I had never met?" The words just tumbled out now, as I find foreign languages come to one in moments of great stress. "And do you think I carry cyanide around in my purse? I would have no idea where to get cyanide, especially not in a strange city."

Something in this speech finally had an effect. "You are related to the king of England?"

"Yes. I'm his cousin," I said.

"I see." He sucked through his teeth, now weighing up whether he should go on questioning me or not and what diplomatic repercussions there might be if he did. "It appears that you only wished to do a kind deed."

"That's right," I said. "And if you want to find out who might have killed the poor lady, I suggest you locate her champagne glass and see if there are any suspicious fingerprints on it, because you will not find mine."

Now he did look at me in astonishment. "You suspect the champagne glass, then? You saw something suspicious?"

"No, I saw nothing. But if she was given cyanide, then the champagne glass would be logical, wouldn't it? How else could it be administered? I understand that cyanide has an effect that is almost instantaneous."

"You are well informed, milady. I have seen the effects of cyanide for myself," he said. "It is not a pleasant death but very rapid."

"Quite correct," the doctor added. He had been sitting silently until now and I had forgotten he was there. "Cyanide is a most unpleasant death. The victim dies by suffocation before the heart stops."

"So the champagne glass may still contain traces of the poison," he said. "And, as you say, fingerprints. I trust they have not been cleaned and put away since?"

"No, I suggested to Madame that they be put aside in case you needed to examine them."

"You are a thoughtful young woman, I see." He went to pull back the curtain and summoned Sergeant Lapin. I didn't hear what they said but he came back, looking satisfied. "My men will have the necessary materials brought to test the champagne glasses. And examine them for fingerprints."

I nodded.

There was a pause. Clearly the inspector had lost his train of thought and he wasn't sure how to go on. Then he said, "Where were you sitting with these programs beside you?"

"I was here," I said. "I had to remain in this room until Madame Chanel came for me."

"You were in this room?"

"I was."

"Looking out? Watching the show?"

"Yes."

"So let me ask you, milady. Did you notice anybody else creeping around when all eyes were on the models?"

"I'm afraid I didn't," I said. "That's just the problem, you see. The spotlights were on the runway. The rest of the room was in shadow and we were all watching the models. Anybody could have sneaked around, pretty much unseen."

"That is true, unfortunately," he said. "Well, I have no further questions at this moment. We will be making additional inquiries into the dead woman and also into the German woman who was supposed to be occupying that seat. I trust you have given my men all the information on how to contact you and you should not think of leaving Paris without getting permission from us. You understand?"

"Yes, Chief Inspector, I understand," I said. Then something occurred to me. "You asked if the dead woman was here alone. She was not. She had a companion here with her. A niece who traveled with her."

"No. I was not told of this. Where is the niece? Why did she not come forward when I asked?"

"I escorted her to this room so that she could see her aunt's body," I said. "I don't know where she can have got to."

He looked around.

"I believe she went down this staircase," the doctor said, indicating the small spiral in the corner.

"There is another staircase? Another way out of the building?" He stood up, going over to it, bristling. "Why was I not told of this? Does it lead to the outside of the building?"

"Yes. That was the way I was admitted," the doctor said.

"Then anybody could come and go without being noticed." The inspector paced now. "This changes everything. We could be dealing with an international assassin."

"I don't think so, Chief Inspector," I said. "I was in this room throughout the entire event. Nobody came or went. And an American man was with me the whole time. He would have witnessed my actions."

"An American man? So there were other Americans here. Where is he now?"

"I think he was sitting with his friend, out of the way with the ushers. There were two of them. They were here to help move chairs."

The chief inspector pulled back the curtains in dramatic fashion, looked around, grunted. "First we locate the niece," he said. "Robert? Go down to the street and ask if a young American woman was seen leaving the building."

"Her name, milady?"

"I only knew her as Madge," I said. "She was a rather unassuming sort of person, wearing a brown two-piece suit."

"You hear that, Robert?" he said. "Go now and find this person. She can't have got far. She was staying where?"

"The Plaza Athénée," I said.

"Ah. The woman had wealth all right."

"Ask the hotel to alert us if this Madge comes back."

The policeman took off down the twisting stair. I heard his footsteps clanging against the metal and then the sound of street noise as a door opened below. He was not gone long before we heard footsteps coming up again. The policeman reemerged, followed by Madge.

"I found her, Chief Inspector," he said. "She was just standing outside, waiting."

Chapter 21

STILL SUNDAY, APRIL 26
STILL AT CHANEL.

**Will we be allowed to leave soon? Golly, I really need to spend a
penny.**

Madge looked terrified as the chief inspector bore down on her.
"So, mademoiselle, you try to flee from the scene of the crime, eh?"

Now she looked bewildered.

"I don't believe she speaks much French," I said. "Would you
like me to translate?"

"That would be helpful, milady."

I repeated what he had said. Madge shook her head violently.
"No. I wasn't running away. You said I should cable Uncle Frank.
I saw there was a way out down these stairs so I went to see if I
could find a post office. But then I realized I had no idea how to
send a cable and I couldn't speak enough French. So I came back
but the door was locked and I couldn't get back in."

I duly translated this. He nodded. "You were visiting France with your aunt, mademoiselle?"

She understood that much and nodded. "Auntie was doing a grand tour. We were going on to Switzerland and Italy. It was something she'd dreamed of."

"And you were her favorite niece that she took with her?"

This made her smile when I translated. "Not at all. My father lost all his money. We lost our home. My aunt took me in to be her companion. I carried and fetched for her."

"So she treated you like a servant?"

"More or less," she said. "She liked to be waited on. She was a very demanding person."

"This clearly irritated you," he said.

"It did, sometimes."

Oh dear. Couldn't she see she was being led into a trap? Suddenly she must have realized. "But not enough to want to kill her. I couldn't kill anybody. I'm a good Christian. 'Thou shalt not kill.' It says so in the Bible."

"Very well," he said. "You were seated where during this fashion extravaganza, mademoiselle?"

"Out of the way, next to the stairs with the other maids and less important people."

"Could you see your aunt from where you were sitting?"

"I saw where she was sitting. After that it was too dark and I was watching the models like everyone else."

"She was not feeling ill before the show started?"

"Not at all. In fact she was in fighting form." (I had been translating as we went along, but "fighting form" had me stumped. "She was very healthy," I translated.) "She was annoyed that she had been put at the back when she felt she was more important than that. So she took a chair that was empty and when the lady tried to claim it she told her to go away. And she wouldn't budge."

The inspector nodded as this confirmed what he had been told.

"You have a purse with you, mademoiselle?"

"Yes." She held it out to him. It was a rather old, fake leather purse.

"May I examine it?"

She looked surprised but handed it to him. He rummaged through it, then handed it back to her. "You carry a lot of money, mademoiselle," he said.

"It's my aunt's money. She likes me to do the paying since she doesn't quite trust foreign money and is afraid that French people will swindle her."

This wasn't easy to translate politely. The inspector grunted. "All is in order, mademoiselle. And your aunt? She also had a handbag?"

"It's right here, Inspector," I said. "I brought it to this room when we thought she had taken ill."

I gave it to him and he went through it, finding nothing that appeared suspicious to him. Then a thought seemed to occur to him. "Would you say that your aunt was in a pleasant frame of mind?"

"Pleasant?" Madge looked surprised. "She wasn't a very happy person, sir. Always found something to complain about."

"Ah. So is it at all possible that she took her own life?"

"Aunt Elsie?" Madge tried to suppress a grin. "Not possible. She thought an awful lot of herself. The world had to revolve around her."

"I see no evidence that either of you carried a means of transporting cyanide," he said. "It would have been in crystal form, do you think, Doctor?"

"Most likely," the doctor said. "It could possibly have been injected from a syringe, but I didn't see a mark. Of course, it has been a most cursory examination. When we take her to the mortuary maybe we shall find something different."

The chief inspector was staring down at the dead woman, who now lay looking quite peaceful. "So someone brought cyanide with her. Someone knew where to obtain it and came with murder in her heart. We now know that this staircase leads to a back entrance, so it's possible that this person was an outsider and not one of Madame Chanel's guests."

"I don't think that was possible, Inspector," I said. "As I said, I was in this room the whole time."

"A person could have gained access before the show and hidden until the right moment?"

I shook my head. "I can't think where anyone could have hidden while we were all rushing around with last-minute preparations before the show." As I said it, I realized I might be making myself the only suspect.

He was staring out past me now, trying to organize his thoughts. "This is not a casual thing to do. Not an impulsive act of anger. It is planned carefully and cleverly by a brilliant mind. The person knows when to strike and that all eyes will be on the models and afterward a room with at least fifty women in it. Important women. Women who could make it difficult for police if we question them."

As if on cue the curtains were wrenched apart. Mrs. Simpson stood there. "Just how long am I to be held prisoner here, Inspector?" she demanded.

"Everyone will be permitted to leave when I say so and not before," he replied, making me aware that he actually understood English.

"You do know who I am?" she asked.

"Oh indeed, yes, madame. I have seen your picture in the papers. I realize you are an important lady. But a murder has occurred in this room. If I let you go, every lady will expect to leave also. So I beg you to be patient a little longer. My men will need to take fingerprints from each of you."

"Fingerprints? You want to treat the future wife of the king of England like a criminal?"

"Indeed no, madame," he said, eyeing her with interest now, as if this was news to him. Until now she had just been a "friend" in the French press. "Simply to rule you out when we test the champagne glasses."

"The champagne glasses?" Wallis Simpson looked horrified. "So that's how it was administered? But we all took our champagne from a tray. It could have been any one of us. It could even have been meant for me."

"I think it highly unlikely, madame. Now if you would be so good as to wait with the other ladies a few minutes longer . . ."

"I'll be phoning the British ambassador," she said. "And the king, of course. This investigation is being run in a most slipshod manner."

"I assure you that the investigation will be most thorough," he said haughtily. "We shall not rest until this criminal is brought to justice, I promise you. Now please leave, I beg of you, so that we may bring this swiftly to a close."

She swept out in dramatic fashion. The inspector turned to Madge. "You too may go for now. But I shall want your fingerprints, plus the details on your aunt. Everything you have done since you arrived in Paris. Everybody you met. And you are not to think of leaving Paris."

Madge shot me a desperate look, not having understood the command in French. I duly translated.

"How can I possibly leave Paris when I will have to make the arrangements to transport my aunt's body back to America?" She put a hand up to her mouth, her voice shaking with emotion. "Oh dear. It's going to be awful."

"I'll be happy to help," I said. "I'll come round to your hotel if you like and see if there is anything I can do."

"Oh, would you really? I'd like that. I don't know how to do anything. How to send a cable. Any of that stuff."

"I'm sure the hotel will be happy to send a cable for you," I said.

She put a hand to her mouth again. "Uncle Frank will be devastated. He'll be so angry. He'll blame me for not taking care of her properly."

"Of course you can't be to blame," I said. "Nobody goes to a fashion show expecting to be poisoned, do they?"

"But who'd want to kill Auntie?" Madge wailed, near to tears now. "I know she could be rude and annoying, but she doesn't even know anybody here. She's never met these people before."

"I think we may find that it was a case of mistaken identity," I said. "You said yourself—your aunt was in the wrong place."

"What is this?" The inspector had understood the English and was looking at me sharply.

"Chief Inspector, if Mrs. Rottenburger was sitting in another woman's seat, is it not possible that the poison was meant for the other woman? She was just unlucky."

He hadn't considered this. "It was meant for this other woman? A German lady, yes? And the Germans made sure they had left before the police came. That in itself is suspicious."

I nodded.

"I have heard of what goes on in Germany now. It is rule by fear and ruthless means. But questioning them will be difficult, especially now that we know that Göring's wife was among them." He sighed. "It may be that we'll never know the truth." There was a pause while he processed these facts. Outside the curtains the level of conversation (or was it complaint?) had risen. I suspected the two young policemen were having a hard time manning the staircase.

"So," the chief inspector said. "Somebody has instructions to kill this German woman. They know she will be at Chanel today. They gain entrance and do the deed in the darkness."

Oh dear. I'm afraid that was exactly what I was thinking. Someone had been instructed to retrieve the canister of microfilm at all costs. Possibly a member of her own party.

"Of course there are still bad feelings about the war, here in Paris," he went on, rambling now. "It is possible that someone has a grudge against Germans in general and chose this woman because she was wearing a Germanic style of dress."

"Would you come to a fashion show carrying cyanide on the off chance of killing a German?" I asked. "And look at Chanel's guest list. It is half the most influential women of Europe."

"But don't you see, madame, it is because of that that the killer feels she will be safe." He wagged a finger at me. "She knows the police will not be allowed to pry too deeply and risk insulting the wrong people. You have already seen your Mrs. Simpson plans to make the trouble."

I nodded. He was right, of course. Suddenly a thought struck him.

"You, milady—you have connections to Germany yourself, perhaps?"

"Golly, no," I said. Then I corrected this. "My great-grandparents, Queen Victoria and Prince Albert, were German, of course. But not since then."

"So no connection to the visiting German party?"

Oh gosh—I realized I was falling into a trap. "My mother is with them, as you know."

"Now this is interesting, is it not?" he said, staring intensely at me now. "Your mother, she has a disagreement with a member of her party. No, more than a disagreement. A member of the party has done something to insult your mother. She demands revenge but she can do nothing herself. But her beloved daughter, who would do anything for her mother, waiting in the shadows for the right moment to slip out . . ."

I'm afraid I burst out laughing. "You don't know my mother, Chief Inspector. If something insulted her she'd let them know it right away. She's a feisty woman. And I may be her daughter, but we're not close. We've hardly seen each other since I was two. So what she does in Germany is none of my business—except she'd not be the sort to poison anyone. She is not subtle in any way. If she wanted to kill someone she'd stab them or shoot them." I paused, tired of speaking so much French and fishing for words. "But in this case, she hardly knows the other women in this group and she certainly doesn't mix with them." I wanted to say he was barking up the wrong tree, but I didn't know what the saying might be in French.

He sighed, still looking at me with an intense gaze. "I get the feeling there is more to this," he said. "But you also don't come across to me as a murderer."

"Of course I'm not," I said.

"We shall perhaps know more when the champagne glasses have been examined." He sighed again.

"Which brings us to an interesting point," the doctor said. I had almost forgotten again that he was in the room. "How was the cyanide placed into the glass? It is not an item one handles lightly. Highly dangerous, in fact."

"Do you know who handed out the glasses?" the inspector asked me.

"They were taken around on trays," I said. "By the ushers. From what I saw the women helped themselves from the tray."

The inspector sighed. "The ushers. Young men, all of them, correct? We must question them. Perhaps one of them lost a beloved father in the Great War. Or a farmhouse burned down by the Germans . . ." I could see his brain was already trying to form a case. "Where was the champagne poured, do you know?"

"I do," I said. "I saw it happen. It was on the table right there beside you. The American man helped open the bottles and poured, and the ushers carried it out."

"Aha!" He looked excited now. "This American man—what is he doing at a fashion show? And he offers to pour the champagne, does he? His name, please?"

"Harry Barnstable. He's sitting over in the corner."

"Lapin," the inspector called. "Bring me the American Harry Barnstable."

Chapter 22

I am so tired and overemotional that I'm afraid I might burst into
tears at any moment. If only I could sneak down those back
stairs and find Darcy. But I'd never make it down that staircase
in this dress and I have no way of getting changed, apart from
going up a similarly twisty staircase and exposing my legs to the
world. I'm stuck, as I believe the inspector is too. We're going
around in circles and getting nowhere.

Harry was ushered into the room. He looked around with interest,
saw me, and grinned.

"Have they browbeaten you into confessing yet?" he asked.

"Take a seat, please," Chief Inspector Mauville said. "Your name?"

"I think she already told you. Harry Barnstable."

"You speak French, I see."

"I should. I've lived here for eighteen years now."

"From where do you come in America?"

"New York," Harry said. "But I haven't lived there since before the war. I'm actually a French citizen now."

"I congratulate you on your good taste, monsieur," the inspector said. "I would like to ask you a few questions."

"Certainly. Go ahead." Harry sat on one of the chairs and leaned back.

"This young woman tells me that you poured the champagne."

"I helped," Harry said. "I work in a bar sometimes. I'm used to opening champagne and I could see the usher wasn't too comfortable with it, so I volunteered to open them for him."

"Did you then pour the champagne?"

"A couple of times I did. To help speed things up."

"The glasses were where?"

"They were on trays. We filled one tray, the ushers took it out and then we filled another tray until all the guests had been served."

"Monsieur, think carefully. Did you notice anything in any of the glasses when you poured?"

"What kind of thing?"

"A small white crystal, perhaps?"

Harry chuckled. "I certainly didn't. I might have thought it was a lost diamond and picked it up."

"Did you help with the distribution of these drinks?"

"No. I'm not properly dressed, you see," he said. "Chanel only employed Arnie and me to help with the humble tasks, like moving furniture. The ushers are all pretty boys who look the part. We look disreputable and not in keeping with the atmosphere of the day."

"Think carefully again, monsieur. Did you notice how the drinks were distributed?"

"Of course. The ushers took the trays around. They offered the drinks. The women helped themselves from the trays."

"So can you see any way that a particular woman could have been handed a particular glass?"

Harry sat up straight again. "So that's it, is it? She drank poison from a champagne glass?" Then he shook his head. "I don't see how that could have happened. I mean, how would anyone know the right glass to have given her?"

"How, indeed?" The inspector shook his head. "A pretty puzzle, is it not?"

"Is it possible she was poisoned before she got here?" Harry asked. "And it took that long to have an effect?"

"I do not think so." The doctor spoke up again. "The effect of cyanide is usually instantaneous."

"Right," Harry said. "Well, perhaps it wasn't in the champagne glass at all. Isn't cyanide also a gas? Someone could have switched her smelling salts or her perfume?"

"She had no smelling salts in her purse," the inspector said. "We will know more when the glasses have been fully examined."

Harry went to stand up. "Is that all you wanted from me? I've left my name and address with your man. I wish I could help but I can't think of anything else."

He started to walk out of the room.

"One more thing." The inspector grabbed his arm. "I have not yet asked you if you know this woman."

"Know her? Why should I?"

"You were one of the only other Americans in the room."

"America's a big place, Chief Inspector," Harry said with a rather patronizing grin. "And I haven't lived there for half my life. Besides, from what we've been told, she was stinking rich and I am rather poor. We're not likely to have crossed paths." He patted the inspector's sleeve now. "Sorry to disappoint you. Besides, I don't think Americans go around using cyanide to kill people. We much prefer good, old-fashioned guns." With that, he left the room.

"So. We are no closer," Chief Inspector Mauville said. "But you mentioned another American?"

"Yes. He came to help out with Harry and he brought his camera because he's a keen amateur photographer."

"Bring him also, Lapin," Chief Inspector Mauville said.

Arnie came into the room looking rather nervous, I thought. But he answered in good French with only the trace of an accent, gave his name and address easily enough and said that he'd also lived in France since the Great War. He said he had no desire to live in a country that glorified violence and he found France more civilized.

He told the inspector he came to help set out the chairs, having been asked by Belinda. He was outside with his camera when the champagne was handed around, taking pictures of the arriving women and hoping to sell one to a newspaper. Then he had stood at the back, just beside this room, also trying to take pictures and hoping that he wouldn't be noticed by the professional newspapermen, who might have objected.

"I will ask you what I asked your friend. Was this woman known to you?"

"She wasn't," Arnie said; then he reconsidered. "I met her at Gertrude Stein's place. She claimed she knew my family, but I think she was just a social climber who liked to feel important."

"So your family is socially prominent?"

"Not really. They're a big military family. My dad was a general in the army. My brothers went to West Point. I'm the black sheep who didn't like fighting. That's why I came here." He paused, considering this. "I believe she also said she was from Pennsylvania. Pittsburgh, was it? Or Philadelphia. So it's possible she might have encountered my parents. But not me, I assure you. I run away as fast as possible from anyone like that."

"Like what, monsieur?" the inspector asked blandly.

Arnie sighed. "You should have seen her at Gertrude Stein's. First she tried to grab Hemingway's attention, then she wanted to buy Gertrude's paintings. Gertrude was fuming."

"I see." The inspector paused again. "So you two Americans were at Gertrude Stein's and coincidentally met the deceased woman there?"

"That's right."

"As a policeman I find it hard to believe in coincidence."

Arnie gave an exasperated laugh. "Hey, now you're not going to try and pin this on us, since we're the only Americans present and we bumped into this woman before? And we carried cyanide around with us, hoping we'd run into her again? Because I can assure you, Chief Inspector, that we had no idea who was on the guest list for this event. We don't usually move in Chanel's circles."

This seemed to satisfy the inspector. He nodded. Then as Arnie was leaving he said, "You said your last name was Franzen?"

"That's correct."

"A German name, is it not?"

"That's right," Arnie said. "My ancestors came over from Germany in the mid eighteen hundreds."

"And you still have ties to Germany?"

Arnie frowned. "Not really. I mean, we know what region the ancestors came from, but that's about all. I've never visited myself. After what we went through in the war, I stay away from anything to do with Germany."

"You bear a hatred for Germany?"

"For their politics," Arnie said, "but not for the poor bastards we fought against. They probably hated it as much as we did. Thank God it's all behind us. I just hope that Hitler is not spoiling for another fight. Luckily I should be too old to get involved this time."

The chief inspector moved closer to him. "Did you have a chance to converse with any of the German women who attended?"

Now Arnie looked surprised. "Me? I wasn't allowed to converse with the guests. In fact we were told to keep well out of the way. And I told you—I was outside taking pictures when they arrived, then I sneaked up with the rest of the press photographers and made myself inconspicuous at the very back of the room."

Now the inspector looked interested. "So let me ask you this— did you happen to see anyone creeping around during the show? Going up to another guest? Handing her something?"

Arnie frowned. "I can't say that I did. Apart from Georgie, and you already knew that."

"Georgie?"

"Lady Georgiana here. I saw her come out at one stage and go up to the lady and then come back to ask for help in carrying her to this room."

"And what did this Georgie do when she got to the woman?"

Arnie shrugged. "I can't say I noticed too much. There was a spectacular dress on the runway. All gold. I wanted to get a good picture of it. But I did see she was carrying a program, I believe."

"You see," I said to the inspector. "I took her a program. As simple as that."

The curtains parted and Chanel came in. She looked flustered, not her usually poised self. "How much longer is this to continue, Chief Inspector?" she asked. "My clients are becoming increasingly angry. I can't afford to offend these women. They are my bread and butter."

"I understand, madame," he said. "It seems, from my investigation, that we may be looking for an assassin who came with the party of Germans."

"Germans?" Then the light dawned. "Oh. I see. You are suggesting that this unfortunate woman was sitting in the wrong seat, wasn't she? So you think the poison was meant for a German woman?"

"It seems highly possible, since this particular woman was unknown to your other guests and thus nobody would have a motive to want her dead."

"How very difficult," Chanel said. "These German women are connected to the highest levels over there. If they sense you have any interest in them, they'll be whisked off back to Germany, where you can do nothing."

"That is all too true, madame. So—we have collected information on all present?"

"I believe so. And fingerprints too, much to the annoyance of my guests."

The inspector moved to the doorway and stood examining the room. A hush fell on the conversation as the ladies observed him. "Madame, you have a seating plan?"

"Of course." She snapped her fingers and an assistant brought it over to her. The inspector studied it.

"And the dead woman was sitting where?"

Chanel pointed.

"So the women with positions on the other side of the runway had no easy way to reach the place where Mrs. Rottenburger was sitting."

"That is correct," she said. "During the show it would have been impossible for them to move around the room."

"But before the show?"

"They were escorted to their seats as they entered. The lights were fully on. Any movement would be noticed."

The inspector took a deep breath. "Then I think, madame, that we can excuse now the women who sat on the far side of the runway."

"That is good because they are my most influential clients." She went out into the room. "Those of you who sat on this side of the room during the presentation are now free to leave," she said. "I do apologize most deeply for the inconvenience. I'm sure you all wish that justice is served for this unfortunate woman. We all do. And please, all of you ladies, if this worrying occurrence distressed you too much today to examine the outfits properly, do let my assistants know and they will try to fit you in another of the showings, later in the week. If not, then please return when fashion week is over and I personally will assist you in choosing the correct outfits for you. I thank you again for coming."

"Finally." Mrs. Simpson rose and strode toward the stairs. "You'll be hearing about this," she called in the direction of the inspector. "Keeping an important woman hostage is not a wise move. The king will hear about it."

Other eyes followed her, not all of them knowing who she was, I suspected. There was the scraping of chairs as the women to my left got up, brushed themselves down, collected their handbags and made for the stairs. I saw that Mummy was among them. She was about to leave, then turned and came over to me. "Bye-bye, then, darling. Don't worry about all this. You know what the Continental police are like. Absolutely useless. Come to lunch with Max and me at the Ritz. Any day you like. And we'll go shopping for some lovely outfits for you, all right?"

"All right," I echoed, feeling that absurd sense of loss and disappointment I always felt when my mother left. As soon as she'd left the thought occurred to me that my mother was part of the German party. I would definitely go and visit Mummy at the Ritz. I might have a chance to meet Frau Goldberg socially and find a way for her to pass across the film and plans. This seemed like a clever idea until I remembered something—a woman in Frau Goldberg's seat had been murdered.

Chapter 23

STILL SUNDAY, APRIL 26
FINALLY OUTSIDE CHANEL.

Can I really go back to enjoying Paris after this? I'm afraid I'll be looking over my shoulder, not knowing if the assassin is coming for me.

It was approaching six o'clock before we were released. Chief Inspector Mauville told the remaining occupants of the salon that they were finally free to go, for the moment. He went on to say that the champagne glasses were being tested and the police now had the fingerprints of all the attendees on file. He hoped that this would shed more light and they would be able to narrow down a suspect. This produced some outrage.

"You insinuate that one of us might be guilty of this terrible crime?" a voice demanded, and I saw that it was Louis-Philippe's mother. A thin, colorless woman with a haughty expression sat beside her. Was that Jacqueline, whom Belinda's recent beau was to marry? In which case, he was getting what he deserved and no wonder he wanted a mistress like Belinda. In other circumstances I'd have been interested, wanting to share the information with Belinda, perhaps even to giggle about it. But I was emotionally exhausted and all I could think of was going home and having a comforting cup of tea. Not that that would happen since the French idea of a cup of tea was a pale, light beige liquid with a piece of lemon floating in it, or, worse still, an herb and flower tisane—not real tea at all. I found I was chewing on my lip—obviously having chewed away my carefully applied lipstick. Not that it mattered anymore.

Another dowager, even more impressive than Louis-Philippe's mother, approached the detective. "I think you have made a terrible mistake here. This doctor is a quack. There was no crime. The woman died of a seizure or a heart condition. You'll see. Do the proper examination and you'll find no crime was committed and we have all been kept here for nothing."

"Nobody hopes that is true more than I, dear madame," the inspector said. "Because if this really was a case of murder, then I'm afraid it may never be solved. The criminal may walk free among you."

"Then what exactly do we pay you for?" this same woman demanded. "I know your superior well. Believe me, I shall be speaking to him about this."

"Speak all you wish, madame," he said defiantly. "Perhaps there is another man at the Sûreté who can make sense of a crime that happens in the presence of a hundred people and nobody notices it."

"But you have the answer in front of your eyes, don't you?" a third woman joined in. "This young English person. She was seen to approach the victim. Who is to say that the woman wasn't alive and well when she was approached? This young woman could have administered the poison, which one understands has an instantaneous effect, then claimed that she had found this poor lady had fainted. We only have her word."

"I assure you this is being taken into consideration, madame," he said. "There did seem some . . . irregularities in her response, but then I discover she is related to the king of England and has no connection to the American woman, so I have to take her at her word."

"There have been royal assassins before now," this woman said.

I could keep silent no longer. "I assure you that I am as distressed as you are at finding this woman dead. This has been very upsetting for me."

Zou Zou came to my side. "I personally know Lady Georgiana," she said. "She is a person of great integrity and impeccable character. To implicate her is an insult to the entire British royal family."

"And not good for my friend when she is in such a delicate condition," Belinda added.

Chief Inspector Mauville now saw that guests might be ganging up on him. He looked around warily. "Ladies, please. Let us leave the investigation to the professionals," the inspector said. "Now go, please. You are free to leave."

There was the scraping of chairs as women rose from their seats and the murmur of voices rose as they made for the door.

"Don't worry, dear girl," Zou Zou said. "Go home. Have a lovely hot bath and forget all about this. Have Darcy take you out to dinner. He'll be furious, of course. He'll let the police know that he does not appreciate what has happened to his wife."

I didn't like to say that he was the one who got me into this mess in the first place.

"And come over to me at the Ritz anytime you like if you need cheering up," she said. "I'll be staying a few more days to have some fittings done. I bought the gold dress, you know. I saw that Mrs. Simpson wanted it and I couldn't resist."

She gave me a wicked smile then kissed me on both cheeks. "Go on, go home."

I SANK BACK onto a chair, suddenly completely worn out. Belinda put a comforting hand on my shoulder. "I'm sorry, Georgie. This has been ghastly for you. Let's get you out of the dress and back into your street clothes then we can go home and have a nice glass of wine."

"I'd prefer a cup of tea," I said. "But I don't think French dishwater would do it."

We went through to the back room. Mrs. Rottenburger's body and the doctor had now gone, as had Madge, presumably with her aunt's body. Arnie and Harry were already stacking chairs and piling them against the wall. I hitched up my skirt in a most undignified fashion again and climbed back up to the workroom. There the models were changing into street clothes and removing makeup. They looked at me with suspicious interest, making me blush.

"What exactly happened?" one of them asked Belinda.

So we had to go through the whole thing again. They nodded with sympathy as I explained my ordeal.

"The French police, they are impossible," one of the models said. "Don't worry, I'm sure nothing will happen to you. If necessary, make for the Channel and go home."

"I can't do that," I said. "Then I'd look guilty."

"But your relative the king will protect you."

This now seemed to be on the verge of turning into a major

international incident. I must admit going home seemed awfully tempting. But Darcy was here and I wasn't going home without him. Also I wasn't the sort to run away. We Rannochs had stood and fought to the last man in every Scottish battle, changing hands when arms had been hacked off. I wasn't going to let the side down now.

Belinda helped me out of the dress and into my own clothes. Then she hung the dress back up. "Ready for tomorrow," she said.

"Oh no. I'm not supposed to be wearing this again, am I?"

"There are three more showings," she said. "I'm sure Chanel will want you to model at each of them."

This was getting more horrible by the minute. I wondered if any of the Germans would come back to another showing, if Frau Goldberg would find a way to come back. But then if I were her and someone had died in my seat there was no way I'd come anywhere near the place. If she was the intended victim there would be other opportunities to take the microfilm, and to kill her if necessary. I felt awfully worried for her.

"If you don't mind," I said to Belinda, "I'm exhausted. I'll take a cab home now."

"I won't be that long," Belinda said. "I think we're more or less finished for today."

"But I want to telephone Darcy," I said. "He has to know what happened here. He'll be worried about me."

"Of course." Belinda put an arm around me. "Are you sure you don't want to sit and wait until I'm finished? Then I can help you into the cab and take care of you."

I had a sudden awful feeling I might cry.

"No, thank you. I just want to get out of here."

"Off you go, then, darling." She kissed me on the cheek. "I'll tell Chanel you weren't feeling well."

I made my way down the twisty stairs, hoping not to encounter Chanel. I didn't feel up to it at the moment. I had a feeling she might blame me for ruining her fashion show. If I hadn't touched the dead woman perhaps nobody would have discovered until after the show that she had died. I didn't think the chief inspector was quite happy with my explanation of why I went to Mrs. Rottenburger at that point in the show. It was fairly near the end, after all. I didn't think I was quite happy with it myself. Oh golly. I promised I wouldn't say that word anymore, but I couldn't think of a better one at this moment.

I came into the back room and was just about to continue down to the street when I realized I hadn't done what I had planned to do—search to see if Mrs. Goldberg could somehow have left the plans for me to find. I went into the salon. It was empty. Chanel must have escorted some of the women downstairs to the boutique and remained down there, as I heard voices. I went over to the area where Mrs. Goldberg must have been sitting. I checked along the walls. I checked in the big floral displays and among the potted palms. I even got down to look under the drapes surrounding the runway. As far as I could see there was nothing. I was just trying to stand up—not always easy with a baby sticking out in front—when a voice said behind me, "What exactly are you doing?"

I jumped, scrambled to my feet, my face now bright red. Oh gosh, I'd never make a real spy. My face would give me away instantly. I gave a sigh of relief when I saw it was just Harry and Arnie, carrying trays of glasses toward the back room.

"Did you lose something?" Arnie asked. "Need help?"

"Oh no. I'm fine. Everything's fine," I said. "It was just—an earring. It must have come off when I helped move the dead woman." This was the first thing that came into my head. I don't normally wear earrings. I hate the way they pinch my ears. But by luck Belinda had put some on me to complete the outfit. I'd taken them off again now and they were sitting upstairs, but Harry and Arnie weren't to know that.

"Okay, let's take a look," Harry said, already getting down on his hands and knees. "You think it might have gotten under the stage here?"

"I thought so at first but now I know that was impossible," I said. "The fabric goes right down to the floor. So it must have fallen off somewhere else. In the back room, maybe. Don't worry. It was only paste, not expensive, and I'm sure the cleaners will find it in the morning. I have to come back and help Belinda tomorrow."

"You're going home?" Harry asked. "If you wait awhile until we've put out the last of the glasses we can take a taxi together."

"I thought I'd pop round and see my husband first," I said.

"Your husband's still in Paris?" He gave me a surprised look.

"Yes. But he's here on business, so I took the opportunity to stay with Belinda. We hadn't seen each other in ages and we're such good friends."

"Okay. I get it," he said. "Right. Off you go, then. Are you going out this way?"

"I am. I don't want to face Chanel or any of the ladies who might not have left."

He nodded as if he understood this sentiment. "See ya, then."

The bottom of the stairs was in darkness and I felt uneasy as I stood there, groping for the handle, then turning it to emerge into the street. Suddenly everything seemed menacing. Nothing felt safe. I stepped out into a glowing red sunset. I had completely forgotten the time of day and expected it to be dark. But here was a normal Sunday scene with couples strolling, babies in prams, dogs on leads, everyone enjoying a balmy evening. Now what should I do? I looked around. Anyone who had been waiting to take the film and the plans from me would have gone long ago, having seen Mrs. Goldberg get into a car.

I had to see Darcy. Could I negotiate a French telephone kiosk and telephone his hotel, I wondered? If he wasn't there I could leave a message for him. But would he risk coming to see me at Belinda's? It was all rather tricky. Now that the plan had not worked, I presumed I was off the hook. It was unlikely the canister of film could be passed across now. If Frau Goldberg had deduced that the cyanide was meant for her, I wondered what she would do. Would she suspect one of her party? Would she go straight home to Germany and back to her husband? Would she seek protection from her friend Frau Göring? What would I do in her place? Try to escape to England? But then she'd be deserting her husband to certain imprisonment, and I'd never do that to Darcy.

I stood on the street, trying to decide what to do next. If I went back to Belinda's I could telephone Darcy from there. We could arrange to meet somewhere. As if someone could read my mind, a taxi pulled up beside me. "Do you require a taxi, madame?" the driver asked.

"Oh yes. Thank you. I'm going to 38 Rue de Lille."

I opened the rear door and sat down, gratefully. It was only when the cab drove off that I realized I was not alone in the backseat.

Chapter 24

I really hope the worst is over and I am not involved anymore.
Frankly all I want to do right now is go home and play with my
naughty puppies.

I gasped as I was aware of the man sitting beside me. He reached
out a hand to touch my leg. "It's okay, Georgie. It's only me," he
said.

"Oh, Darcy. You don't know how glad I am to see you." I fell
into his arms, feeling the tears flooding out. "It's been an absolutely
beastly day."

"What happened?" he asked. "What was going on? I've been
watching the place for hours. I saw the German women come out
ages ago. And then nobody else. And the police went in through a
back entrance?"

"It was awful, Darcy," I said. "A woman was murdered."

He was instantly alert. "Not one of the Germans? But no. I counted them all. I saw Frau Goldberg come out with the others."

"It was an American lady. A Mrs. Rottenburger. And I think she was killed by mistake."

"Mistake?"

"Yes. You see, she was sitting in the seat that Frau Goldberg should have had. This American lady was horribly pushy and demanding. So Chanel's assistants put her in a chair at the back and she was furious. She tried to take Mrs. Simpson's seat to start with, but Chanel wouldn't let her. Then she found another vacant chair and took it." I looked up at him; our eyes met. "It was Frau Goldberg's place."

"Oh God." He gave a sigh. "So they did know about her, after all. Somebody found out."

"So it seems. Frau Goldberg tried to get the American lady to move but she wouldn't, and then the show started. So she had to go and sit down elsewhere."

"And somebody killed this woman during the show? How?"

"Cyanide," I said. "It must have been in her champagne, although we can't work out how it was put into the glass."

"That would be a classic German method of murder." Darcy nodded. "But why would they want to kill her, I wonder?"

"To get the canister of film?"

He shook his head. "If this was known to the German authorities and they wanted the film back, why not search her room? Take her to the embassy? Ship her back to Germany? What would killing her achieve?"

"Maybe they suspected she was about to flee to England? Or thought she had information she was going to turn over verbally?"

"All the same, there would have been easier and less risky ways to stop her. But now she's still alive and safe, but for how long? I can see we need to rethink rapidly. I'll drop you off at Belinda's house and then make some phone calls to London. I'll need new instructions on how to proceed." He paused, staring out of the window past me as we crossed the Seine, then shaking his head. "Frau Goldberg must have realized that the poison was meant for her. In which case, what does she do next?"

"After the show I searched the salon to see if she could have left the film and the plans for me, but I didn't find them."

"No. I don't think she'd have risked doing that," he said. "Especially if she suspected somebody in the party was watching her. We'll have to find a way to contact her, although they will be watching her every second, I presume."

"Darcy, do be careful," I said. "These are ruthless people."

"I'm well aware of that. But don't you worry. You can keep out of this now. Go back to enjoying yourself with Belinda."

"I'm not sure that I can," I said. "I seem to be the prime suspect at the moment."

"What's this?"

I shrugged. "I was the one who found she had died. I went to exchange programs, as we'd planned. She didn't respond. I touched her and she fell forward, dead."

His hand gripped mine. "That must have been awful for you." He suddenly seemed to realize that he was not talking to a fellow spy, but to me, his wife. He took my face in his hands. "Georgie, I'm so sorry I got you involved in this. I'd never have suggested it if I thought I was putting you in danger. It seemed so simple. God, I feel awful. Can you forgive me?"

"Of course I can." I gazed up at his worried face. "I was happy to help and be part of what you do—until things went so horribly wrong."

He nodded. "We certainly hadn't expected anything like this. So when you went up to her, you didn't notice it wasn't the German lady?"

"No, I didn't. She was sitting in the correct seat. She was wearing a hat with feathers and a cape. Exactly what I'd been told. And it was too dark to see her face." I took a deep breath that was half sob. "And I couldn't come up with a good explanation for why I crept out in the middle of the show. I babbled about giving her a new program because champagne had been spilled on hers, but it sounded implausible even to me. So I'm sure that police inspector suspects me, Darcy." I leaned close to him, feeling the comforting warmth of his jacket. "If they question me again, what am I to say? I presume I'm not allowed to mention that a German woman was supposed to be passing state secrets to me?"

"Absolutely not. We still have a chance to get our hands on those secrets. And we don't want to risk putting her life in more danger."

What about my life? I wanted to yell. I had moved from being scared to being angry. My husband had, after all, put me in this horrible position.

"So what possible excuse can I give for creeping around in the dark?"

"You better not change your original story or it will sound more suspicious."

"Oh golly." I rested my head against his jacket sleeve. "Darcy, you really have got me into a pickle this time! What am I going to do?"

He wrapped an arm around me.

"Maybe you should go straight home. Maybe I should take you back to England myself so I can have a chat with the boys in London."

I shook my head. "I'm not allowed to leave Paris. None of us are. The police are testing the glasses for traces of cyanide and for fingerprints. I should be all right because I didn't touch any champagne glasses, but . . ." I broke off and gasped. "Oh golly, yes I did. Harry was helping to pour the champagne, and at one point the tray wobbled and some glasses fell over and I helped straighten them again. I had completely forgotten that. Oh no. What am I going to do?"

"You're going to go back to Belinda's and not worry tonight, and by tomorrow things may have sorted themselves out. I'll get in touch with the British ambassador and we'll decide what is the best course of action. If the French police do their homework, they'll find out that you have no connection whatsoever to the American woman."

"But they know I've a connection to the German lady," I said. "My mother is staying with them at the Ritz. She's part of their group."

Darcy gave an impatient little sigh. "Yes, that could be tricky."

"She told them she has little to do with the rest of the party, but they may not believe her. The whole thing will come down to a motive, and we can't tell them, can we?"

There was a long pause. Motorcar horns honked as we came through a busy corner. "We may be able to have a chat with the French secret service. They are our allies, after all. It's in their interest to do all that we can to stop Hitler."

"And they could tell the police to back off?"

"They could. But I don't think you have to worry, Georgie. You told them you were related to the royal family, didn't you?"

"I did. But the particular inspector is clearly anti-aristocrat. When Chanel told him half the important women of Europe were in the audience, he said that France had no more aristocrats and all were equal in the eyes of the law."

"I see. One of those. Well, let's take it easy until I get directions from London. I may have to go back across the Channel myself,

Georgie, so please let the police see that you are an ordinary tourist in Paris—that the horrible incident has nothing to do with you."

"I'll try," I said. "It won't be easy. Chanel wants me back there tomorrow for the next fashion show."

"Why? Is she parading you around as a royal coup?"

"No. She designed a dress for my current shape. I had to come out and model it. It's ghastly, Darcy. Mummy said it makes me look like an elongated Humpty Dumpty, and it does. It's only a few inches around at the feet and I have to take tiny little steps."

"Then just say you don't want to model it again, thank you."

"You don't know Chanel. It's impossible to say no to her."

"The American woman . . ." Darcy interrupted this last sentence. "What was her name?"

"Mrs. Rottenburger. From Pittsburgh or Philadelphia. I can't remember which."

"What do we know about her?"

"Not very much," I said. "I met her at Gertrude Stein's salon."

"Gertrude Stein? My, we are moving in artistic circles." He chuckled.

"And Ernest Hemingway was there. The American woman practically threw herself at him and he made a hasty exit."

"So this woman was in the art world?"

"Not at all. She's very rich, or rather she was very rich. She wanted to buy some of Gertrude's paintings. She wouldn't take no for an answer. She said she'd be back and Gertrude muttered 'over my dead body.'"

"Interesting," Darcy said. "And the dead body turned out to be your Rottenburger woman. I wonder if there was a connection?"

"You're suggesting that somebody killed her because she wanted to buy paintings? That doesn't make sense. You just say no and you don't let her in again."

"If she was rich, there will be family who inherit. Did she have anyone with her?"

"A niece who is a kind of unpaid companion. I was suspicious about her, but she's a timid little thing and I hardly think she'd have the nerve to kill her aunt in the middle of a fashion show. Besides, she was with her aunt all the time on the trip. There would have been better chances to kill her, surely? Also I gather the money was Mrs. Rottenburger's husband's. He's some kind of industrialist and he's very much alive. So no motive there for the niece to bump her off. Besides," I continued, "from the way her aunt treated her she wouldn't be the favored one to inherit any money. There is a beloved son."

"At home?"

"Yes. I gather he's rather frail—both physically and mentally. He had a traumatic experience in the Great War and has never been the same since. But the niece says her aunt babies him and stifles him and he could do much more than he does."

"It's hard to say," Darcy said. "The Great War left so many men shell-shocked and mentally damaged beyond repair."

"Anyway," I said. "Is it worth pursuing this line? A rich American woman, at a fashion show where she knew nobody. It's far more likely that the poison was intended for the German woman who was about to pass across secrets."

"I agree," he said, "but your grandfather's old boss at the Met always told him to start with the obvious, didn't he? And the obvious is that someone killed Mrs. Rottenburger. I agree there is no apparent motive, and only one person who might have any reason to want her dead."

I had to chuckle. "I can think of several people she crossed paths with who would not have been sorry about her death. She had annoyed the assistants at Chanel. She wanted to see the collection before anyone else. She was caught trying to sneak up to the work-room. But not weeping about her death is not the same as planning to kill her. And it must have been planned, Darcy, mustn't it? You don't go around with cyanide on you, in case someone annoys you."

"That's true," he said. "It sounds as if this was meticulously planned. She was alive before the show. When all eyes were focused elsewhere, the killer struck. It sounds like a professional job all right."

"But it was a room full of women," I said.

"That isn't to say that one of the women with the German party was not a member of the secret police and a trained killer."

I shuddered. "Don't. It's horrible. And to think that my mother lives there. I wish she'd get out before it's too late."

"It may be too late if she marries Max," Darcy said. "If she marries him she'll have to surrender her British passport."

"Oh golly, will she? Then she'll be trapped. I'm going to try and talk to her, Darcy. Make her see sense."

"As if anyone has ever made your mother see sense." He gave a sort of chuckling snort. "If she'd listened to anyone she wouldn't have bolted from your father with the Brazilian polo player."

"Argentinian," I corrected. "And he was very handsome. And Scotland does require some getting used to."

"You're sticking up for the fact that she abandoned her only child?"

"I'm saying I know how she thinks. Mummy's always had a way with men. Even the chief inspector was gazing at her with interest. But she does like Max's money, and maybe she realizes she's no longer young and may not have many chances in the future." I sighed. "I'll try to have a word before she goes back to Germany."

"We've arrived," Darcy said. "I'll say good-bye, then."

"When will I see you again?" I heard my voice wobble.

"It may not be for a few days," he replied. "I may have to pop back to England. But you're with Belinda. She'll take care of you. And if there is any problem, leave it to Madame Chanel. Everyone in Paris is terrified of her." He took my hands in his. "But there won't be a problem, I promise you. The police will do some investigating and conclude that you had nothing to do with this woman's death. Go and enjoy yourself."

"Enjoy myself?" I snapped. "You're not about to be hauled off to a French jail."

He took my face in his hands and kissed me gently. "Georgie, I really am sorry I put you through all this. I feel terrible now. I suppose I take this sort of thing for granted, and I should never have . . ." His voice faltered. He looked so anguished that I put my hand to his cheek.

"You did what you thought was best," I said. "You had no idea it could go so wrong."

"I promise I won't involve you again," he said. "Go back to Belinda and don't worry," he said as he leaned across to open the cab door for me.

Easier said than done, I thought as I stepped out onto the pavement and the cab sped away.

Chapter 25

I am trying to put this afternoon's drama behind me, but it's hard. I
realize how easily I appear to be the prime suspect—except that
I didn't know the woman. But if my fingerprints were on her
glass? What then? I wish I was home in my lovely, comfortable
house with my puppies. And my grandfather. He'd know what
to do. I'd even be grateful to see Queenie at this moment.

I had just put the kettle on to boil to make a cup of tea when Belinda and Harry arrived home.

"You beat us," Belinda said cheerfully. "You must have found a
taxi right away."

"I did," I said.

"How are you feeling? You looked awfully pale at the salon. I
thought you were going to pass out," she said, taking off her coat as
she talked and hanging it on a hook in the vestibule.

"Still a bit shaky, if you want to know. It's not a pleasant experience being considered a suspect in a murder."

"Don't worry about it," Harry said. "The French police are useless. They make stabs in the dark but they rarely catch anybody. Besides, you've got the power of the British monarchy behind you. They are not going to risk arresting you, knowing that your cousin is the king. And you didn't even know the woman. We can all prove that you never met her before."

"I didn't actually speak to her ever, but she did show up at Gertrude Stein's when I was there. The police may find that too coincidental."

"Everybody bumps into everyone else in Paris. It's a small city if you move in the right circles," Harry said.

"I can attest for you," Belinda said, now taking over the tea-making from me. "I can swear that Harry and I have been showing you around ever since you arrived and that you've never spent time in Paris before. And you never had a rendezvous with that woman."

"As long as they don't think we're all in on the crime together."

"With what motive?" Belinda demanded. "You and I have only been to America once and that was on the West Coast, not wherever she came from, which was somewhere on the East, wasn't it?"

"I've lived away from the States for almost twenty years," Harry said. "I may sound American, but I don't even have a US passport anymore. And trust me—I would not have chosen to spend time with people like her even if I did live there."

I looked from one face to the other. Should I tell them what I suspected—or part of what I suspected? "I think it may turn out that nobody actually wanted her dead," I said. "She was unlucky. She may have been in the wrong place at the wrong time. She took another woman's assigned seat."

"Really?" Harry was interested now. "Whose seat was it supposed to be?"

"One of the Germans who came with Frau Göring."

"Gosh," Belinda said. "That's a different kettle of fish, isn't it? One does not mess with the Germans these days. So you think that somebody had a reason to bump off one of the German women?"

"I do," I said.

"I wonder why? Political assassination? Rival party? Communist?"

"She's just a wife, not a political candidate," I pointed out.

"There aren't too many communists who get into Chanel fashion shows," Harry pointed out. "They don't spend enough money."

This made us all laugh, breaking the unbearable tension.

"Probably someone who drew a silly cartoon of Hitler," Belinda said. "You know how vain he is."

"But why not do it at home in Germany, then?" Harry wagged a finger at her. "Why wait until they were in France with all the complications of foreign police? I bet people get assassinated all the time in Germany for disagreeing with the Nazis and nobody bats an eyelid."

"Maybe she's well guarded at home," Belinda said.

"But a fashion show—that seems odd, doesn't it?" Harry stroked his beard. "And horribly risky. And anyway, if someone was sent to do the job, why not make sure they were killing the right person? They must have known what she looked like."

"I suppose in the darkness they both looked similar," I said, trying to sound detached as they were.

"They should find out if any of those ushers are German," Belinda said. "Otherwise, who could get in? You know how fiercely Chanel guards the door."

"The newspapermen," I said, as this suddenly occurred to me.

"There were quite a few, weren't there? What if one was from a German newspaper and had been sent to do the job?"

"That's a good thought," Harry said. "They moved around quite a bit trying to get the right picture, didn't they? And if they had just used a flash, then everyone around them would have been blinded for a second."

For the first time I felt a glimmer of hope. Maybe we were getting somewhere. I wanted to share this new idea with Darcy. It might just be important. I wished I could just stroll over to the Hôtel Saville anytime I felt like it. But he said he might be going to England this week. I tried to remind myself that it was not my case to solve. As long as it didn't involve me, I'd leave it to the French police. Then I realized that it did involve me. I was still their number one suspect.

"I hate to say it, but it served Mrs. Rotten-whatsit right for stealing another woman's place." Belinda shook her head. "She really was a horrid person, wasn't she? Pushy, demanding. I bet if she'd died at home there would be a whole ton of suspects with a motive for wanting her dead."

"Starting with her family, do you think? If you had to put up with her all day and every day?" Harry suggested.

"She seemed to hint that her husband adored her."

"No accounting for taste." Belinda chuckled. "Did she have children?"

"A son," I said.

"I do feel for him," Harry said. "So many young men were damaged by the war. Not just their bodies, but their minds."

"Her companion said that his mother stifled him, so maybe he'll be able to improve now," I said, wondering as I said it whether life would be better for him or whether the loss of his mother might be a final straw for his damaged brain.

"I'd be looking into that companion of hers," Harry said. "It's always the quiet ones who are most lethal. I can just see her re-searching poisons."

"Oh, I really can't see poor little Madge dropping cyanide into her aunt's glass," I said. "Something like that takes nerve and a cool head. She almost went to pieces when the inspector questioned her."

"How does one obtain cyanide, anyway?" Belinda asked. "You can't just go into a chemist's shop and say, 'Can I please have a le-thal amount of cyanide?' Can you?"

"I believe you can extract it from fruit pits," I said. "Cherry, apricots? Isn't that right?"

"I hate to point this out, but it's April. Too early for any stoned fruit," Belinda said.

"You must be able to buy it in refined form," Harry said. "There are certain industries that use it. But presumably you'd have to sign a poisons book before they'd sell it to you at a pharmacy. And the police will be checking on that."

"Except it is most likely that if the killer was German, he or she brought the cyanide with them."

The other two nodded.

"And they will presumably be heading back to Germany before the police can put two and two together," Harry said.

"Anyway, it was horrible, but there's nothing we can do." Be-linda stood up and went to take the boiling kettle off the stove. "We'll go on enjoying our lives. Georgie will go home and have an adorable baby. Harry will write the great American novel and I . . ." She paused. "I'm not quite sure what I'll do. I can't stay here forever. It's been fun and I've learned a lot, but . . ."

"Maybe you want to go back to Cornwall and work on your house there?" I suggested.

"Yes, maybe," she said. "Now I know that I have no desire to become a French count's mistress."

"What's this?" Harry asked.

Belinda gave an embarrassed little grin. "You know Louis-Philippe, who has been showering me with gifts recently? It turned out that he's been engaged to someone else for most of his life. So he had no intention of marrying me and even went as far as to suggest that he'd set me up in a nice little flat somewhere close and convenient." She looked from my face to Harry's. "The nerve of it! I was almost tempted to run off with Paolo just to show him."

"Hold on." Harry lifted up a hand. "This is getting too complicated for me. Who is Paolo?"

"He was her former beau," I said. "An Italian count. Very handsome."

"And he's here in Paris?"

Belinda nodded. "He is actually staying with that rotter Louis-Philippe. Two men who have ditched me in one room. I mean, really, it's awfully bad for a girl's ego."

"They must need their heads examined to ditch you," Harry said.

"You are very sweet." She came across and stroked his hair. "Why can't all men be kind and considerate like you?"

Harry slid an arm around her waist. "I'd make you an offer myself, only there is no way I'll ever be able to give you the kind of life you are used to."

She bent and kissed the top of his head. "As I said, absolutely sweet. But I'm afraid I have expensive tastes. And there is another chap at home, if I can stop him from being horribly sensitive about our class differences."

"Do people still think that class matters?" Harry demanded. "After what we went through in the war when the sons of lords were dying beside the sons of chimney sweeps? It's utterly ridiculous."

"I know it is, but it still matters," Belinda said. "I wish it didn't, but at home in England it does. How you speak, where you went to school . . . they all matter."

"But if you love someone enough, you should be able to get around that, shouldn't you?" Harry said. "I know if I loved someone enough, I wouldn't care a damn what people thought."

"Have you ever loved someone enough?" Belinda asked as she broke away from him and went to pour cups of tea.

"Once. Long ago. She was snapped up by my best friend. We were both very young. And since then—well, there have been odd flings here in Paris. But in some ways I feel that my ability to love and to be passionate died on that battlefield in the war. I sort of shut off who I had been before and became an observer rather than a participant."

"That's too bad," Belinda said. "I'll make it my mission to find a suitable girl for you before I go back to England."

"You'd better make her rich," Harry said dryly. "Because I can't afford to feed her."

Chapter 26

MONDAY, APRIL 27
BACK AT CHANEL.

Today we have to return to Chanel for the second day of fashion
shows. I am absolutely dreading it, but I can't seem to find a
way to get out of it. Belinda said that Chanel will be miffed if I
don't model the dress again, and I realize there might be a
chance to pick up a clue or two. I'll be watching the press
photographers this time to see how easily one of them could
have slipped cyanide into a glass.

I was feeling positively sick as we sat in the taxicab heading for the
Rue Cambon.

"Don't look so worried," Belinda said. "Nobody's going to be
murdered today. It was a onetime occurrence. And the German
women won't even be here today. It will be a whole new group of
ladies who know nothing about yesterday and are dying to spend

lots of money. And all you have to do is walk out and let everyone admire your dress."

"They must be half blind if they admire it," I muttered.

Belinda looked surprised. "You don't like it? But it's haute couture."

"Mummy said it makes me look like Humpty Dumpty and I tend to agree with her. Besides, I can't walk with that tight skirt around my ankles. I'm terrified I'll trip and land in someone's lap."

"You're just worried because that happened to you once before at a fashion show," Belinda said.

"Well, yes. I remember what it was like dealing with unpleasant French policemen. There's an equally unpleasant detective now and I have no wish to have to face him again."

"You won't, darling." Belinda put a reassuring hand over mine. "You are not a suspect. He knows you're related to the king. And you don't know any Americans. So relax. Enjoy it. Have a glass of bubbly."

"I'll try," I said with a sigh.

The preparations weren't quite as frantic as the day before. There was a certain amount of bustle, Harry and Arnie straightening chairs, the ushers carrying up champagne bottles, but it didn't have that first-night feel to it. Upstairs the models were equally less tense. One was even smoking and the herby smell of a French cigarette made me feel queasy. Again Belinda did my makeup and helped me into the nightmare dress. Again I had to hitch it up above my knees before I could make it down the stairs to the back room. It was empty. Trays of glasses stood on the table. Buckets of ice contained champagne bottles, just like yesterday. The only thing missing was Mrs. Rottenburger's body, laid out on the floor. I stared at the space where she had lain and I shuddered.

One of the ushers came in and started opening champagne bottles. He didn't do it quite as smoothly as Harry, and I wondered where Harry had got to. Maybe gone outside for a smoke again. The usher filled the glasses on the first tray, then started on the second one. Voices down below announced the arrival of the first guests. Chanel came up the stairs escorting a lady draped in a dark mink, a small black hat tipped provocatively over her eyes. "I must apologize again about yesterday," Chanel was saying. "What an unfortunate occurrence."

"As you say, most unfortunate." And the woman following Chanel came into view. It was Mrs. Simpson again.

"Did the police ever get an idea who might have done it?" Mrs. Simpson asked. "Someone must have been awfully desperate to want to kill at a fashion show, in front of so many people. Surely there would have been better opportunities. I mean, it wasn't a random act. It must have been someone the murderer knew. At the very worst you follow them to the Place de la Concorde and push them under a bus."

I had been thinking the same thing. There must have been an easier opportunity, unless . . . unless the German party was well guarded and the killer was an outsider. Sent directly from Berlin, maybe, when they discovered that secret documents had been taken out of the country? Or from Hitler himself to get rid of a woman who dared to marry a Jew? I wondered how the chief inspector had fared when trying to question the German women. Not too well, I suspected.

"I wasn't going to come back," Mrs. Simpson said. "I decided I'd never come here again. After all, Schiaparelli is designing the most daring numbers this year. Have you seen her mermaid dress? My dear—how does one walk in it? But then I telephoned the king last night and told him about that gold lamé dress, and he said, 'Wallis, if you want it, you have to have it. Only someone with your figure could carry it off.' So I thought I'd take another look."

Chanel snapped her fingers impatiently for the usher to bring out champagne. He picked up the tray and crossed the room, offering a glass to Mrs. Simpson. This was exactly how it had been done yesterday, I thought. The ushers hadn't touched the glasses. They had offered the tray. Mrs. Simpson accepted the glass and took her place as other women started to arrive. The room filled. I saw mainly unfamiliar faces, not many who had attended the day before. I spotted Zou Zou, who had returned, and felt a rush of relief that I now had one ally in the audience. Other women were now sitting where Mrs. Rottenburger and her neighbors had sat. I watched them take champagne glasses from the tray. Most puzzling, unless an usher had ignored instructions and actually handed Mrs. Rottenburger her glass. I wondered if the police had checked on the background of the ushers. If Harry and Arnie were working here, then was it possible some of the ushers were also American and therefore knew the lady? It all seemed highly improbable.

Just before the show started, the gentlemen of the press were allowed to come in. They stood around the walls, taking pictures of famous faces in the audience. But they kept well back from the two rows of chairs, and . . . I realized . . . they were not allowed on the far side of the room, away from the windows, where there was a third row of chairs against the wall. So any press photographer who tried to approach Mrs. Rottenburger would have impeded the view of ladies sitting against the wall. They would have noticed and been told to get out of the way immediately. Another theory dashed!

Someone must have done it. The ladies sitting on either side of the murdered woman would have had the best opportunity. It would have been easy to drop something into Mrs. Rottenburger's glass while her eyes were glued to the models on the runway. But they both seemed to have impeccable backgrounds in French soci-

ety and no reason at all to kill an American intruder or, more sig-
nificantly, the wife of a German scientist.

The lights dimmed. The spotlight shone on the mirrored staircase as Chanel made her grand entrance. She gave a similar speech
to the day before, omitting the mention of the tragedy that had
occurred. Presumably it wasn't yet in the newspapers, so nobody
knew except those who had attended both days. The show started.
Models strutted down the runway toward where I was peeking
from my room. Today there was no sign of Harry or Arnie, since
they had finished putting out the chairs. I suspected they had
slipped out to a café until they were needed again—no need for two
men to watch a fashion show twice. I wondered whether Arnie had
managed to snap any good pictures and . . . I stopped breathing for
a moment . . . whether Arnie's pictures had captured anything we
hadn't noticed yesterday. Why hadn't that occurred to me before?
Had he developed them yet? I couldn't wait to find out.

The show progressed. Nobody moved along the right side of the
room. Flashbulbs exploded and I had to agree that they temporarily
blinded me. So it was just possible that someone could have moved
swiftly right after the flash went off. The gold dress appeared, to
loud applause. Flashes from around the walls. But nobody moved.
And . . . I would have noticed if anyone had passed in front of me.

The moment I was dreading came closer. The models all pa-
raded out onto the runway to enthusiastic applause. Chanel gave
her final speech, then crossed the room to take my hand. Today I
came more willingly as there was no dead body to explain. It was
still impossible to walk in the dress, but women crowded around
me, congratulating me. There were Englishwomen among them,
some of whom I knew from my days as a deb.

"The first thing you must do is hire a decent nanny, my dear,"
one of them said. "I have three of the little monsters now, but for-

tunately I only have to see them for an hour a day and the oldest is about to go off to boarding school. Nannies do make life a lot smoother."

This was exactly what I was not going to do, I thought. I intended to be a big part of my child's life. He or she was not going to be stuck in a lonely nursery while I went off to Paris to enjoy myself. Zou Zou fought her way over to me. "Darling, you still look so worried," she said. "That episode yesterday must have upset you terribly."

"It did," I agreed. I leaned closer. "Also I can't walk in this awful dress."

"I didn't like to say anything because I thought you'd chosen it," Zou Zou whispered back. "But my dear, it's the most ghastly thing I've seen in ages. Burn it instantly."

This made me smile and some of the tension lifted. I had just decided that I could disappear into the back room again and then attempt to climb the twisty stairs when there was a commotion at the mirrored staircase. Confusion, gasps of surprise, as Chief Inspector Mauville and several colleagues appeared.

"What now, Chief Inspector?" Chanel demanded testily.

"Just a few more questions, if you don't mind. And we especially want to talk to the young English lady. Is she here?"

"Lady Georgiana? Yes, she's . . . ah, there she is." And Chanel pointed at me.

If I'd had a wider skirt I might have been tempted to flee. As it was, I was trapped. The inspector came toward me. "A few words, if you don't mind, my lady."

"Of course not." I was not going to let him know that I was rattled.

"Have you made any progress, Chief Inspector?" Chanel asked.

"A little," he said.

"Did you have a chance to question the members of the German party?" I asked, thinking that attack is the best form of defense.

"I was able to speak to one of them, a Frau Bruhler, who told me it was ridiculous to think that anyone would want to harm Frau Goldberg, who was a beloved friend of Mrs. Göring. But she would not allow me to speak to this Frau Goldberg, saying the lady had a headache."

"But what about how the poison was administered?" Chanel asked.

"Traces were found in one of the champagne glasses," he said. For some reason his eyes strayed in my direction.

"And were there any fingerprints on the glass?"

"The American lady's prints were on the glass," he said. "And also this young woman's."

And he turned back to stare at me.

Chapter 27

Every eye in the room was now looking at me. I felt my face turn bright red. I was trying to think clearly, but thoughts were flying around inside my head so fast that I couldn't capture them. There must be some mistake.

"This is ridiculous, Inspector," I said. "Are you accusing me of killing a woman I didn't know with a poison I have no idea about?"

"I'm not accusing you of anything," he said. "All I'm asking is how your prints are on the glass that killed this woman."

"I remember now," I said, relief flooding my face. "I was in the back room when the young men were pouring champagne. Some empty glasses fell over, so I picked them up and held them out for the champagne to be poured. You should find my fingerprints on several glasses. Besides," I went on, "I watched carefully today. The ushers offered the tray to the ladies and the ladies took their own glass. Nobody could have had a chance to slip anything into a particular glass."

"Nevertheless, the cyanide did manage to get inside somehow."

"I understand that, but I certainly didn't put it there."

"Yet, you were the only one seen approaching the dead lady." He actually raised an eyebrow as he looked at me.

Anger was overtaking anxiety at this point. "I've explained that to you," I said. "And I've told you before that I did not know this woman, had no interaction with her—nor had I any interaction with the German lady who was supposed to be sitting in that seat."

"And yet your mother is one of that woman's group from Germany?" He smiled now, as if he had scored a point.

My gaze scanned the room, trying to find where Zou Zou might be sitting. At this moment it would be good to have an ally. Then another voice spoke, loudly and firmly. "Inspector, you had better think carefully before you start accusing a member of the British royal family!" It was Mrs. Simpson. She had risen to her feet and was actually heading in my direction. "I've known Lady Georgiana for years and I can tell you that the king, her cousin, is very fond of her. And to accuse her of a murder of some American lady is absolutely ridiculous. You'll have the British ambassador coming after you before you know what's what."

She had started in her bad, American-accented French but lapsed into English in the middle. I wasn't sure if the chief inspector understood, but it seemed that he did.

"I assure you, madame," he said, "that I am not accusing anybody of anything. At this stage of the investigation I am merely gathering facts. And the facts that I have at my disposal, at this moment, are that a woman was killed during a fashion show in this very room. She died of cyanide poisoning. Traces of cyanide were found on the glass and . . . this young woman's prints were found on that same glass. You tell me, what am I to think?"

"You are to think that you have a clever murderer on your hands who leaves no trace," she said. She came right up to me now. "Georgie, honey, are you okay? You shouldn't be going through this in your condition. Why don't I take you home with me?"

Mrs. Simpson being nice to me was almost a last straw. I was horribly afraid I'd start crying—my emotions being so near the surface during the time I was expecting. She had never shown any inclination to be nice to me before, but I suspected we were now united against a common foe. She adored David. David was fond of me. Hence she was going to defend me. At this moment I could almost have hugged her. Almost, but not quite. Wallis Simpson is not a very huggable sort of person.

"Nobody is to leave until I say so." The chief inspector felt he was fast losing his grip on yet another set of rich and powerful women.

I suddenly realized I had a trump card to play. "Inspector, a thought occurred to my friends and me when we were discussing this last night." I gave what I hoped was a dramatic pause. "The cameramen were taking photographs the whole time. Is it possible that one of those pictures might have captured someone tampering with the lady's champagne?"

I could see I had now scored a point. "Ah. You may have something there, young woman." He nodded, digesting this. "I presume Madame checked the credentials of these newspapermen before they were allowed in?"

"Of course," Chanel said testily. She had clearly had enough of the police. "I don't allow any riffraff into my salon. Only the leading press of the world, you know."

The inspector gave a little bow to acknowledge this. "Then if

Madame Chanel can provide me with a list of which newspapers were represented here, I will have my men examine all the photographs they took. Would you be able to do that, madame?"

"I will have to ask my assistant. She was the one who checked their credentials and admitted them to the salon," Chanel said. "I will find her for you."

"And the rest of us, are we free to go?" an imperious woman's voice asked.

"Madame, I hope you will stay long enough to examine the models at your leisure and make your selection," Chanel said hastily.

"I see no reason to detain anyone," the chief inspector said. "You ladies were not present yesterday, therefore you have nothing to contribute to my investigation, unless one of you knew either a Mrs. Rottenburger from America or a Frau Goldberg from Germany."

There were various shrugs as neither name rang a bell.

"Thank you for coming to my aid," I whispered to Mrs. Simpson.

"Anytime, honey." She patted my arm. "I can't stand bullies. And I know darned well that you'd never go around dropping cyanide in someone's glass." She gave me a wicked grin. "I couldn't vouch the same for your mother."

"Neither could I!"

And we both chuckled. It was with a feeling of relief that I headed for the back room, thence to climb the stairs and change out of the dress. But I had only gone a few steps when a large woman in mauve, trailing scarves, stood up in front of me and pointed at me excitedly. "I remember you!" she said. "You were at Chanel's fashion show in Nice a few years ago, weren't you?"

"Uh—yes, I was," I stammered.

"And you modeled an outfit then. And you tripped and fell off the runway, and . . ." And she paused. "A valuable necklace you were wearing simply vanished."

"What's this?" Chief Inspector Mauville rushed over to us. "A necklace vanished, you say?"

"It did." The woman was waving her hands in animated fashion now. "I thought something about you looked familiar and then I remembered where I had seen you before." She was almost dancing up and down with excitement now.

"This young lady was wearing a valuable necklace and it vanished when she tripped and fell? How convenient." He approached me now, looking large and menacing. "So now it begins to become clear to me. You attend a fashion show. A necklace vanishes. And maybe now the object was not the murder but to obtain a piece of jewelry from the deceased woman."

"That is ridiculous," I said, but he waved me off before I could say any more.

"Ah yes," he continued, now pacing in animated fashion. "I have seen it before. The gentleman thief, or rather, in your case, the gentlewoman thief. Nobody suspects because she is of the right class with the right pedigree. She lives in a grand house. But . . . it costs money to keep up this lifestyle, does it not? Did you not say you encountered this Mrs. Rottenburger at the salon of Mademoiselle Stein? *Eh bien*, you spot a large and valuable piece of jewelry she is wearing and when you find out that she is going to attend the fashion show at the House of Chanel your plan is made. You will poison her, then when she dies, you will appear to help with the body and quietly remove the jewels you want, just as you did in Nice."

"If you would stop talking and listen for a moment," I finally managed to interrupt him. "Somebody else planned for me to trip and fall that time in Nice. Someone else stole the necklace. A clever and accomplished thief stole it."

"We have only your word for that, I presume?"

"Except that the necklace was later posted back to me, anonymously. It was returned to the queen of England, from whom it had been borrowed, and all is well. You can telephone Buckingham Palace and ask her yourself. . . ." I broke off, realizing that Queen Mary was no longer at Buckingham Palace. Her son was now king.

"You must admit, Lady Georgiana," he said slowly, as if savoring my name, "that it is a great coincidence that you were attending functions at Chanel when two outlandish incidents took place. Me, I do not believe in coincidence, so I say to myself there must be a reason."

"Then I suggest you conduct an inventory of Madame Rottenburger's jewelry from her companion and see if anything is missing," I snapped, my tension rising to the breaking point. I could see all too clearly how easy it would be to pin this murder on me now. The fingerprints, the fact that I was seen approaching the dead woman. I was the one who found she had died. And I had been at a previous Chanel event where a necklace vanished. Together these would make a good case. I found myself wondering if the French still used the guillotine and if it hurt.

"This would prove nothing. Maybe you were disturbed before you could remove the piece you desired."

"As far as I remember she had horribly flashy jewelry and it was probably all paste," I said. Wrong thing to say. I saw his eyes light up.

"Ah, so you did notice the jewelry she was wearing. And you say this is a woman unknown to you!"

"I noticed it after she was dead, when I helped bring her into the back room," I snapped. "Really, Inspector, this is going too far. You can ask my husband. He will tell you I am incapable of killing. I don't even like to kill mice."

"You said your husband is also in our city?"

"Yes, he has been here."

"Doing what?"

"Meeting some people."

"Your husband—what kind of business is he in?"

Oh dear. I could hardly say he was a spy. I resorted to my best Queen Victoria impersonation. "He is an aristocrat, as I am. He doesn't really have a business."

"Ah. I find this interesting. An aristocrat who travels abroad, who keeps a nice house but has no business. He must need money to fund this lifestyle. Perhaps you are in this together. A clever pair of jewel thieves who will stop at nothing . . ."

I was now quite ready to punch him, although I realized this would not aid my cause. "Perhaps you should work harder at trying to find the true murderer," I said. "I have enough witnesses in this room to attest to my good character. Important people who can complain about your treatment of me. My cousin, the king . . ."

"Need I remind you, madame," he said, "that you are now in France, where we got rid of kings many generations ago. When you are here, you are an ordinary person, like everyone else."

He paused. I could see he wasn't quite sure what to do next. The guests were now murmuring. Some were standing and heading for the door.

Chanel came over to me and put an arm around my shoulders. "This is enough, Chief Inspector. The young lady has already told you about the unfortunate incident in Nice and a brazen jewel thief. She is a sweet girl, and she is expecting a baby too. She should not be upset like this—it is bad for the child. She should go home now."

"She may go for now," the inspector said, "but she had better not think of leaving Paris. She will be watched. And I will be in contact with my colleagues in the South of France."

Chanel beckoned to Belinda. "Come. Take this poor child home before she is locked in the Bastille."

"I have to change first." I felt dangerously close to tears now.

"Nonsense. Camille—fetch Lady Georgiana's clothing from upstairs. Belinda, escort her down the stairs."

Now I had no other option than to cross the room, under the scrutiny of many eyes, and then to descend a mirrored staircase in a dress that was impossible to move in. As I neared the dreaded stair, Zou Zou stepped forward and took my other arm. "Come, my darling," she said. Then she whispered, "I could fly you home right now, if you like. My little plane is waiting at Orly."

Chapter 28

This is turning into an absolute nightmare. That horrid policeman
seems fixated on proving me guilty and I'm not sure what to do
to prove my innocence.

Zou Zou and Belinda bundled me into a taxi.

"Do you want me to fly you home?" Zou Zou asked.

"As tempting as that sounds, I don't think I dare leave now," I
said. "It would create an international incident. Besides, I have to
prove my innocence."

"How do you intend to do that?" Belinda asked.

"I don't know. I need to see Darcy," I said. "I want to be
with him."

"Of course you do," Zou Zou said kindly. "At which hotel is he
staying?"

"Hôtel Saville," I said, leaning forward to give the address to the taxicab driver.

"I do not know this hotel. Is it new?" Zou Zou asked.

"On the contrary. Rather old," I said.

"Good heavens," Zou Zou exclaimed as we pulled up in front of the dilapidated building. "What on earth is he doing there? It looks ghastly."

"Saving money, I suppose," I admitted.

"Nonsense. Nobody could be that poor." Zou Zou waved a hand, having never been that poor herself. I almost had to smile. Any hotel in Paris would have been out of my reach until recently.

I was about to exit the cab when I remembered. "Oh golly, I'm wearing the dress still. I can't possibly climb stairs in it."

"I'll come with you," Zou Zou said. "And give that boy a piece of my mind about leaving you alone in Paris and in your condition."

She tucked her arm firmly through mine as we went in through the front door. The proprietor came out as the bell rang. "*Bonjour, madame*," she said.

I asked her if Mr. O'Mara was in. She looked surprised. "But no, madame. He is gone. He left this morning. He told me he would be keeping the room and he would be returning later this week."

She must have observed my stricken face. "He did not inform you of this?"

"He said he might have to go back to London," I said bleakly. "When he comes back, would you tell him to come and see me immediately?"

"Of course, madame." She gave me an understanding look. I suspected she was thinking he had slipped away for a few days with his mistress, leaving his pregnant wife. I said nothing as we returned to the cab and headed for Belinda's flat. Everyone was very kind. Belinda made me tea and toast. Zou Zou threatened to visit the ambassador if she couldn't fly me home.

"Do you want me to fly to London and drag Darcy back here?" she asked.

I shook my head, smiling. "He has important meetings," I said. "Very hush-hush."

"Your husband needs a good talking-to. He should start acting like a country gentleman and go out shooting and fishing."

"We do need an income and his assignments do bring in money."

"You live on a lovely estate," she said. "Let it pay for itself. Breed cattle. Plant cash crops. Keep pigs."

I had to laugh now. "I can't see Darcy keeping pigs," I said. "But you are not wrong. We do have a lot of land that is just sitting there."

"There you are, then." She patted my knee as if she had just solved everything.

I wished it were that simple. As I lay in bed that night, listening to the sounds of a strange city through my open window, I found it hard to harness my racing thoughts. It seemed quite possible that this was a murder that would never be solved. I suspected that a trained assassin had been sent from Berlin to dispatch Frau Goldberg and thus take the secret documents from her. He would no doubt strike again and there was nothing I could do to prevent it. Or to prove my own innocence, for that matter. I had helped solve other crimes in the past. How had I done it? As I looked back it seemed more by luck than brilliant deduction. I had usually noticed something not quite right, some small detail that had sent me on the right track.

So what had I noticed here? The truth was that I had been in such a panic about wearing a dress that was liable to trip me up when I was receiving secret documents that I hadn't noticed much. I tried to recall champagne being handed around. Surely the ushers had gone out with trays, offered them to ladies either as they came in or were already seated. If one of those glasses contained cyanide, how could anyone make sure that the right person took it? The answer was that they couldn't. And the drinks had been poured in the back room, assisted by Harry while I looked on. Nobody could have slipped anything into a glass. We would have noticed. If only the photographs taken revealed a slinking figure who was not me! And if only Darcy would come back. I was sure he'd know what to do.

I must have drifted into disturbed sleep eventually, but I awoke with bags under my eyes and a sick feeling in my stomach. Belinda was up bright and early, bustling around and looking horribly cheerful as she handed me a cup of coffee. I have never done well with coffee in the early morning and immediately the familiar nausea returned.

"You look terrible," Belinda said kindly. "Why don't you spend the day in bed? No need for you to come back to Chanel. I'm sure she understands what a strain this has put on you."

"I don't want to stay in bed," I said, "but I would prefer a day away from everything to do with Chanel. Just to sit watching the boats on the Seine sounds heavenly at this moment."

"Do that, then, darling," she said. "I must rush, if you don't mind."

"But the show isn't until late afternoon."

"I know, darling, but I have a date with your divine mother. Remember she wants me to design a trousseau for her, so I have to take the measurements and make some sketches before she flees back to Germany. I thought I'd go over this morning."

Flashes were going off in my head. Mummy. At the Ritz. Probably close to the other Germans, if they hadn't left Paris already. Maybe a chance for me to find out more or even to meet Frau Goldberg.

"You know what," I said. "I'll come with you. You don't mind, do you? I see my mother so seldom."

"Of course. That would be perfect. She'll be more relaxed with her darling daughter there. And you can keep Max entertained if he's in the room. I always find men are a confounded nuisance."

"Not always," I reminded her.

She sighed. "Not always. You're right. I had a note from Paolo yesterday. I didn't mention it. He'd really like to see me again. He realizes how special I was to him. And we're both mature adults and alone in Paris, so why not make the most of it?"

"Oh golly. Not another one. You're not going to, are you?"

"In spite of the fact that I'd love to hear more about my son and in spite of the fact that I once adored Paolo, I think I'm going to be strong. I don't want to be anyone's mistress. I don't want any more one-night flings. I want to be happily married like you."

"Can you see yourself doing that with Jago?"

She gave an embarrassed little smile. "Maybe. If he can get over the class difference thing. Can you see me as a Cornish housewife?"

I had to laugh. "Darling Belinda. As if you could ever be a housewife. But I could see you as lady of the manor in your grandmother's old home, hosting parties for the Cornish nobility."

"Yes. I think I like that," she said. "And popping up to London to show off my latest collection."

"With no murders," I pointed out.

She chuckled and agreed. "No murders."

HAVING DECIDED TO go to Mummy and do a bit of sleuthing, I splashed cold water on my face, washed and dressed in the new outfit Zou Zou had bought me. I managed a piece of baguette with jam and off we went. Mummy, of course, had only just stirred at ten o'clock. She was still in her black satin robe looking horribly like a film star, reclining on a chaise longue, the morning papers around her. The suite might have been made as a stage set for my mother—large displays of flowers everywhere, a dark mink thrown casually over the back of a chair, reminding me sharply of the different lives we had always led.

"So early, darlings," she said, reaching out a languid hand to greet us. "I'm really not at my best at this hour."

"Belinda wants to get started on your clothing designs."

"Oh, of course." A dramatic sigh as if this might be a huge burden to her.

"Where's Max?" I asked.

"Gone to a stupid meeting, of course. Probably getting an order for a million more motorcars. Certainly not guns or tanks in France. Those are all going to the homeland."

There was a tap at the door and a tray was carried in with coffee and croissants on it. She poured herself a cup, black, then sank on the chaise again in a languid pose. "Thank God for coffee."

"So where are the rest of the German party?" I asked, innocently. "Did the other ladies end up ordering any outfits from Chanel? They disappeared in a hurry on Sunday."

"I couldn't say. We only exchange a polite greeting. Between us girls, I can't stand them. And I'm sure they don't like me because I'm a foreigner, although I'm blond and Aryan. And Hitler quite fancies me." She gave a cheeky smile.

"Are their rooms nearby?"

"On this same corridor," she said.

"And what about Frau Goldberg? Have you seen her recently? Spoken to her?"

"We have hardly exchanged more than a nod," she said. "I be-lieve she has the room next door to me, but I haven't seen her recently. She certainly wasn't at dinner last night. Someone said she wasn't feeling well. Why this interest in Frau Goldberg? I'd say she was the least interesting of the group. Quite dowdy."

"Only because she was supposed to have the seat that the American lady took—the one who was murdered."

"Oh God, Georgie, you're not trying to play detective again, are you?"

"Trying to clear my name," I said. "That policeman has all but made up his mind that I'm the guilty party. I'd really like a word with Frau Goldberg. I think I'll go and tap on her door. See if she's all right."

"Good luck with that," Mummy said. "There is some kind of security person who lurks in this hallway. Didn't you encounter him as you came up?"

"There was a man at the far end of the hall," I said. "I thought he was some kind of hotel lackey."

"German, darling. Great big brute. Keeps watch over the flock."

"How frightening."

"One gets used to it. And of course Max is a favored son, so I'm not under as much scrutiny as others." She reached for the bowl of pastries. "Now stop talking and let me get on with my breakfast. I like my croissants while they are still warm."

Belinda waited patiently until Mummy had finished her breakfast. "Now, Your Grace. Tell me what you had in mind," she said, taking out her sketchbook.

Meanwhile I went over to the windows. They were tall and elegant, opening onto wrought iron French balconies with the view of the Place Vendôme beyond. I opened one and stepped out. There was a nice wide ledge running to the next balconies, which, if Mummy was correct, belonged to Frau Goldberg. I glanced back into the room. Belinda and Mummy were completely engrossed in dress design, poring over a sketch on the table. I didn't waste another second, but hitched up my skirt (thank goodness it was wide enough today), and climbed over the balcony railing. The ledge might be wide but it was still rather intimidating to realize I was on the third floor and it was a long drop. I reached out for a convenient drainpipe and eased myself along, suddenly remembering that my stomach now took up more room than before.

My heart was beating awfully fast as I climbed over the railing onto the next balcony. The curtains were half drawn and it was hard to see into the room. I tapped on the window.

"Frau Goldberg," I whispered through the glass. "Are you there?"

Perhaps she didn't understand much English, and my German was nonexistent. I tapped again, not wanting to shout too loudly in case I alerted any of the other German women. There was no reply. From what I could see between the curtains there was no movement in the room. I had a vision of Frau Goldberg, lying dead, the poisoner having found his mark at last and the microfilm gone. I jiggled the handle of the window and, to my delight, it turned. The window swung open and I stepped into the room. The bed was made. There was no clothing about, no sign of any presence at all. I went across to the wardrobe. It was empty. I opened the bathroom door. No toothbrush, no comb. Nothing. Frau Goldberg had gone.

Had she been whisked back to Germany? I wondered. Or had she been killed, as I feared, and her body quietly disposed of? I'd have no way of finding out. I felt a great surge of disappointment that we had failed in our little transaction. Now Britain would never have the valuable formula. And poor Frau Goldberg—well, she had paid for being brave.

I looked around the room. Was it possible she knew she was being shipped back and had left at least the microfilm for one of us to find? I moved around the room, looking under the bed, in the bathroom cabinets, on top of the wardrobe . . . but the room was spartan, unlike my mother's, and there was no good hiding place that I could see. I went back into the bathroom, wondering where housemaids might not clean well. Behind the lavatory? Up in the cistern? I was standing on the lavatory seat, fishing around, when I heard a sound behind me.

"You see, the window is open," said a voice in accented French. "Somebody has entered here."

I looked around. There was no place to hide. I held my breath and turned to see Chief Inspector Mauville staring up at me with the ferocious Frau Bruhler, the German watchdog, behind him.

Chapter 29

TUESDAY, APRIL 28
IN A DARK, DANK FRENCH PRISON.

I can't believe what is happening to me. It's like a nightmare that
goes from bad to worse. The guillotine can't be far away. Oh,
Darcy, why did you have to go away?

"The young English milady who protests her innocence," he said.
"I might have known it. And what, may I ask, are you doing here?"

What could I say? My brain refused to work. If I told him Frau
Goldberg was a spy who had plans to hand over to the British and
she had been transported back to Germany, then her life would be
worth nothing and I might have endangered a whole British net-
work. But one must obviously have a good reason to climb from a
balcony into another guest's room. And then to be found standing
on a lavatory seat with one's hand in the tank.

"My mother occupies the next room," I said, pleading that she
might just have the sense to play along with this if questioned. "She

has lost a diamond bracelet. She didn't want to make a fuss but she found her window open and thought that a thief might have taken it and got away through the window."

It was the first thing that came into my head. It wasn't very convincing, I could hear as I said it.

Chief Inspector Mauville was frowning as he held out his hand and helped me down. "And if this thief took the valuable bracelet, why would he or she want to hide it in a toilet tank? Why come into another room that until very recently was occupied by another lady and thus risk alerting the authorities? Why not just walk out with it? It is, after all, small enough to slip into a pocket."

"I don't know," I said. "My mother sometimes has strange whims. She is a famous actress, you know. She has a vivid imagination."

"She is obviously lying," said Frau Bruhler, taking a threatening step toward me. "Clearly she is part of some criminal enterprise. She enters through the window, intending to rob Frau Goldberg, not knowing that the lady has become ill and been taken home to Germany. Or worse"—and she gave a dramatic pause—"she came here intending to kill poor Frau Goldberg, as you suggested that the poison at the fashion show may have been intended for her, and we have now caught her in the act of hiding a vial of cyanide in the toilet tank."

Chief Inspector Mauville barked out a command and a uniformed officer of the Paris police pushed past me, climbed onto the lavatory seat and fished around with his hand. "Nothing," he said, climbing down again.

"And why would I hide a vial of cyanide in a toilet tank when I could easily toss it from the window into the bushes beneath?" I said, trying to show that I was not in any way cowed by this woman. In truth my knees were knocking beneath my skirt.

"She clearly came in here to do no good," Frau Bruhler said. "I want her arrested. Either she is a clever thief or she is deranged and bears a hatred toward Germans because of the Great War."

"I would hardly do that," I said, "since half my ancestry is German."

"What ancestry is this?" she demanded.

"Queen Victoria and Prince Albert," I said as belligerently as I could. "They are my great-grandparents."

This did take the wind out of her sails, just a little. But not enough. "At the very least she is trespassing in a room paid for by the German government. She can come up with no good reason for being here, and she is your one suspect in the murder of an innocent tourist. What are you waiting for, Inspector? Do your job. Remove her at once."

He turned to me. "English lady, I must ask that you accompany me to the Sûreté. I will not put handcuffs on you, in deference to your status, but I ask that you come with no fuss."

The young policeman took my arm and started to lead me from the room. I wanted to confront Frau Bruhler and demand to know what she had done with Frau Goldberg. Was she still alive? But of course I couldn't, without giving my reasons. As we came out of the door I stopped. "Wait," I said. "I have to tell my mother that I am being taken away. She will panic if I'm missing."

"Very well," the chief inspector said.

I tapped on her door. Belinda opened it. Mummy was still languishing on the chaise. "The police are taking me away," I said, the words tumbling out in a rush. "They found me in the next-door room. I told them about your missing bracelet, Mummy, but they don't believe me. You thought someone might have climbed in from next door, didn't you? So I was searching the room, but they don't believe me."

"Missing bracelet?" Mummy asked, those wide blue eyes trained on the inspector. Then she looked at me. Our eyes met. "Oh, that bracelet," she said. "It wasn't really that valuable. I'd almost forgotten. You were sweet to look for it for me." My mother might play dumb sometimes but she was really quite sharp. I saw the inspector frowning.

"Nevertheless," he said, "we have questions for this young lady. Why were her fingerprints on the glass that contained the cyanide? Why was she the only person seen to approach the chair of the dead woman? And now why is she in the room of the woman who should have been occupying this chair? Too many coincidences and we want answers. We are prepared to wait for answers and give the young lady time to think in a more suitable environment." He looked past me to my mother. "Let us hope we do not find out that you are somehow involved in this . . . this scandal, madame."

I had to translate.

Mummy stood up and came toward him, the black robe sweeping out behind her. "I am not involved in anything other than accompanying my fiancé to Paris on behalf of the German government," she said. "And I resent your implications."

I duly translated her reply. He didn't look very happy.

"Come," he said. "We go now."

"Belinda, get in touch with Darcy, and Zou Zou and even Mrs. Simpson," I said. "Tell them I'm being hauled off to the Bastille."

"We have not taken prisoners to the Bastille for over one hundred years," Mauville said dryly.

It was almost in a dreamlike state that I was taken down in the lift, then led through the foyer with curious eyes on me, out through the front door and into a waiting police motorcar. We drove across the Seine to the Île de la Cité. The building fronting the river looked grim, austere, medieval—remarkably like my version of the Bastille. I half expected to see a guillotine standing in the central courtyard. I kept telling myself that I was innocent and that they would have to release me, but I was so scared that I could hardly walk up the steps beside the policeman. I was ushered into a small room containing a table and four chairs. No window. Black painted walls. Terrifying. I was told to sit, which was good as my legs wouldn't have held me much longer.

I don't know how long I waited. It seemed like an eternity. It felt cold and damp in the room. I wanted a handkerchief and realized I had left my purse in Mummy's hotel room. Would that give her an excuse to bring it to me? Was Belinda doing what I asked her? Was someone, somewhere, working on my behalf? Eventually the door opened and Inspector Mauville came in, together with another older man. They pulled out chairs across the table from me.

"This is Chief Inspector DuPont," Mauville said. "He was brought into this case since it might possibly have involved a member of an important German trade delegation."

"Does the young lady speak French?" DuPont asked.

"She does. Fluently. And since we have been told about a robbery in the South of France that also involved her, we must assume she is frequently in our country."

"I speak French because I was at school in Switzerland," I said. "And this is only the second time I have been in France, apart from passing through it by train."

"This robbery, in the South?" This was clearly news to DuPont.

"I was asked to model in a fashion show put on by Chanel," I said. "I was wearing a valuable necklace loaned by Queen Mary. The outfit I was asked to wear came with impossibly high-heeled shoes. I tripped, fell from the runway and when I stood up the necklace had been taken. It was later returned anonymously. You can check with Inspector Lafite in Nice if you want the details."

"Have we done that?" DuPont asked.

"I believe we are waiting for a response from Nice."

DuPont shrugged. "What do you expect? The South. They take their time, don't they?"

"You can ask Madame Chanel," I said. "She was there. She had borrowed the necklace from Her Majesty the Queen. She saw everything. I am no thief."

"Then what," said Inspector Mauville, "were you doing, breaking into a woman's hotel room? There can be no explanation except for criminal intent."

During my time alone I had come up with something vaguely plausible. "I came to see if Mrs. Goldberg needed my help," I said. "My mother told me that she thought Mrs. Goldberg might be being held prisoner as she was no longer seen with the others at meals. And since we know that she was supposed to be sitting where the American woman was killed, I thought something might be wrong—knowing that her husband is Jewish and how they are treating the Jews in Germany."

"And how do you know this?" DuPont asked sharply.

Oh golly, I'd said too much. How did I know it? "Goldberg is a Jewish name and I believe she mentioned to my mother that her husband was not allowed to travel with her." There. That sounded convincing, didn't it?

DuPont was still staring at me with interest. "And may one ask why you took it upon yourself to be the rescue mission for this woman? Do you make a habit of this sort of thing?"

"I just wanted to see if she needed help. I knew the corridor was being monitored so I couldn't enter through her door. Then I got into the room and there was nobody there, and I wondered if she'd been abducted and maybe left a message."

It wasn't brilliant but it would have to do.

"Lady Georgiana," DuPont said slowly, "I believe there is more that you are not telling us. It would not be the first time that the British government has used an aristocrat to assist in international intrigue."

"But the murder," Mauville cut in. "Her fingerprints on the glass. And she was the only one to approach the dead woman during the performance. How do we explain those, I'd like to know?"

"I have explained them," I said. "When the champagne was being poured several glasses on the tray were knocked over. I picked them up and held them out to help with the pouring. I also explained that the champagne was passed on trays and each lady helped herself. I don't see how the cyanide could have been put into the glass."

"You believed that the German lady, Frau Goldberg, should have been occupying that seat?"

"That is correct," I said. "So I wondered at the time whether she had been the intended victim. I understand that things like that happen in Germany these days."

"Very true," DuPont said. "So let me ask—did you know either of these women?"

"I did not," I said. "I was at the fashion show helping my friend Belinda Warburton-Stoke, who is now designing clothes with Chanel. I had never met Mrs. Goldberg. I had seen the American woman once before when she showed up at the salon of Gertrude Stein, but I did not exchange any words with her. She seemed very assertive, shall we say, and Mademoiselle Stein was most upset with her."

"Ah?" DuPont glanced at Mauville. "Do you think it's possible that this woman upset other people?"

"I think it's highly likely," I said. "But, as I said, that was the only time I encountered her."

"Interesting," DuPont said. "Mauville, have we questioned those who knew this lady?"

"There was only her niece who traveled with her," Mauville

said. "She seemed very upset about the death of her aunt. The husband is on his way from America."

There was a long pause. DuPont cleared his throat. "Well, Lady Georgiana, that will be all, for now. You have given us food for thought. I will not say you are free to go. Some of the things you have told us will need to be verified. But I see no reason to detain you any longer. You understand that you are not to leave Paris?"

"Yes, I understand that," I said, trying not to let the relief show on my face. As I was escorted from the room I heard a commotion going on in the foyer. A woman's voice shouting.

"I demand to see her right away! You'll hear about this." An American voice. To my astonishment it was Mrs. Simpson, with a distinguished older man standing behind her, looking extremely uncomfortable.

She saw me and rushed toward me. "Georgiana, honey, are you all right? Did they interrogate you? They didn't torture you, did they? I came as soon as your friend telephoned me. I telephoned David and he got right on to the British ambassador."

"Lady Georgiana, I am sorry for this regrettable incident," the man, who was obviously the ambassador himself, said. "I must demand that this relative of the royal family be released immediately."

"Don't worry, I'm already free to go," I said. "Just not free to leave Paris until they've sorted out who was responsible for the murder of the American woman."

"The king of England was most upset to hear how his young cousin was treated," Mrs. Simpson cut in.

"The king of England?" DuPont was digesting this information.

"I'm his fiancée," Mrs. Simpson said triumphantly.

On that note we left.

$\mathcal{C}$hapter 30

I can't just sit back now. I have to get to the truth somehow,
otherwise my name will never be cleared. Please hurry back,
Darcy.

Everyone was most kind. Mrs. Simpson and the ambassador returned me to the Ritz, where I found Mummy and Belinda trying
to work in spite of the distractions. They both flung their arms
around me.

"Thank you for rescuing me," I said, hugging them both back.
"You must have contacted Mrs. Simpson. She came storming in,
bringing the British ambassador with her, and whisked me away.
She was magnificent. I never thought I'd say this, but maybe I've
misjudged her."

"You mean we actually have to be grateful to Wallis Simpson?"

Mummy asked. "I know I'm a great actress, but that really will be stretching my abilities."

"But she saved your only daughter, Mummy."

Mummy sighed. "In that case, I suppose." She took my face in her hands, examining me for signs of trauma. "Darling, I was worried out of my mind. Did they mistreat you horribly, the brutes?"

"They were really quite civilized," I said. "Luckily there was a superior officer who seemed to believe me, or at least partially believe me. For now, at least. But I still have this cloud hanging over me." I looked at Belinda. "Did you find Darcy?"

"I left a message in several places, including your house," she said. "Also the foreign office, where no one would admit to knowing him. I didn't quite know what else to do."

"There is nothing else," I said. "His dratted secret life is infuriating at times. I'm going to insist he settle down and work in a bank!"

This made them chuckle.

"Why don't you go back to the flat and rest?" Belinda said.

"Or should I order some food for you here?" Mummy suggested. "You are looking quite pale."

"You'd look pale if you had been in the headquarters of the Sûreté in a little room with no windows," I said. "It was actually quite terrifying. I had a horrible urge to go to the loo."

"Sweetheart. Let me take you straight back home and have Mrs. Holbrook look after you," Mummy said. "You've had enough excitement in Paris."

"I can't. I'm not allowed to leave."

"Stuff and nonsense," Mummy said. "I'll telephone the ambassador myself and insist that you are escorted home."

"No, Mummy. Don't you see—then I'd look like a fugitive. I have to get to the truth."

"And just how are you going to do that?"

I shrugged. "I should talk to the lady who sat beside Mrs. Rottenburger again. She might remember some small detail that she had overlooked. And I promised I'd see if Mrs. Rottenburger's niece needed help with the paperwork for her aunt's death. That would give me a chance to talk to her again. Although I can't say I suspect her of having anything to do with it. She wasn't sitting anywhere near her aunt." I sighed. "I just feel terrible about Frau Goldberg. Did you have any idea she was leaving? Did you hear anything?"

"What sort of thing?"

"I don't know. A scuffle?"

"Certainly not. The Ritz makes rooms that are soundproof. What a thought."

"So I'll never find out if she was taken back to Germany or if she was killed here and her body taken away."

Mummy looked confused. "Why on earth should someone want to kill her? Or kidnap her?"

"Mummy, she was supposed to be in that chair. It was dark. One has to assume . . ."

"But why? She seemed a most innocuous sort of woman."

"Because her husband is a Jewish scientist."

Mummy's eyes narrowed. "You know more."

"I can't tell you more. But there might be a reason to want her dead."

"Poor woman. If only I'd known I'd have been more friendly."

If only, I thought. If I'd trusted Mummy and been allowed to tell her, they could have become chummy and the microfilm could have been passed across. Now it was too late. But that didn't mean I had to give up. "Belinda," I said. "Can you find me the name and address of the woman who sat beside Mrs. Rottenburger?"

Belinda glanced at her watch. "I have to go to Chanel soon anyway. Stay here and I'll telephone you."

Mummy decided I needed feeding up and ordered a rather large amount of food plus a bottle of champagne. "Wonderful pick-me-up, darling," she said.

Belinda departed and I found I was hungry after all. I worked my way through a clear soup, an omelette aux fines herbes and a crème brûlée. I was just finishing when Belinda telephoned, giving me the name and address of the woman who had identified me at the fashion show. I asked at the reception desk and was told it was a street in the first arrondissement, not far from the Seine. "A very good address, madame," the clerk said with a nod of his head. I took a taxicab and we drove along the river until we turned onto the Rue François Premier. It was lined with sycamore trees, sporting bright new leaves, and instead of apartment buildings there were houses on either side—big stone houses with wrought iron balconies, very like the one occupied by the disgusting Count Louis-Philippe. The taxi pulled up in front of one of these.

"Should I wait, madame?" he asked.

I thought, rapidly. "Oh yes, please do." Mummy was close by. I need not worry about money for a change.

I took a deep breath before I went up to the front door and rang the bell. It was answered by a severe-looking maid in a black uniform, starched white apron and cap. I realized, too late, that I should have handed her my card.

"Yes?" she said, eyeing me with disapproval.

"I am Lady Georgiana Rannoch," I said, deciding against the simple Mrs. O'Mara. "I need to speak to your mistress if she is at home. It is a matter of great urgency."

"Concerning what?"

"We were at the House of Chanel together. A lady died. . . ."

"We heard. The mistress was most distressed."

"Your mistress was seated beside this unfortunate woman. We are trying to get to the truth. May I come in?"

Grudgingly she allowed me to enter a rather splendid foyer. A white marble floor, sweeping curved staircase on one side. A Roman bust on a plinth, a huge display of spring flowers, a gold-framed mirror. I was still looking around when the maid returned.

"The mistress will see you," she said.

I was ushered into a sitting room. A fire burned in a marble fireplace. There were swaths of velvet at every window. The furniture was gilt and silk. All very French. One half expected Louis XIV to be sitting there. Instead Madame de Moret was sitting beside the fire, dressed in a simple wool skirt and white blouse. She did not give me a friendly smile.

"I have no idea why you would want to see me," she said. "If you wish me to change my report to the police, I am afraid you are wasting your time."

The hostility took me by surprise. "Madame, I have no wish to influence what you saw or what you said. I do not deny that I approached the woman and found she had died," I said.

She shook her head. "I have been most upset by what occurred and have no wish to revive that day."

"I am really sorry to disturb you," I said, "but I really need your help. Because you saw me approach the dead woman, they are trying to accuse me of killing her. I didn't even know her, let alone kill her, so I need to prove my innocence. I wondered if there was any small detail you might have overlooked that could help me."

I saw her expression soften, just a little. "I'm afraid I can be of no help," she said. "My attention was on the activity on the runway. Once I realized that I did not know my neighbor and indeed took her for a rather objectionable woman, I paid no further attention to her."

"But if we could just go through the stages of that afternoon," I said. "You arrived. You were seated by one of the ushers?"

"That is correct."

"And nobody was sitting in the chair to your right at the time?"

"Also correct."

"And you were offered champagne at this point?"

She frowned. "No. First the dead woman came and took the seat beside me. She made rather a fuss about it. Settling herself and muttering something I did not understand. I concluded she was not French as she did not greet me in the way one should." She paused, frowning as she tried to remember. "Then the champagne came around. I took a glass from the tray. The woman drank hers immediately. Gulped it down. Most uncivilized."

"She drank all her champagne immediately? Before the show started?"

"She did."

This gave me pause for thought. Surely cyanide had an almost instantaneous effect. Had she been dead from the very beginning of the show? But no—she had an interaction with the German woman after that.

"Then she snapped her fingers and said she wanted a refill."

Now we were getting somewhere. "And someone refilled her glass?"

"No. You must understand that I did not wish to look in her direction. I found her distasteful. But I believe one of the ushers took her glass away and handed her a new glass."

"Handed it to her?" I heard my voice quiver a little.

"He offered the tray to her. She took a glass and this time she did not drink it because the German lady approached at that moment."

"I see." I nodded.

"She tapped the American woman on the shoulder and said that the seat was hers. But the American lady clearly spoke no French. So the German lady repeated what she had said in English. 'You have the wrong seat. This chair is for me,' she said. But the American said, 'Too bad. I got here first,' or something like that. It was most unpleasant. At that moment the lights dimmed and Madame Chanel started to speak. The German lady had no alternative. She went away."

"And then?"

"Then the show started. We were all watching the runway. I would not have seen you approach if you had not found the lady had died."

"So nobody else came near you the whole time?"

"Nobody that I observed. The press photographers were moving around behind us, setting off those nasty flashbulbs. In fact one was so close that I was startled at the sound of the bulb going off. And was blinded for a second too. Most unpleasant. Chanel should keep those men in their place, not let them wander around, disturbing the guests."

"This was before I found the lady had died?"

"It was."

I took a deep breath. "Madame, did you not notice her in any distress before she died?"

Madame de Moret considered this. "You know, she was the sort of woman who moved around a lot. Fidgeted. Shifted around in her seat. Most annoying. So I tried not to look in her direction. I think she did make little noises. She gasped once but it was when one of the models appeared and I took that to mean that she was surprised by the outfit. I wanted to concentrate on the show, you know. After she had been hauled away I felt distracted. Unable to concentrate any longer. It quite spoiled my afternoon, I have to tell you."

"Mine too," I agreed. She actually smiled.

"You are a British aristocrat, are you not?"

"I am."

"Related to the king, I am told."

"This is true."

"So I can see now that you would have no interest in killing an unpleasant American woman."

"No interest at all." We exchanged a smile.

She sighed. "I wish I could tell you more, something that might help your cause. But I am sure the police will soon get to the truth and you will not have to worry."

"I really hope so," I said.

I was clearly being dismissed. I came out of the house and climbed back into the taxicab. Had I learned anything I didn't know before? Only that Mrs. Rottenburger had taken a second glass of champagne. Then that a photographer had come up too close behind Madame de Moret and for a moment she was temporarily blinded. So would everyone else around her have been? Could the killer have taken that moment to strike? Or, was the photographer himself planting the cyanide in the champagne glass? It would have been simple for someone sent by the German government to show newspaper credentials, to let off a flashbulb and plant the cyanide. Unfortunately we'd have no way of proving it. I wondered if we'd ever find out if Frau Goldberg really went back to Germany. I wondered if I'd ever be free from suspicion. I prayed Darcy would return soon.

Chapter 31

Everybody is being really kind. Mummy offered to take me
shopping today. Belinda said she'd try to skip today's fashion
show to keep me company. Zou Zou offered to fly me home in
her little plane, but I think that would have been just as
terrifying as waiting here for the police to haul me back for
more questioning. Besides, I'm not allowed to leave. I'm not
sure how they could stop me but I suspect there is a policeman
watching the flat. And I don't want to be a fugitive all my life.

I awoke to find someone standing over my bed. A man. A strange
man in black. I gasped and tried to sit up, but the person put a hand
on my shoulder to hold me in place. "Don't get excited," said a familiar deep voice. "It's only me."

"Darcy!" I exclaimed. "You scared me to death. I thought it was
the killer coming to find me."

"You silly old thing." He sat down beside me and brushed my forehead with his lips.

"When did you get back?" I asked.

"I took the night train. I just got in and came straight to you. I received a rather convoluted message that seemed to come from Belinda. Something about you being in jail?"

"I was," I said. "They arrested me yesterday and I'm still not in the clear."

"Arrested you? For what?"

"A series of coincidences," I said. "All so stupid. Because I was the only person seen to approach the woman who was murdered. And then at Chanel another woman recognized me from the fashion show in Nice several years ago and told the police how I had fallen and then a valuable necklace I was wearing went missing. So the inspector immediately jumped to the conclusion that this murder was a robbery gone wrong."

"Idiots," Darcy muttered. "Didn't you tell them who you were?"

"I did. The inspector said there have been cases of the 'gentleman thief.' But the worst thing was that they caught me in Frau Goldberg's room and I couldn't really explain why I was there."

"What?" Darcy reacted, glaring at me. "What in the blazes were you doing in Frau Goldberg's room?"

"She had the next room to Mummy," I said, feeling rather foolish now. "I thought I might get a chance to speak to Frau Goldberg, so I climbed over the balcony and got in through her windows. But I found that she had gone. No trace of her. So I wondered if she might have left the microfilm for us to find, and then I was standing up on top of a toilet when the chief inspector, along with that horrible Frau Bruhler, who is their watchdog, caught me."

"Georgiana, what were you thinking?" Darcy sounded very angry. "Firstly you are pregnant and you climb over balconies, secondly you go into the room of a person who is of interest to the German government and may have been the object of an assassination attempt. Did you not realize if the watchdog, as you put it, had caught you with Frau Goldberg it would have been even worse for her and extremely dangerous for you?"

"I suppose I hoped to speak to her privately, without anyone seeing," I said, lamely. "And I did regret climbing over balconies. It was silly of me." I gave him an appealing look. "I just wanted to help, Darcy. I felt so badly that I had not been able to carry out the one assignment you had given me."

Darcy took my face in his hands. "My dear girl, do you not realize that you are far more precious to me than any damned assignment? What if you had lost your balance and fallen? What if a German agent had been waiting and decided to dispatch you on the spot?"

"I suppose I wouldn't be here with you now," I said, giving an embarrassed grin.

"I am so angry with myself for getting you into this in the first place." He got up and started to pace around my room. Since the room was tiny it was rather like watching a panther in a cage at the zoo. "There's not much we can do," he said. "We now know that Frau Goldberg has been taken back to Germany. It's unlikely she'll be able to meet up with any of our chaps in future. Her husband will almost certainly be taken to a camp, and now she might very well too."

"Oh dear." I stared at him bleakly. "So the microfilm has gone back to Germany with her?"

He nodded. "Unless she found a way to post it, which I very much doubt, given the surveillance."

"Poor lady. Was there nothing you could do to rescue her? To take her to England?"

"We offered," Darcy said. "We told her we could transport her to safety if she wished, but she made it clear she was never going to leave her husband, especially not now."

"Golly. What a brave woman." I paused, thinking. "But then I would never leave you either."

"I hope you would if that sort of situation arose," he said. "But the point is that the matter is out of our hands. However, there is another point. My contacts tell me that there was never an attempt on Frau Goldberg's life. She was taken back to Germany because they thought there was an attempt by the British and French to contact her and they weren't sure how much information she might have to share. But never a plan to kill her."

I sat watching him, my mouth open now. "So," I said, "do we conclude that the murderer actually planned to kill Mrs. Rotten-burger?"

"It would appear that way."

I went to say "golly" again but swallowed back the word at the last moment. "So who could possibly have wanted to kill her?"

"You tell me." He came to sit on my bed again. "You say she knew nobody at the fashion show?"

"Apart from her niece, Madge. Oh, and she had had a brush with several of Chanel's assistants when she tried to get a sneak peek at the garments. But among the guests nobody admitted to knowing her."

"She was the only American in the room?"

"Apart from Mrs. Simpson—who has been brilliant, by the way. I never thought I'd say this, but I'm deeply in her debt. She grabbed the British ambassador and hauled him to the Sûreté to rescue me. Wasn't that nice of her?"

"Amazing," Darcy said. "So she does have a softer side after all.

Who would have thought it? And who would have thought that she was in any way fond of you?"

"Because of David," I said. "She wouldn't have wanted anything bad to happen to his cousin."

Darcy nodded. "But I hardly think we can see her as a suspect in the murder."

"Oh no. Absolutely not," I said. "For one thing she was on the wrong side of the runway. She could not have come around to where Mrs. Rottenburger was sitting during the show. And anyway, I don't think she's the sort to bother with poison. If she wanted someone dead she'd have simply shot them."

Darcy had to smile at this.

I was still thinking of the implications of what Darcy had said. It all pointed rather strongly to Madge now, didn't it? Good motive for wanting an objectionable aunt out of the way. She was the sort of person that others overlook—colorless, quiet. Maybe she was the one who brought her aunt a new glass of champagne, and not one of the ushers. How easy that would have been. Here, Auntie, I've found another glass for you. . . .

"We should talk to Mrs. Rottenburger's niece," I said. "She did have motive and means, really. I thought of her as a bit insipid but sometimes it's the quiet ones, isn't it? Silently plotting. Maybe she's studied chemistry . . . and she did say that she loved to read to her cousin. What if she loved to read detective stories?"

"*We* should not do anything," Darcy said firmly. "I want you to stay well away from this in future and leave everything to the professionals."

"But, Darcy." I put a hand on his shoulder. "I have to clear my good name, don't I? And Madge speaks no French, so I did offer to translate for her. I could at least go and see how she's getting on.

You could come with me and we'd get a feel about whether she had anything to do with her aunt's death."

Darcy sighed. "Now that Frau Goldberg has been taken back to Germany this is out of my hands, Georgie. I'd get into trouble if I interfered with a French police investigation."

"So you don't want your wife to prove her innocence?" I said.

"Of course I do. And naturally I'd step in if the police came back for you. I can get our chaps to contact America and find out what we can about Mrs. Rotten-whatsit. See what connections she might have had in Paris, or if her husband was involved in any sort of international crime. But no other Americans in the room, you say? Nobody else she knew?"

"Nobody claimed to know her when the police asked," I said. "Actually, there were two other Americans in the room. The man who lives upstairs and his friend Arnie. Belinda roped them in to help move chairs. However, they've both lived in Paris since the Great War so I don't see what connection they could have. Arnie did meet Mrs. Rottenburger at Gertrude Stein's."

Darcy was instantly alert and interested. "He met her before, you say?"

"Yes. She gate-crashed Gertrude Stein's salon and wanted to buy pictures. Gertrude was furious."

"How furious?"

I gave a nervous chuckle. "Not furious enough to sneak into a fashion show and kill somebody." I saw his expression. "Or even to send a henchman to do it for her. She's very civilized, you know."

"Even civilized people have been known to kill if they have to."

"Yes, but . . . you don't kill someone who wants to buy your pictures, do you?"

"And this Arnie was there? Spoke with her?"

"They were both there but Harry escaped when he saw how

awful she was. Arnie was stuck and she claimed she knew his family, which he said was rubbish."

"So there was a connection, however tenuous," Darcy said. "Give me the names of these two men and we'll have our boys in Washington find out what they can."

"But what possible reason could they have for wanting this woman dead?" I demanded. "They were only roped in at the last minute and they didn't know she'd be attending. You don't carry cyanide around in your pocket on the off chance, do you?"

"All the same, we have to leave no stone unturned," Darcy said. "I tend to agree that the niece had the most plausible motive. But the other two—do you know their full names and where they came from?"

"Harry Barnstable. He told the police he came from New York, although I'm not sure whether that was city or state. But he's been here since the end of the war and he has no contact with his family. He's really nice. Kind. Friendly. Funny."

"And where is Arnie from?"

"I think it was Pennsylvania, like Mrs. Rottenburger. He's from a big military family, which is why he left and came over here. He said they treated him like a hero and glorified war when he had seen what it was really like. Both he and Harry were devastated by what they went through. They are both writers, or trying to be writers."

"How do they survive? They have jobs?"

"They take what they can get," I said. "Harry helps out at a pub and a bookstall and writes occasional pieces for the American newspapers. Arnie is also a photographer. He was trying to take pictures at the fashion show. I'm not sure the real newspapermen let him. I think there was a bit of a kerfuffle and one of them tried to take his camera, and Harry rescued it."

"What was Arnie's name?"

I tried to think back to when I had met him at the café and when he had been interviewed by the police, but my brain refused to work. Something German, right? "I'm not sure. You'll have to ask Belinda. She was the one who hired them to help out."

"Right," he said. "Now you lie there and I'll bring you breakfast. I want you taking it easy today. And I'll have a word with the ambassador to see if we can take you home. I think you've had enough excitement in Paris for now."

"I agree with you," I said. "I keep thinking about the puppies and how I'd like to play with them."

"They have probably destroyed the entire house by now," he said, with a grin. "But it will be good to be home again."

Chapter 32

I feel so much better knowing that Darcy is here. I wanted to move in with him at the Hôtel Saville, but he thought I should keep staying with Belinda as he'd be out and about so much and the hotel wasn't particularly comfortable. But he's going to check on me often, which is reassuring.

Darcy was really sweet and brought me a tray with tea, baguette and jam. I sat up and wolfed down the lot, feeling jolly hungry. Then he left, warning me to take it easy, go for a gentle stroll but nothing more. Belinda informed me she had done some preliminary sketches for my mother and wanted to take them over to her. Did I want to come along? But the Ritz seemed to have lost its appeal, knowing that Frau Bruhler and the Germans were still there.

"Don't worry about me," I said. "I'll just go for a walk. It's a lovely day."

"Be careful," he warned. "Don't do anything silly."

"Of course not." I blew him a kiss. I wasn't intending to do anything silly, just pay a visit to Madge, Mrs. Rottenburger's niece. After all, I had promised to check on her after the initial shock. But, in my defense, I had been otherwise occupied.

After Belinda had gone off to the Ritz I put on my coat and started out along the Seine. It was a blustery day, more March-like than April, with the hint of a future shower. I turned up my collar as I crossed the Seine toward the Place de la Concorde. Then I turned left, taking the route my taxi had taken to Madame de Moret the day before. And there, on the Avenue Montaigne, was the Hôtel Plaza Athénée, looking very splendid with flags blowing in the wind. I was not greeted with open arms but rather with suspicion when I asked for Mrs. Rottenburger's niece. The fact that I looked rather windswept and didn't know her last name did not help my cause.

"I can telephone her suite for you," the reception clerk said. "I do not know if mademoiselle is in residence. You no doubt heard of the tragedy that befell her aunt?"

"I did. I was there. I witnessed it," I said. "I have come to see if Mademoiselle Madge needs any help. She speaks little French, you see, and I'm sure there are a lot of formalities."

He nodded now, deciding I wasn't quite as undesirable as I looked. "And who shall I say wishes to speak with her?"

"Lady Georgiana Rannoch," I said and noticed his reaction with satisfaction. I really was going to have to get used to being Mrs. O'Mara. My child would only be Master O'Mara, or Miss O'Mara, since I couldn't pass along my title. When Darcy's father died he would become Lord Kilhenny and the children would then be honorables. Until then, we were ordinary folk. But the title was certainly useful at times.

"Of course, milady," he said now, with a little bow. "Please take a seat. I will check if the lady is available."

A few minutes later Madge appeared from the lift. "Georgie," she said, rushing toward me with open arms. "Oh boy, am I glad to see you. It's been a nightmare. All those papers to fill out in French. You said you'd help but I didn't know how to get in touch with you."

"I've had a few problems of my own," I said. "The police are half convinced that I killed your aunt."

"Why, that's so silly! You didn't know her."

"Exactly. I told them that."

"They've been questioning me too," Madge said. "And most of the time I couldn't understand what they were saying and I was terrified that if I said '*oui*' or '*non*' at the wrong time I'd be admitting guilt."

She sat beside me, pulling her chair up close. "I'd invite you upstairs but I'm in the middle of packing up Auntie's things. I didn't dare touch anything in case the police wanted to take a look. And now Uncle Frank is coming and I don't know what he'll want done with all her stuff. No point in shipping it home, is there?"

"Not that I can see," I said. "So your uncle is on his way?"

"Yes. He was taking the ship that sailed out of New York yesterday. He'll be here by the weekend."

"In the meantime where is your aunt's body?"

"The police took it. They did an autopsy, I gather, and they are not ready to release it yet."

"Did they give you the results?"

She shook her head. "They haven't told me anything. They did go through my things, looking for anything that might have held cyanide. How silly is that? I told them I hadn't a clue about poisons. I couldn't know where to buy it or how to use it. Besides, why would I want to kill my aunt? If she hadn't taken me in, I'd have had nowhere to go. I'd have starved by now."

"I suppose people might say she was a little . . ." I paused, searching for the right word.

"Bossy?" Madge asked, the hint of a smile on her face. "Oh yes. She wasn't the nicest person in the world. But being in Paris was sure better than starving or working in some god-awful job and living in a boardinghouse."

I examined her face. No trace of nervousness. She was quite at ease with me. I phrased the next question carefully. "From what I saw, she was rude to people. Can you think of anyone else in Paris whom she might have upset?"

Madge gave a little laugh. "Oh, tons of people. It was horribly embarrassing. Trying to buy that lady's paintings, wanting the best table at a restaurant. And taking another lady's seat at the fashion show. That's just how she was. But these were all just casual encounters. You don't kill someone because they annoy you, do you?"

"No, you don't. And cyanide is a planned crime too."

She shuddered. "It's horrible. Only someone really nasty would do that."

"Or desperate," I said. "So tell me—did she bump into anyone she knew in Paris? Because it had to be someone she knew, someone with a good reason to want her dead. Can you think of a good reason?"

Madge frowned. "I don't think we met anyone we knew. She didn't exactly move in high society at home, although she'd have liked to. She was on lots of committees, charity stuff, you know. She loved being important." She stopped, thinking. "She was excited that she met that young guy at the salon."

"Arnie?"

"I can't remember his name. She said she knew his family. She said she couldn't wait to go and visit and tell them she'd seen their son."

I felt a rush of excitement go through me. For the first time we were getting somewhere. What if Arnie did not want to be found? What if he had left America under a cloud? Run away? Fled from a crime and established a new life for himself?

And then I thought of something else. Arnie was a photographer. Didn't they use cyanide to develop photographs? He was right there, standing in the background with his camera. He wouldn't have been noticed if he had moved around, come up behind Mrs. Rottenburger and dropped a cyanide crystal into her drink. I have to tell Darcy, I thought.

"I'm so glad you're here," Madge said. "I've got forms to fill in—all in French. They've been really helpful at the hotel but I can't keep pestering them. Can you see if you can help me? Perhaps you can come up to the room after all, and never mind the mess."

I was dying to visit Arnie, to get to the truth, but I couldn't very well leave Madge now. I got up and followed her to the lift. As we were going up, the two of us in the little cage together, it struck me to wonder whether I was being foolish, going to a room where I would be alone with her. She seemed so open, so friendly and naïve. But what if she wasn't? What if she had planned to kill her aunt during this trip? The lift came to a halt. The operator opened the door for us and I followed Madge along the corridor. The room was, as she had said, in disarray. There were two beds, one now heaped high with clothes. The wardrobe was open and more clothes hung there.

"Do you see any point in taking all this back to America?" Madge asked. "I wish I could get in touch with Uncle. I don't like to pack it all up without asking him. Do you think he'll want to donate it to the poor?" She gave a nervous little smile. "Besides, I'm not sure Auntie's clothes were suitable for the poor. She did like to be . . . noticed."

I had been observing that the clothes on the bed were all of the brightest colors, many with beads, sequins, fur trim, feathers. Mrs. Rottenburger was not a woman who was easily overlooked. I found myself wondering if anyone might have come to visit her at the hotel—the staff would have noticed. But then Madge said she knew nobody in Paris, apart from Arnie. Madge had gone over to the desk by the window. "So these are the forms," she said. "I suppose I could wait until Uncle gets here, but he speaks absolutely no French so I thought I'd get a start—prove to him I'm not entirely useless." There was a hint of panic in her face when she looked up to me, and I saw what was going through her mind: She had been Mrs. Rottenburger's companion. Would she now still be welcome in their home? If not, where would she go? So Madge had actually a good reason to keep her aunt alive.

We struggled with the various forms. Even I, speaking good French, was stumped by the complexity and number of legal terms.

"I'm sorry," I said at last, "but these are a bit beyond me. There are too many legal words I don't know."

"You were kind to come," she said. "I appreciate it. To tell you the truth, I've been feeling horribly alone and scared. And wondering what will happen next. That policeman hinting that he suspected me hasn't helped."

"You know what?" I said at last. "It might be the simplest thing when your uncle arrives to hire a solicitor to complete all these for you. Or a notary—I believe they use them for legal stuff in France. That way you'll know you are not making an error."

I saw the relief on her face. "Oh, good idea," she said. "I'll ask for recommendations at the front desk."

"And here's my telephone number at my friend's flat," I said, writing it out for her. "Do feel free to telephone me if you need me."

She gave me a shy little grin. "Maybe you and I could go out together for a meal. I have all this money of Auntie's. I'm sure nobody would mind."

"Of course. Why not?" I said. "You should make the most of your time before your uncle arrives."

She nodded. "Who knows, I may never have the chance to get back to Europe after this."

"You could always stay on in Europe," I said as the idea just came to me. "Find a job over here as an au pair or a companion. The Depression doesn't seem to have been so devastating here."

"Gee, do you really think so?" Her face lit up. "That would be amazing. I'll think about it. So—do you want to go out for a walk? Take a look at the fancy stores and maybe get some lunch?"

I thought about visiting Arnie. Surely that was the important thing to do. But then it would not be wise to visit him alone. I'd need Darcy with me—or maybe Harry might be a better idea, since he and Arnie were good friends. If we just chatted, I'd get a feeling as to whether he was uneasy. I made a decision. I'd ask Harry to take me back to the café with his friends.

As these thoughts were going through my head I glanced around the room. On the desk were several photographs in silver frames. One of a younger, slimmer Mrs. Rottenburger standing beside a tall, bullish-looking man. Then one of a pair of boys— sitting on a jetty, both in swimming trunks. They were skinny, with hair flopping across their foreheads and cheeky grins on their faces. One of them was holding a cigarette in his hand and his look said that he knew he was too young to be smoking.

"Is one of those your cousin?" I asked, pointing at it.

Madge nodded. "The one on the left."

"And who is with him?"

"That was his best friend who was killed in the war. Blown to pieces beside him. He's never recovered, poor thing."

I couldn't stop looking at those hopeful young faces. There was something about those eyes, that defiant sparkle, challenging the person who was taking the photograph. Before the war they expected a good life, full of possibilities. And then they were plunged into a horror beyond belief, and the one who survived would never be the same again. I put the photograph back on the desk. "Let's go shopping," I said.

Chapter 33

Madge and I actually had an enjoyable morning, window-shopping along the Rue Saint-Honoré, where neither of us would ever be able to afford the items. We had lunch at a little café in a side street—a bowl of hearty stew that cost pennies. I found myself contrasting it to the Ritz: Had the meals there been so much more enjoyable? Certainly they had been presented with elegance and flair. But our lunch had been satisfying, and it reinforced what I had always known—that one does not need money to be happy. Although one does need enough to survive. Madge must also have been thinking this because as we walked back to her hotel she said, "I'm trying to take this all in, every sight, sound, smell and taste of the city, because I'll probably never be able to travel again." She stopped, staring out across the Seine. "I have to confess I'm scared, Georgie. I don't know what will happen to me."

"I'm sure your uncle won't just throw you out into the cold," I said. "He couldn't be so heartless."

She chewed on her lip. "You don't know Uncle Frank. He's a bullying sort of guy and he takes it out on people who cross him. I'm scared he'll blame me for Auntie's death."

"How can he do that?" I looked at her curiously.

She shrugged. "He'll think I was only here as her companion. I should have taken better care of her. If I'd been watching out for her, I'd have seen if someone slipped poison into her glass."

"But that's silly," I said. "You wouldn't have known. Even if you'd been sitting with her, you wouldn't have thought twice if someone came up and handed her another glass, or stood behind her to take a photograph. And cyanide is so fast-acting that she'd have been dead before you could do anything."

"Really?" she asked.

I nodded. "So tell me—the American she claimed she knew from home, did you see him at the fashion show?"

"I'm not sure. I wasn't even sure who she was talking about the other night."

"He's tall and skinny, rather gaunt-looking with grayish hair. He was trying to take photographs at the salon. I don't know if he succeeded after the lights were dimmed."

"Oh yes. I did see him. I thought he looked familiar."

"Did you happen to see him taking photographs close to your aunt?"

"I don't think so. After the show started I wasn't looking in my aunt's direction at all. I was watching the models."

There it was again. The perfect opportunity. Nobody was watching when the killer moved up behind Mrs. Rottenburger and quickly dropped a cyanide crystal into her glass. I was now anxious to leave Madge and talk to Darcy. But she begged me to come back to the hotel room. "Why don't you take a look at Auntie's clothes. If I'm asked to get rid of them all, you could see if there is anything you'd like."

I had to smile. "I don't think your aunt's taste is mine," I said. "I'm more the simple country girl in tweeds. Your aunt was rather— flamboyant."

"She did have a nice mink."

"In that case why don't you decide which things you'd like? And if there is any item of value, why don't you sell that—give yourself money to tour Europe?"

"Oh gee. That would be swell, wouldn't it?" she said. "I've been thinking about what you said. About staying on here and getting a job, maybe. The problem is that I don't speak any foreign languages."

"You should come to the café where the Americans hang out," I said. "Maybe one of them will have a good suggestion for you." As I said this I realized it would give me a perfect excuse to meet Arnie again. I'd be able to bring up Mrs. Rottenburger's death and see how he reacted. At the very least find out if he took any photographs. "Come this evening," I said.

"All right. I will." She gave an excited smile. "Gee, Georgie, it was a stroke of luck meeting you. I'd have been completely lost and wouldn't know what to do, and worried sick about meeting Uncle Frank. Say—you don't think you'd come over to the hotel when he's arriving, do you? I'd sure appreciate the company. You'd know what to say."

"If I'm still here," I said. "When is he getting in, again?"

"By the weekend," she said. "You'll still be around, won't you?"

"I'm not allowed to leave yet," I said.

"Why not?"

"The police still have me pegged as a suspect in your aunt's death."

She laughed. "But that's so silly. Why would you kill someone you don't even know?"

That was a good question. Only a psychopath would kill a stranger. Whoever killed Mrs. Rottenburger had to have known her well.

I went home for a rest before meeting Madge at the Odéon metro station. I had invited Belinda along but she said she had to work on Mummy's trousseau designs. She sounded really excited about the prospect. "If your mother wears my designs they will be in all the papers," she said. "I'll make my name as a designer."

"Is that what you want—to be a working woman? Look how hard Chanel works and how she has to fawn over all those women."

Belinda sighed. "You're right, of course. I can't see myself working with a room full of seamstresses day in and day out. But it's nice to know that I have the flair for it." She patted my shoulder. "Go on. Off you go. Have a fun evening with Harry and co."

That's when I realized that I hadn't asked Harry to escort us to the café. Of course I should have done so. It was, after all, his special place. "Was he not working at the showing today? He'll be tired."

Belinda shook her head. "Neither he nor Arnie showed up today. Chanel was livid. So were the pretty-boy ushers who had to do the heavy work."

I went up to Harry's flat and tapped on the door. No answer. So I left to meet Madge. There was no sign of Harry or Arnie when we reached the café. The morose Swede was there with a glass of bright green liquor in front of him. So was the other American, Dan, and a couple of Frenchmen. Pierre saw us arriving and came over to join us, pulling up a chair beside me again.

"So how was the fashion show?" he asked.

"You haven't heard from Arnie or Harry?"

"They have not come here all week," he said.

"They've been busy processing Arnie's photographs," Dan, the American, said. "Apparently he got some great shots and he wants to sell them to American magazines. Magazines that pay real money."

Two thoughts were going through my head. One was that maybe those photographs might reveal a clue—someone slinking around in the darkness, a hand slipping cyanide into Mrs. Rottenburger's drink. Then a second, more alarming, thought. One that had occurred to me before. Cyanide was used in the development of photographs. Just as I was thinking this the door opened, with a rush of cold air, and Arnie himself walked in, followed by Harry.

"So we're being honored again with a visit from the aristocracy," Arnie said, as he joined us at the table. "Are you drinking absinthe again, Sven? It will rot your guts, and your brain."

"Sometimes one needs to forget," Sven said.

"So how was today's fashion show?" I asked innocently.

"We played truant," Arnie said. "I had so many good photographs to process. Harry's been a great help and we've contacted several American magazines who are interested. This could be my big break." He looked suddenly young and excited.

"Those photographs—" I began. "Do you think I could see them? I'd love to know what sort of candid shots you managed to get."

"Sure. Come round tomorrow," Arnie said. Then he noticed Madge. "Who's this? Another member of the royal family?"

"This is Madge," I said. "Mrs. Rottenburger's companion. You know, the lady who was murdered? Now she's not sure what's going to happen to her as she no longer has a job. She was thinking of staying on in Paris if anyone can come up with a way of making money for her."

"What talents do you have?" Pierre asked. "And do not say that you can cook because Paris has too many cooks, as I have already discovered."

"I'm quite handy with a needle," Madge said.

"There you are, then," Pierre said. "Belinda knows Chanel. You could get a job in her workroom."

"Oh, I don't think I'm good enough for that," she said. But a brilliant idea struck me.

"Belinda is making some outfits for my mother. She'll need someone to sew them, if you think you can handle it," I said.

Madge's eyes opened wide. "Gee, that would be swell," she said. "Do you really think so?"

"We'll ask her," I said.

Harry touched her arm. "Sorry about your aunt," he said. "A rotten thing to have happen."

"It was awful." She looked as if she might cry. "And to have those horrible policemen insinuating that I might have wanted to kill her."

"They seem to be clutching at straws looking for a suspect," I said. "They tried to pin it on me."

Arnie chuckled. "They must be very dense, or desperate."

"Both. Have the police bothered you again?" I asked. "About the American lady's death?"

"Not for the past couple of days."

"Why would the police be interested in Arnie?" Sven asked. "He doesn't look like the murdering type to me."

"I suppose it was because he was the only person who actually knew the dead woman," I said.

"You knew my aunt?" Madge asked. "What's your last name?"

"Franzen," Arnie said. "And I didn't know the woman. Just because we both come from Pennsylvania does not mean we were bosom buddies. And I haven't been home since 1920. That's quite a while."

"But she recognized you," I went on, wondering as I said it if I was stepping into dangerous territory.

"I doubt it," he said. "She would recognize my family name. We're quite a prominent bunch. But not me, personally."

He looked so relaxed as he spoke. I found it hard to believe that he had just killed a woman.

"Mind you," he went on. "She was pretty obnoxious, from what I saw. I bet someone would be tempted to do away with her." And he chuckled. "Maybe it was Hemingway. Remember how she threw herself at him at Gertrude's. He's a trained killer."

"But he would have throttled her with his bare hands," Dan said.

Arnie was still chuckling. "True," he said, and then his face sobered. "I'm sorry." He turned to Madge. "This is most distasteful. You're obviously upset."

"She wasn't a very nice person," Madge said. "But she didn't deserve to die."

"Neither did all those boys in the Great War," Arnie said. "It still haunts those of us who survived."

Pierre got up and went to bring food to the table. A coarse pâté, fresh bread, olives, cheese. The men tucked in as if they hadn't had a meal in weeks. I found it hard to eat. Now I was confused. Arnie seemed so relaxed and unconcerned about Mrs. Rottenburger's death. So maybe my hunch was wrong. Madge seemed devastated. Which brought us back to square one. But there was something . . . something was nagging at the fringe of my consciousness. Something that had been said tonight. . . .

Chapter 34

WEDNESDAY, APRIL 29
BACK AT BELINDA'S BUILDING.

I'm going to stop trying to be a detective. I'm obviously no good at
it. Everyone I suspected seems to be completely in the clear.

The group broke up at last. Harry escorted Madge and me to the
Metro station. We said good-bye to her, promising to meet the next
day, and then we walked along the Seine to Belinda's building.

"How long do you think you'll be staying?" Harry asked. "Has
your husband concluded his business yet?"

"Pretty much," I said. "Actually I can't wait to go home. I miss
my house and my puppies and my quiet life."

"Yeah," he said. "You should go back where you belong. You're
lucky. Some of us can't."

He opened the front door for me with his key. The concierge
scurried out of her cubbyhole. "Oh, it is you," she said. "Your husband was here, madame. He left you a note. He said it was urgent."

"Thank you."

I took the envelope from her and opened it:

Just heard from America. There was no Harry Barnstable on the roster of soldiers from New York. Nor a record of his death.

That was when I remembered two things that had been troubling me. When we first met Harry I was sure he had told me he came from Pennsylvania. But he told the police he came from New York. Pennsylvania. Where Mrs. Rottenburger came from. And the other thing . . . He had told Madge this evening that he was sorry about her aunt. But I had introduced her as Mrs. Rottenburger's companion. How did he know, unless he had overheard when she was being questioned by the police at Chanel's? And he had said something about her son being wounded in the Great War. I was pretty sure I hadn't mentioned that when he was around.

While I was processing these thoughts Harry held open the lift door for me and I stepped inside. So did he. The lift door slammed shut and the little cage started to ascend. I looked up to see him staring directly at me. And those eyes . . . he was now older, with a shaggy beard. Transformed. But the eyes hadn't changed. I had seen them on a photograph on Mrs. Rottenburger's desk. Harry was the friend who had supposedly been killed in the war.

I think I must have gasped. Anyway, he saw my reaction.

"You know, don't you?" he said quietly.

I was in a small cage with him. I had to keep stalling until I was safely out. "Know what?" I asked.

"You're a terrible liar." He actually laughed. "You figured it out. I saw how you were asking Arnie questions when all the time you knew it was me. I thought I was safe here. I thought nobody would ever recognize me. Never realize I was still alive. But she did. I saw how she looked at me. She half recognized me. She hadn't quite figured it out, but she would. And then she'd go home and blab to the whole world."

"I don't know what you're talking about," I said. "Blab about what?"

"That I hadn't died in the war. That I was a deserter. That I was responsible for her son's mental breakdown. That I was a disgrace to my proud family. I couldn't let that happen, could I?"

"I suppose not," I said cautiously, trying to appear calm and sympathetic. We passed the first floor, then the second.

"I get off here," I said, reaching for the button.

"No, you don't," he said. "Sorry, Georgie. I really hate to do this. But I can't let you go."

"They know about you, Harry," I said. "It's too late. My husband has already been in touch with the American authorities. They know you're living under an assumed name."

"Henry Cunningham III," he said. "One of the illustrious Pennsylvania Cunninghams. Barnstable was where we had a summer place. I couldn't take it anymore, Georgie. In the trenches, I mean. Night after night of being shelled. Being sent over the top and waiting to be blown to pieces. So when a shell landed near me and threw me into the mud, I took my chance. I was so glad to find I was all right. I got up, tossed down my dog tags near the remains of some poor guy and I crawled away into the darkness. I made it to a field, then a barn, and some French peasants hid me."

The elevator continued to rise. We passed the third floor. I wondered if Belinda would hear if I yelled loudly. I knew I had to keep him talking, to let him see that I understood, I was sympathetic. It was my only chance.

"That was why you changed your mind and came to the fashion show," I said.

"Absolutely. I knew I had to strike quickly. Luckily Arnie roped me in to carry his flash attachment. I helped myself to a cyanide crystal from his lab. I followed him around while he took pictures, and when we were close enough to Mrs. Rottenburger I dropped the crystal into her drink. Nobody saw. Nobody thought it was strange because the press photographers were all moving to get better shots."

The lift was passing the fourth floor. There was not a soul around. If I shouted for help would the concierge hear me? Would she do anything? Did she have a telephone to summon the police? But I'd probably already be dead.

"What are you planning to do with me?" I asked, and to my annoyance I heard my voice wobble.

"There will be a malfunction of the elevator, I regret to say." He was still speaking calmly but I saw his eyes darting nervously. He was not a natural killer. Hurting people did not come easily to him. I had to play on that.

"I'm going to have a baby," I said. "Don't you want to give it a chance to be born? Haven't you seen enough killing and suffering?"

"Of course I have." His own voice cracked now. "I have nightmares every single time I fall asleep. Boys of eighteen with a look of terror on their faces right before they are blown apart. How can I ever forget that?"

"And your best friend Richie," I said. "He's suffered all his life believing you were killed. Wouldn't you like to put his mind at ease? One good thing you could do. To make up for killing his mother."

"You don't understand," he said. "Henry Cunningham really is dead. And Harry Barnstable will be too. When I leave here I'll shave off the beard, dye my hair, and become someone new. I have no bank accounts, no way of being traced. I might go on to Italy. Switzerland. Lots of possibilities when you have nobody but yourself."

The lift ground to a halt on the top floor. Harry grabbed me and shoved me out. Then, still holding on to my arm, he wedged the door open and sent the lift down again. I saw now what he was going to do. He was going to push me down the lift shaft. I looked around. A narrow landing with several doors, all of which were shut. We heard the clunk as the lift reached the ground floor.

"I'm sorry," Harry said. "If there was another way, I'd do it. But there isn't."

I shook myself free of him and headed for the staircase down. Not fast enough, of course. He grabbed me by the hair and jerked me back so violently that I almost fell over backward. Then we both froze as we heard a sound. The lift had closed far below and it was starting to come back up. For a moment Harry stood motionless, unsure what to do next. Did he want to push me onto the roof of the ascending lift, and would that fall be enough to kill me? Then I heard another sound—the most welcome one in my entire life.

"Georgie? Where are you?" Darcy's voice echoed up the stairwell.

"I'm up here, Darcy! Top floor." I screamed as Harry tried to put his hand over my mouth. "Harry's going to—"

Harry wrenched open the cage and yanked on a red lever. The lift ground to a sudden stop. I heard an alarm bell go off, shouts from down below as occupants emerged from various flats, and then, miraculously, feet coming up the stairs, echoing from the marble. Feet coming fast. But not fast enough. Harry looked around, then opened a door with a sign on it: *To the Roof.* He was still holding me around the neck and tried to drag me with him. I fought with all my might, bracing myself against the doorway. Then Harry let go and slapped my face hard. I staggered for a second and he pushed me, sending me sprawling ahead of him into the darkness of a narrow stair. He was about to slam the door shut when Darcy appeared, gasping for breath.

"You take your hands off my wife," he said coldly and landed one brilliant punch on Harry's jaw. Harry's head jerked back and he went over like a tree. Darcy scooped me into his arms. "It's all right, my darling. You're safe now," he said.

Chapter 35

Golly, I never want to go through that again. From now on I want a
quiet life at Eynsleigh, looking after my baby and tending the
garden.

Later that evening we were finally alone. The police had come and
taken Harry away. A doctor had been called to examine me and
declare that the baby and I had suffered no lasting damage but
should rest. Belinda had been incredibly solicitous, going out to a
café to bring me consommé with egg and a glass of brandy.

"How did you manage to get here just in time?" I asked Darcy
as I lay propped against his shoulder.

"I found out from Belinda that you'd gone to the café where
you would meet Harry and his friend, so I went there as quickly as
I could. But you'd already left."

"We came back a different way because we took Madge to the Metro station," I said.

"I got here just as the lift was taking you up," Darcy said. "I told the old biddy to call the police. She didn't seem too willing. I had to be rather forceful. That delayed me a couple of seconds."

"He was going to throw me down the lift shaft," I said and gave a shudder.

"Desperate men do desperate things. I suspect he was really a decent bloke who would be horrified at what he had done. That war damaged so many men."

"Let's hope there is never another one," I said.

"Amen to that," Darcy muttered.

I lay back against him, feeling safe and content.

"So what would you like to do?" he asked. "Stay here for the night and then we could go to a nice hotel in the morning? I could give you the trip to Paris that you deserve. We could see the sights together."

"You know what I'd really like?" I said. "I'd like to go home. To my house. My puppies. I've had enough excitement for now."

Darcy laughed and stroked my hair. "Sometimes I feel the same way," he said. "I'm quite ready to go home, although I'm so frustrated that we did not manage to obtain those things from Frau Goldberg—unless she did somehow post them and they'll be arriving in England."

"I think she was too closely watched all the time," I said. "If only Mrs. Rottenburger had not taken her place . . ."

"We can't worry about if-onlys," Darcy said. "We have to chalk up some losses and move on. The next big thing will be to try and get them both out of Germany before they disappear into one of the camps that are springing up all over the place."

I grabbed his wrist. "Darcy, you won't be involved in that, will you? Not going into Germany and trying to rescue somebody?"

"I doubt it," he said. "It will be someone with good German. And more training than I've had." He sat up. "So do you want to come back to the Hôtel Saville with me or stay here tonight?"

"I'd rather stay where I am," I said. "But I don't want you to go."

He sat on the edge of the bed, examining it. "It is a small bed for two people," he said. "But I suppose for one night . . ."

⁂

AGAIN BELINDA CAME up trumps. She offered us her bed and she slept in the guest room. So we had a lovely peaceful night and in the morning Darcy went out for fresh pain au chocolat. I began to feel that Paris wasn't such a bad place after all.

"I'll need to check out of the Hôtel Saville," Darcy said, "but if we hurry we could catch today's boat train, if they've any more first-class seats left."

I considered this. I wasn't in the mood to do anything in a hurry. "I should go and say good-bye to Mummy first," I said. "And I'd like to see her trying on the outfits that Belinda is making for her."

"Very well," Darcy said. "In that case I'll see if they have a room for us tonight at the Ritz. We might as well go out in style."

"Darcy—how can we afford the Ritz?" I demanded.

He gave me that adorable, wicked grin. "Expenses. Surveillance, you know. Nobody's going to query one night."

And so we took a taxi across the Seine and moved into a glorious room overlooking the Place Vendôme. Darcy went off to arrange for train tickets while I joined Belinda for Mummy's fitting. I thought the outfits were gorgeous and Mummy certainly seemed pleased.

"So different," she said. "I love the trousers in that striped silk. They make me look tall and elegant. And the ivory ballgown. I could be married in that, maybe. Close enough to a white wedding, don't you think? And white makes me look too pale."

After so many marriages that I had lost count, I hardly thought that a white wedding was appropriate, but I said nothing. Instead I sat in the armchair by the window, looking alternately at my mother and around the room. My nose started twitching and I sneezed.

"I hope you're not coming down with a cold now," my mother said.

"It's all the flowers," I said. "So many flower arrangements, Mummy. Do you really need so many?"

"Max loves to spoil me with flowers all the time," Mummy said. "See that lovely mimosa? He had it sent up from the South of France. And the orchids . . ." She paused, smiling. "And that display next to you came from my neighbor."

"Your neighbor?"

"That German lady you asked about. Frau Whatsit. The room boy brought these to me when she was leaving. Apparently she said it was a pity to throw out such lovely flowers and she knew how much I liked them. Wasn't that sweet of her? Of course, they are not as lovely as the bouquets Max gives me. . . ."

A strange thought was crossing my mind. "What exactly did she say? Can you remember what the room boy told you?"

Mummy shrugged, the way she always did when she didn't consider something important. "I really can't remember. Why does it matter?"

"It might, Mummy. Just think. Why did she think you should have the flowers and not another of the German party?"

She recoiled at my forcefulness. "Because she knew I liked flowers, I suppose."

"How did she know that?"

"I suppose she was passing in the hall when one of my flower arrangements was being delivered. Yes, that was it. The other ladies were with her and one of them said, 'So many flowers. It's good you are not allergic to them like me.'"

"So that was why the room boy delivered Frau Goldberg's to you?"

Mummy frowned again. "He said she immediately thought of me because the English love their flowers and perhaps I'd like to share them with my daughter."

I didn't wait another second. I started delving into the base of the flower arrangement.

"What are you doing? You are destroying it," Mummy snapped.

"With good reason." My fingers closed around a cold, hard cylinder as I lifted out the roll of microfilm. "So she did manage to hand it over after all."

"What is it?" Mummy was staring at me now.

"Nothing. Just some snapshots," I said. "Do go back to your fitting."

THAT EVENING DARCY and I strolled along the Seine. The roll of microfilm was safely hidden in my toilet bag, wrapped inside my soap dish. We would deliver it in London tomorrow. We dined at a simple bistro where the food was outstanding: lentil soup, veal chops, floating islands for dessert and then a cheeseboard to follow.

"I must say the French really know how to cook," Darcy said, pushing his plate away with satisfaction. "I shall miss this when we are back to Queenie's stodge. We really must do something about a proper cook, Georgie."

I suddenly had a brilliant idea. "I think I know a chef who might like the experience of working in a big country house," I said.

"Really? Where is he?"

"Right now he's a waiter," I said. "Because he can't get a chef's job."

"Can he cook?"

"He can't be worse than Queenie," I said. "And he does know French food."

"Then let's go and see him."

PIERRE DID NOT need much persuading. He agreed to come to work for us for a trial period. His friends at the café teased him about going off to a land where they did not appreciate fine food, but he said he could put "related to the royal family" on his résumé. He promised to start on May 1. I kept my promise to Madge and helped smooth things over with her uncle. She was going to stay on in Paris for a while and might even visit us in England. And Darcy and I . . . we boarded the train home. Lots of hugs from Belinda and the promise that she'd come to visit soon. Hugs from Mummy and a similar promise to come when the baby was born.

When the boat train arrived at Victoria Station, Darcy delivered the soap dish to a certain office while I waited at the station café. Then we took the train to Haywards Heath and finally on to Eynsleigh. Eynsleigh had never looked more inviting. Apple trees in blossom, spring flowers blooming in the borders, the fountain splashing. I gave a sigh of content as we opened the front door and walked in.

We had hardly got inside when two large puppies came bounding up to us, barking, tails wagging madly.

"Oh, you're home, my lady." Mrs. Holbrook appeared. "That is good news. Quiet, you brutes. Get down." (This to the dogs.) "Oh, my lady, you won't believe what these two have been up to. They need taking in hand and some serious training."

"Don't worry, Mrs. Holbrook," I said. "We'll get to it right away."

Epilogue

It was later that month that we received word that the Goldbergs had been to visit relatives in Bavaria and had safely made it over the mountains to Switzerland.

Author's Note

You're probably cringing every time Georgie takes a drink of alcohol. At that time it was not frowned upon. No research had been done on the dangers; in fact a pregnant mother might be instructed to have brandy and hot milk to fortify her. My mother-in-law instructed me to drink plenty of beer so that the milk would come in.

And my mother, pregnant during World War II, was also encouraged by her doctor to smoke—to calm her nerves during the bombings!

Acknowledgments

As always I'd like to thank Michelle Vega and her wonderful team at Berkley for making these books such a joy to write, as well as Meg Ruley, Christina Hogrebe, and my brilliant team at Jane Rotrosen Agency.

And I can't forget to thank my husband, John, and my daughters, who are forced to be first readers.